D1398595

The Curious Incident at CLARIDGE'S

Also by R. T. Raichev

The Hunt for Sonya Dufrette
The Death of Corinne
Assassins at Ospreys
The Little Victim

The Curious Incident at CLARIDGE'S

AN ANTONIA DARCY AND MAJOR PAYNE MYSTERY

R. T. RAICHEV

SOHO
CONSTABLE

Constable • London

Constable & Robinson Ltd
3 The Lanchesters
162 Fulham Palace Road
London W6 9ER
www.constablerobinson.com

First published in the UK by Constable,
an imprint of Constable & Robinson, 2010

First US edition published by SohoConstable,
an imprint of Soho Press, 2010

Soho Press, Inc.
853 Broadway
New York, NY 10003
www.sohopress.com

A copy of the British Library Cataloguing in Publication
Data is available from the British Library

UK ISBN: 978-1-84901-122-8

US ISBN: 978-1-56947-633-8
US Library of Congress number: 2009044017

Printed and bound in the EU

1 3 5 7 9 10 8 6 4 2

Mixed Sources
Product group from well-managed
forests and other controlled sources
www.fsc.org Cert no. SA-COC-1565
© 1996 Forest Stewardship Council

To Kirstin – the very best of literary devotees

Author's Note

This is a work of fiction. All the characters are imaginary and bear no relation to any living person.

R. T. R.

Contents

1

The Military Philosophers

'Gentlemen – the Queen.' Major-General Hailsham held up his glass.

'The Queen!' They all raised their glasses.

'His Royal Highness, the Duke of Edinburgh.'

'The Duke of Edinburgh!' They drank again. They had already toasted the regiment, twice.

'Shame HRH couldn't be with us today.'

'Terrible shame. No question of him *not* wanting to be with us.'

'Of course not. Circumstances beyond his control.'

'HRH sent a message, saying he'll be with us in spirit.'

'How frightfully thoughtful. Couldn't have wished for a better patron, what?'

'Absolutely. Sound on every topic. The Army, the Navy, women, the Chinese, what's to be done about blacks, the *Cutty Sark*, the French, the global whatsit – am I missing something?'

'Rain forests, the General Dental Council, the Mussulman menace, horses?'

'Thank you, Savil. Yes. List as long as my arm. Practically endless. Horses? Horses *are* important, dammit. Can be a bit radical on occasion, true, but they *listen* to him, that's the bloody marvellous thing. They're not supposed to, they wouldn't admit to it, but they listen to him. HRH has ideas. Knows exactly what's to be done about things.'

'They listened to him about Diana –'

'Of course they did. And a good thing too, Ormsby. They said they didn't, but of course they did. MI5, MI6, the Ministry of Defence, the old HO, the old FO – they all listened to him.'

'Confounded incompetents, but he's got them all eating out of his hand.'

'Thank God for that.'

'Thank God for that. There'd have been no end of trouble if they'd let things take their course. "Lady Diana Al Fayed", that's what she would have insisted on styling herself, some such nonsense.'

'Doesn't bear thinking about. The mother of the future King of England!'

'Couldn't allow that sort of thing.'

'Of course not. Pretty girl, good colour, but quite mad. Completely bonkers. Mixing with the wrong crowd and so on. Well, HRH saw to it. Knew where to draw the line.'

'He is often misunderstood, mind, the liberal press tries poking fun at him, calls him gaffe-prone, a Nazi and I don't know what else, but he doesn't let that bother him one little bit. Well, there's nothing wrong with being radical, dammit. *Au contraire*. Somebody's *got* to be radical these days, wouldn't you say? Somebody's got to save us from tipping over the edge.'

'Quite.'

'Absolutely.'

'There's one subject HRH never broaches.' Colonel Speke cleared his throat. 'Sometimes a fellow asks an oblique kind of question, drops a heavy hint, but d'you know what? *He never gets an answer.*'

'You mean . . .?'

'*Yes.*'

'Of course not. Out of bounds. Not the done thing.'

There was a pause as they all once more regarded the portrait on the wall.

'Did – what was the chappie's name now? – do that one?' Brigadier Fielding asked. 'Namby-pamby sort of chap. Never cared for him much, to tell you the truth, but they thought the world of him. Kept asking him over to Buck House. The sort of chap the Queen Mum favoured. You know. Beaton, that's it. He did them all, didn't he?'

'It's an Annigoni, actually.'

'Is it? Is there anything you don't know, Payne?' Colonel Weldon glowered boozily at him.

'Payne knows all the answers.'

'No, not really.' Major Payne made a self-deprecating grimace. 'Wish I did.' He was sitting at the distinguished 'top table'.

'How he manages at his age I have no idea.' Colonel Speke shook his head. 'No, not Payne. Payne's a young man. I mean HRH. How he manages to do *so much*. Where does he find the *energy*? He's two years older than me, you know.'

'They give him *something*. Regular course, I am told.' General Savil lowered his voice. 'German medico practically lives at Buck House now. No one's supposed to know. Top secret. Reliable source – lady-in-waiting – friend of m'wife's – play bridge together – sensible woman – got a head on her shoulders – talks in her cups – only way to get her going. They put him on a drip for two days, she says. He doesn't like it, grumbles a bit, but he submits, then he gets up and marches out, head held high, as good as new. As bright as a button. Roses in his cheeks and so on. Would create a stir, if it got round, so mum's the word. Regular as clockwork, I am told. On the highest authority.'

'The last time he was here you could hear a pin drop the moment he opened his mouth. He hates it, absolutely hates it, terribly unassuming, wants things to carry on as per normal. Expects no credit. Wants everybody to have a good time What was it he said last time, d'you remember, Somerville? Ha-ha. It made us laugh. Remember? What *was* it?'

'*What d'you take me for? Some bloody oracle?*'

'That's it, Denham. Ha-ha. How we roared. We weren't here then, actually, were we? Completely different place.

3

The Savoy, I think. How we roared. It *was* the Savoy, wasn't it?'

'The good old Savoy. Building like a 1930s radio set, you almost expect Lord Reith to toddle along in his dinner jacket and give you a lecture. *Some bloody oracle.* That was damned funny. Can't quite say why but it's damned funny. For some reason. What's this place called? I mean *this* place. Sorry – my memory's completely gone. Total blackout. Memory's gone AWOL. Place has a name, hasn't it? All decent places have names.'

'Claridge's.'

'Claridge's, to be sure. Thank you, Payne. Good to have a young man around. Young Payne knows all the answers. You are such a clever fellow, Payne. The right man to have in a crisis.'

'Not at all.' Major Payne stole a look at his watch. He did not feel particularly flattered to be referred to as 'young Payne', given the average age of everybody was about eighty-five. The amount of drinking that went on around him was quite astonishing, if not alarming.

'Jesty's also a young man, but he's always busy, aren't you, Jesty? Always on the run. Oh, he's gone,' Colonel Speke glanced round in a puzzled manner. 'Where's Jesty gone?'

'Gone AWOL, ha-ha.'

'What's become of Jesty, since he gave us all the slip,' murmured Payne.

'Jesty always disappears without warning, have you noticed? Quite a trick he has. Quite a habit.' Savil cleared his throat. 'The usual, would you say?'

'Most likely. That's the kind of thing he likes to do. Styles himself "Beau", apparently.'

'Beau Jesty, eh?'

'*Chacun à son gout.* I am inordinately fond of clay pigeon shooting myself. Well, Claridge's is as good a place as any other for that sort of thing.'

'One of these days Jesty'll come a cropper, mark my word,' said Livingston-Gore.

4

'Interesting place, Claridge's. The King of Yugoslavia was born on the premises. Back in 1940-something. After Tito did his thing. The Communist takeover. Damned good wine, this. Why d'you keep looking at your watch, Payne? Haven't got a train to catch, have you? Don't tell us your lady wife keeps you on a short leash. Writes murders, doesn't she? Dangerous sort of woman to have round the house.'

'I was here, you know, when the King of Yugoslavia was born. I was chief of security. Had the whole floor cordoned off and declared Yugoslav territory. One of those emergency measures. Real crisis. Checked every bloody waiter – in case one or more of the champagne buckets contained a bomb. Every damned bell-boy too. Ha-ha.'

'Why couldn't HRH be with us today?'

'Bad back, poor fellow – pain more than a human being could bear, I was told – on the highest authority – practically doubled up.'

'Poor fellow. Worried about Harry, that's what's got him down. First they drag the boy back from the Khyber – then they ban him from Knightsbridge!'

'Don't be dramatic, Ormsby. They banned him from some club or other, that's all. Couldn't matter less. Bijou or Beaujolais, some such name. It's a *night* club, or so I understand. In Knightsbridge, that's correct. Good address.'

'Boujis, actually.'

'Is that so? The kind of thing you know, Payne!'

'I glance at the rags sometimes,' Payne said apologetically.

'My niece met Harry once. In Knightsbridge, that's correct. Charming young fellow, she tells me. A little on the boisterous side, pinched her apparently. Full of beans, as we used to say. Enjoys a drink better than anything else, perhaps, but oodles of charm.'

'Oodles of charm. Ahem. That thing they suggested about Hewitt . . .?'

'Tittle-tattle, Livingston-Gore. Rank nonsense. Complete rot. Nothing in it whatsoever. What d'you say, Knatchbull?'

'Fearful piffle. Hewitt deserves to be shot.'

'Charming young rascal, eh? Eye for the girls, like HRH. I mean Harry.'

'That's why HRH has taken it so badly. Damned fond of the boy.'

'Damned fond.'

'Nothing namby-pamby about Harry.'

'Nothing namby-pamby about Harry.'

'That's what we want to hear.' Major-General Hailsham nodded. 'Let's drink to it, shall we? I'd like to propose a very special kind of toast.' He picked up his glass. 'Gentlemen – Prince Harry.'

'Prince Harry. Hurrah.'

'Hurrah!'

'Cry God for Harry, England and St George.'

'Jolly well put, Payne. Has a familiar ring to it . . . Your own?'

The regimental reunion luncheon was exactly what Major Payne had expected it to be – glorious grub, the best of wines, incredibly inconsequential talk – everybody sounded as though they had sat at the feet of Ionesco or Beckett. Virtually interchangeable, if one shut one's eyes and just listened. It didn't matter who said what. Age and the demon drink had something to do with it. Payne didn't exactly *revel* in the company of his brother officers, though regimental dinners were something he was apt to attend, out of habit rather than loyalty or any particular affection. His accounts of past regimental dinners had made Antonia laugh, so now he tried to keep mental notes of what was being said. Was the superannuated army officer an intrinsically British phenomenon? He rather thought it was. They didn't have *quite* the same thing in France or in Germany. Why did they have to shout so? Enough to burst one's eardrums. Well, some of them were quite deaf . . .

Major Payne cleared his throat. 'Would you allow me an observation? At our last reunion most of the fellows had moustaches. Now there are only two chaps with moustaches. Jesty and the Brigadier.'

'By Jove, you are right. You are always right, I can't help noticing.' Colonel Speke squinted around. 'Yes. How perfectly extraordinary. Damned curious, in fact. No moustaches!'

'The mystery of the ... diminishing moustaches, eh, Payne?' Brigadier Fielding cocked a knowing eyebrow. 'Perhaps you should investigate what's behind it? That's what you like doing best, someone said. Investigating. Finding out about things. You and your lady wife. That's what a little bird told me.'

'Not true. Nothing but silly rumours. People like to make up all kinds of stories.'

'I say, Payne, would you like one of my cigars? You strike me as the kind of fellow who would appreciate an authentic Montecristo.'

'Thank you, Fielding, I think I would. If you'll excuse me ...' Major Payne rose.

'No moustaches,' Denham said thoughtfully. 'Payne's absolutely right. Payne's hit the nail on the head, as usual. That's what I've been thinking. *Standards are slipping.* Where are you off to, Payne? No problems with the waterworks, I trust? A young man like you –'

'No, nothing of the sort. Got to clear my head,' Major Payne explained.

2

Conduct Unbecoming

He strolled out of the private dining room and found himself in the foyer. The tall silver-framed mirror told him what Antonia had already pointed out: he looked good in uniform. He twirled an imaginary moustache and looked at his cigar. An authentic Montecristo, eh? Made the Brigadier feel young and dashing, he supposed. Payne didn't smoke cigars often, but sometimes he did feel like it – after a good meal – when he was ever so slightly tipsy – with a good brandy – always made him think of Kipling – went with the uniform somehow. Shame he couldn't smoke it here, though. For some reason his thoughts strayed back to the Annigoni portrait of the Queen. It had been painted two years after the Coronation and blended formality with informality, in a manner that was characteristic of the Queen's style. She wears her Garter robes like a dressing gown, Payne thought. An ordinary woman in an extraordinary role . . .

Not many people around. Lunch hour drawing to a close, too early for tea. Someone standing beside a potted palm, looking furtive. Same uniform as me, Payne thought languidly. The next moment he blinked. Good lord. One of their chaps. Jesty? Yes. The elusive Captain Jesty. Payne had seen Jesty slip out of the dining room earlier on – he'd had a determined air about him, or so Payne imagined. Payne didn't know Jesty terribly well, but they were on friendly enough terms, whenever they bumped into each other. Jesty seemed to be spying on someone. He was standing stock still, head thrust forward, face flushed, eyes bulging –

Not exactly the conduct of an officer and a gentleman. The regiment would most certainly take a dim view of it. What was he up to? With his snub nose and round blue eyes that held a malicious glint, Jesty brought to mind an overgrown boy. Short mousy hair and a little moustache that was not in the least becoming. Physiognomy, no doubt, was an inexact science, but Jesty's face did not invite trust. Jesty had the face of an ageing debauched Puck.

Payne tried to remember what he knew about Jesty. Late forties. Hadn't risen above the rank of captain. Twice divorced. Or was it three times? Something of a ladies' man, nay a professional amorist, if gossip was to be believed. An indefatigable pursuer of the fair sex, in fact. That reference earlier on to the 'usual'. Jesty was reputed to have had affairs with the wives of several of his brother officers. Personally, Payne found it hard to envisage Jesty in the role of an irresistible Don Juan, but then women were funny when it came to that sort of thing. Some women. No accounting for tastes.

What *was* he doing? He hadn't moved. He looked riveted by somebody or something. Payne wondered if he could be witnessing one of Jesty's amorous pursuits . . .

Feeling a little light-headed, Major Payne tiptoed up to him. He was not sure what he intended to say. Something on the lines of 'gotcha' or 'boo'. Jesty, however, turned round before Payne could make a sound. Jesty didn't appear particularly startled. He put his forefinger across his lips.

'Voyeuristic practices are frowned upon at Claridge's,' Payne said sternly. 'Does the honour of the regiment mean so little to you?'

'Something funny's going on, Payne. See that couple over there?' Jesty pointed. 'The old boy and the girlie?'

'What about them? You couldn't possibly be after him, so you must be after her.'

9

'Perhaps I am. Any objections?'

'Are you stalking her?'

'She did something rather peculiar. I'm trying to work out what she's up to exactly ...'

The young woman had a delicate pale face. Hair pulled back in a severe bun. Late twenties or early thirties, Payne decided. Attractive. Practically no make-up. Simple black dress. Intense. Beautiful, yes, in a rather exclusive kind of way. Her bone structure! A model? Something of the head girl about her – the way she did her hair. Made her appear a trifle forbidding. Shouldn't do her hair like that. The old boy was probably in his seventies. Face like a lugubrious bloodhound. Querulous expression. Balding. Smart double-breasted blazer and black tie ... Her grandfather?

There was a coffee pot on the table in front of them with two cups. Also a glass. No food of any kind. Had they been to a funeral? Or were they going to one? A somewhat desolate air hung about them.

'Who are they?' Payne whispered.

'Her name is Penelope, that's how the pantaloon addressed her. No idea how they are related. My guess is he is her aged uncle.'

'May be her aged husband ...'

'Perish the thought! Don't think she likes him very much.' Jesty's eyes narrowed. 'She's a looker, isn't she?'

'She is, rather. Now, steady on –'

'You think I am after her virtue?'

'Aren't you?'

'I want to stroke her hair ... Look at those lips ... She's the kind that puts up a fight ... I'd like that ... Incidentally, the pantaloon is going to a place called Maybrick Manor.'

'Maybrick Manor?'

'Some such name. May have been Maypole Manor. Or Mayflower. Not sure. The acoustics here are awful. Intend to complain to the manager about it.'

'Hasn't it occurred to you that perhaps Claridge's was never meant to accommodate eavesdroppers?'

10

'The old boy said something about it not being his fault the ghastly woman wanted to end it all.'

'What ghastly woman?'

'No idea ... I managed to walk close by their table twice – after I saw what she did. I was curious. Don't think she noticed me. Didn't so much as lift her pretty head. *Distraite.*'

'What did she do?'

Jesty pointed. 'See that little box beside the old boy's cup?'

'What about it?'

The next moment the young woman signalled to one of the waiters and said in a peremptory voice that was loud enough for them to hear, 'Could we have the bill, please?'

'Yes, madam.'

'Looks like a snuff-box.' Payne squinted. 'A silver snuff-box. Seventeenth-century, at a guess.'

The old man spoke peevishly. 'Penelope, my dear, isn't it a bit early?'

She glanced at her watch. 'I don't think you should make the Master wait. It would be bad manners.'

'I wouldn't have minded some more coffee, actually. There's no need to hurry. The Master said, come whenever you want.'

'The Master was only being polite.'

'The Master is *always* polite.'

Payne frowned. 'Who is the Master?'

'A damned fine-looking filly,' Jesty murmured. 'I love her voice. I love her throat –'

'She looks jolly tense. Like a cat on hot bricks.' Payne stroked his jaw with his forefinger.

'She's got a reason to be tense. She did something damned odd.'

'What *did* she do?'

Jesty did not answer. They watched the old man pick up the snuff-box and put it into his pocket.

'What's inside the box?' Payne persisted. 'Not snuff?'

'Not snuff. It contains a pill, Payne. A capsule, rather. A single capsule. All right. She –'

11

'Would you be kind enough to order a cab, please?' The tall young woman called Penelope was addressing the waiter again. 'We are rather in a hurry.'

'We are not, really,' the old man said.

'Name of Tradescant –' She broke off.

'Take cover,' Payne whispered. 'She's looking our way.'

Drawing back sharply, Jesty said, 'She saw us. Hell and damnation. Let's get out of here.' He pulled Payne by the cuff and the two men beat a rapid retreat in the direction of the private dining room. Awfully undignified, Payne thought. Like schoolboys caught in the act.

'She blushed . . . Deep crimson . . . She looked a picture of guilt,' Payne said thoughtfully. 'Penelope Tradescant. It's the kind of name one remembers.'

'Tradescant may be only the old boy's name,' Jesty pointed out.

'Is there any reason for her to look guilty? Come on, what *did* you see? That capsule you mentioned, tell me about it.'

Jesty gave him a sidelong glance. 'Always hunting after a mystery, aren't you, Payne? So it's true what they say about you being a regular Sherlock?'

'Hate it when people use clichés. One should always strive to be original. Why don't you say something like –'

'Ah, there you are, boys, you've decided to rejoin our so – so foolish and trifling banquet.' Major-General Hailsham greeted them with this unlikely quotation from *Romeo and Juliet*. 'We've been wondering what happened to you. Where did you disappear? What have you been up to? You look as though you've surprised a nymph while bathin'! What? What?'

'. . . and then old Wavell asked me if his eye was straight,' Colonel Speke was saying. 'It was *only* then I realized he had a glass eye. Gave me a frightful turn.'

'Some Napoleon brandy, boys?' Brigadier Fielding, his face the hue of a tropical sunset, held up a bottle.

'What *did* she do?' Payne asked again.

Jesty looked at him. 'She swapped the capsules.'

3

Poison in Jest

'Well, I deduced he had poison on his mind some time before he told me the whole story,' Major Payne said in a pleased manner. 'He thought the house was called Maybrick Manor. Would be damned unusual if a poisoning did take place at a Maybrick Manor, if you know what I mean.'

'You believe that was a Freudian slip – an association of ideas? How interesting,' Antonia said. 'Was he really thinking of Mrs Maybrick? Did you ask him?'

It was three hours later and they were in their sitting room in Hampstead. Payne had perched on his wife's desk. He was still wearing his uniform and was twirling an unsmoked cigar between his fingers.

'I did ask him. He said I was probably right. He'd been reading about the case in *Famous Trials* only a couple of days ago, at your old haunt, the Military Club library, of all places. He picked up the book at random. Said he'd actually wondered what it would be like to make love to a poisoner. And now he's fallen for a girl he believes *is* a poisoner! As though the devil made it happen, he said. Incidentally, what was the name of the new librarian lady? I keep forgetting.'

'Mrs Mole – a very nice woman. Something Mrs Maybrick was most definitely not,' Antonia said. 'Mrs Maybrick was accused of poisoning her husband with arsenic.'

'Quite a *cause célèbre* in its day, wasn't it?'

'Yes. So. Captain Jesty was after the girl. He saw her earlier on in the foyer, fancied her wildly and soon after went in hot pursuit?'

'That's the precise sequence of events. Jesty prides himself on being extremely adept in the art of seduction. Got quite a reputation in that department, actually. Life is dull and painful, so why not take one's pleasure where one can? That seems to sum up his philosophy. He is quite incapable of resisting the urge to lunge. He asked if I thought it was one of those self-destructive compulsions and I said yes. It made him laugh. Well, he saw the girl's aged consort produce a little silver box, take out a capsule and swallow it with a glass of water.'

'Any idea what the capsule might have contained?'

'Some anti-dyspeptic remedy, Jesty imagines, but it could have been anything. The elixir of life – a painkiller – royal jelly – an anti-depressant – Viagra. People take all sorts of pills nowadays. Look at poor misguided Michael Jackson. The old boy then rose and started hobbling towards the loo. A second later Penelope did the substitution. She "pounced" on the box. As though her life depended on it, Jesty said. The old boy had left the box on the table. She opened it and took out the remaining capsule –'

'How could Captain Jesty be so sure there was only one capsule inside the box? It wasn't as though he was peeping over her shoulder, was it? He was some distance away, behind a potted palm.'

'He knew because, as luck would have it, Penelope dropped the little box in her nervousness and it fell on the floor. Nothing fell out of it. It was empty. Jesty is certain it was empty. Penelope picked up the box, then opened her bag, pushed the capsule inside, produced another capsule out of her purse and put it inside the box. She then replaced the box on the table where the old boy had left it and leant back in her chair. It all happened very fast. At first Jesty imagined it was some kind of a practical joke. He

14

is fond of practical jokes himself, apparently. At one time, he said, he enjoyed nothing better than spiking fellows' drinks and substituting laxatives for painkillers.'

'Not exactly what one would expect from an officer and a gentleman.'

'No. Well, Jesty is the cad type. Actually I wonder if he is a bounder? He does wear the right kind of signet ring on the right finger, but such details can be easily aped.'

'What exactly was the difference? Cads betray their class – they break the gentlemanly code of behaviour – while bounders are the outsiders?'

'Perfectly correct. Bounders manage to assume the veneer of the real thing –'

'But they keep misbehaving and giving themselves away?'

'Perfectly correct. Now then, if the old boy – the "pantaloon", as Jesty kept calling him – was not to notice anything untoward and become suspicious, the replacement capsule must have looked the same as the rest of the capsules he'd been taking. You agree? Which of course would suggest careful premeditation on the girl's part.'

There was a pause, then Antonia wondered aloud why Captain Jesty was so convinced that the capsule contained poison.

'He didn't think the girl looked the practical joker type. Too serious, too intense. Something in that. Well, she seemed terrified when she realized we had been watching her. She flushed a deep crimson.'

'You thought she looked guilty?'

'I did. Yes.' Payne loosened his collar with his forefinger. 'And now I keep thinking of the fatal capsule gliding down the old boy's gullet. Chances are that he will take it tonight, or has already taken it. *Oh never shall sun that morrow see.* As you can see, my love, my imagination is as bad as yours. You wouldn't set a poisoning case at a house called Maybrick Manor, would you?'

'A name with such a sinister resonance wouldn't be terribly subtle.'

15

'Emblematic names are a bore. Suggests the author has no trust in the reader's intelligence.' Payne clipped the end of the cigar and produced a box of matches. 'Never cared much for Restoration comedies, myself. Did you?'

'No.'

'Don't find Lady Wishfort or Lady Booby in the least comical. Old Dickens was as bad. He had a real weakness for that kind of satirical flag-posting. Mr *Murd*stone – *Do-the-boys* Hall. Then we have Evelyn Waugh and Miles Malpractice. Not terribly subtle, you are perfectly right. That sort of thing is all right in *children's* books. I am sure Mr Nasty and Mr Nice keep toddlers chuckling in an amused enough manner.'

'Something that *sounds* like Maybrick Manor,' said Antonia thoughtfully. 'What could it be? Mayhem Manor? No – that's worse. Were they both going to Maybrick Manor?'

'Only the old boy, or that was the impression Jesty got. "Tradescant" was the name the girl gave to the waiter when she ordered the cab. It would be interesting to know how exactly they are related, if at all. Oh, we also heard her refer to a "master" – she said it wouldn't do to keep the master waiting, words to that effect.'

'A master?'

'Could be a master of hounds. Or a master of a college. Or perhaps some sinister religious order is behind it all?' Payne held up his cigar. 'We may discover that the old boy is a sacrificial victim. He is meant to collapse and expire at the feet of a mysterious masked figure known as "the Master" . . . Penelope and the Master are of course acting in cahoots . . .'

'What if Captain Jesty lied to you? His story of the capsule swap might have been a fabrication.'

'Some kind of malicious joke, you mean? Jesty's . . . jest?'

'He may have decided to live up to his name . . . Is he good-looking?'

'What's that got to do with anything?'

'Merely curious. Cads are usually good-looking.'

'He is not in the least good-looking. He's got round eyes, brown hair and a silly little moustache. He looks annoyingly smug. Well, he seemed familiar with my penchant for puzzles, so a prank is possible, I suppose – though that wouldn't explain Penelope's guilty expression.'

'Didn't you discuss the incident with any other of your brother officers?'

'No, of course not. Awful old buffers. They regard the Duke of Edinburgh as a cross between Maynard Keynes, Professor Moriarty and the Messiah. I don't know why I go to these reunions, I really don't. I always feel a little depressed when I come home.'

'You didn't engage in a single meaningful discussion with anyone?'

'I am afraid not. There are more meaningful discussions taking place in the graveyard at midnight than at any regimental dinner I have ever attended.' He rose. 'I'm going to see if I could persuade Google to locate Maybrick Manor for me, or any similar-sounding houses. I also intend to look up "Tradescant". It is a singular enough name. There can't be that many. Wasn't there a gardening family called Tradescant? There was also a Tradescant baronetcy, I seem to remember.'

'Hugh! Do change, please!' Antontia called out after him. 'You can't sit in front of the computer in your regimental uniform.'

The House of the Lurking Death

'I may last another twenty years, Master,' Sir Seymour Tradescant was saying. 'Or even twenty-five, if I take care. I am not in bad health. Nothing really wrong with me. Heart, liver, blood pressure, all perfectly tickety-boo. If I strike you as a bit off-colour at the moment, it's because of this damned abscess thing, so tiresome. My big toe, would you believe it. Thought it was gout at first, that's why I didn't have my toe seen to sooner. I let it fester. That's how my fool of a doctor put it.'

'Medical men are not what they used to be,' the Master said with a sigh. 'My dentist is Chinese. He treats my teeth as though they were Hong Kong.'

'The abscess was caused by an ingrown nail. Perfectly idiotic, but I might have lost my toe, apparently. At my age it could have been fatal,' Sir Seymour went on. 'One more day and they might not have been able to save it – they would have had to amputate it or something. Terribly gruesome, I know. Reminds one of the worst excesses of the French revolution. Penelope was not particularly sympathetic, I am afraid.'

'I am sorry to hear that.'

'Not at all sympathetic. She insisted it was my own fault. Said I needed to have a pedicure regularly. Hinted that my washing habits weren't up to scratch. Implied that I was mean – that I was saving on soap and hot water. That hurt me. I can't tell you how that hurt me, Master. Pedicures cost the earth, apparently, if one gets the top people to do them.'

Sir Seymour stared ruefully at his left foot. Beside him, propped against the leather armchair, was his ivory-topped cane. Since his arrival he had changed into a plum-coloured smoking jacket, black tie and black velvet shoes with his monogram stitched on the toes in gold braid. The Master, as was his invariable custom, wore a black dinner jacket. Both looked like figures from a bygone age. Dinner over, they were sitting in the Master's study.

'I couldn't wear a shoe on that foot till yesterday, things were so bad,' Sir Seymour continued. 'Feared I might end up in a wheelchair. Ghastly swelling.'

'But you have recovered now?'

'The swelling's gone down. My foot is back to its natural colour, whatever that is. I am no longer in pain, just the tiniest twinge every now and then. I am taking the last of the antibiotics tonight, thank God. It's been every six hours without fail for the past week. Hate the damned stuff. It seems to disagree with me. I have been getting these awful tummy aches – odd rashes. I get depressed too.' Sir Seymour's lugubrious pale eyes fixed on the bronze ink-stand on the Master's desk. 'That may have nothing to do with the antibiotics, mind.'

The Master asked if Sir Seymour was sure he wouldn't like a nightcap.

'Would have loved nothing better, my dear fellow, but I am not allowed alcohol, not while I'm still taking anti-biotics. I may get a reaction, apparently. May balloon and choke to death, or so my doctor tells me. They always exaggerate, these fellows. Terrible quacks. I worry too much, that's the trouble. I wake up in the middle of the night and I have rather grotesque thoughts apropos of nothing in particular. No prospects except pain and penury on this side of the grave. That sort of idea. At one time, I decided Penelope was plotting to kill me. I keep falling into spells of sudden and morbid anxiety.'

'The Tradescants are long-lived.'

'Awfully long-lived, almost indecently so, you may say.'

'I wouldn't dream of saying so,' the Master said primly. 'My great-grandfather lived to be a hundred and two. A biblical age, almost. An uncle of mine is still going strong at ninety-seven. Keeps writing letters to *The Times*. Terribly depressing.'

The Master observed that it had been pleasing to see Lady Tradescant looking so well.

'Oh, Penelope's blooming, blooming. Well, she is *young*. Having a young wife can be a strain, I don't mind telling you, Master. My mistake. Got a bee in my bonnet – wanted a young and beautiful wife.' Sir Seymour shook his head. 'Who was the fellow that kept calling for more of the food of love? Fellow in Shakespeare. Orsino? Nothing but the best would do for me. That was six years ago. I used to set store by that sort of thing. Well, should have known better. *Eros is perfidious and ambiguous, a cheat and a sorcerer, a mixer of . . .* Remember that one? How did it go on?'

The Master stroked his pointed silver beard. '*The mixer of inflaming potions and hemlock, destroyer of human hearts, sensuous and violent, brother to Thanatos.*'

'Hemlock, eh? Oh, it's been a terrible day. Absolute calamity. My housekeeper died this morning. That shook me up. I *was* angry with her but I didn't really want her to chuck herself from the top of my house. That was a bit extreme.'

'From the top of your house? Oh dear!'

'No one can say for sure what exactly happened. No witnesses. Looks like suicide. The police came, of course. Bloody nuisance. Might have been an accident. I'd just sacked her, you see. Mrs Mowbray wasn't a nice woman. Far from it. Vindictive. Had a son called Victor. I didn't like him coming to the house one little bit. Told her off about it hundreds of times. Wonder if he was after Penelope? Then I caught Mrs Mowbray cooking the accounts – that's what did it in the end – the last straw. I'm afraid I lost my temper – shouted – showed her the door – she quibbled over

20

her wages. Didn't strike me as suicidal at all. Tiresome business – tragic too, ultimately. *Not* my fault. No question of me being held responsible in any way.'

'I should hope not!'

'You are a good chap, Master. One of the very few who understand me. For once, Penelope took my side. She was most supportive. Usually, when it comes to that sort of thing, she is no more good than a sick headache, but this time she rose to the occasion. She had no illusions about Mrs Mowbray. Penelope can be a sweet girl – but she tends to be demanding and capricious. Always wants something. I try to keep her on a short leash. She's got a budget she needs to stick to and she resents it. She likes to buy new clothes, you see. Not ordinary clothes, good heavens, no. Haute couture. She's a pretty girl and looks good in expensive rags, so these are the only kind of rags she buys. Hangover from her modelling days, I suppose. Such a lot of nonsense. She's a former model, remember.'

'I do remember.'

'Penelope craves luxury. She'd be snacking on ground-diamond toasties and bathing in champagne, if I ever lowered my guard. Oh yes. She likes foreign travel – holidays abroad. We've got a house in the South of France, but that's proving too expensive to maintain. She's fond of parties, the theatre, something called "gigs". I am afraid I can't keep up with her. Well, perhaps I *am* a little set in my ways, which at my age is not entirely to be marvelled at.'

'You shouldn't blame yourself!'

'Oh, but I don't. Not in the least. Such nonsense. I feel at peace here. Each time I find myself under your roof, I have the sensation of – having arrived. This place feels like home. A proper sanctuary. I hate Half Moon Street. I feel wretched in Half Moon Street.'

'I am so sorry.'

Sir Seymour's lower lip trembled slightly. His voice quavered. Penelope had been brusque with him lately. She spent too much time talking to her friends on the phone. Most of his opinions either annoyed her or made her laugh.

'For example, yesterday I said – what did I say now? No, I can't remember. Never mind. We had a bit of a row this morning. I said I intended to sell the villa in Monte and she said – oh, it was most unpleasant. And to add insult to injury, she then said it was high time I got a hearing aid. Well, that was only an hour before the commotion started – I mean Mrs Mowbray deciding to end it all. Never imagined that class of person ever went in for the final solution, but there you are. A perfectly ghastly day. I do apologize, Master. I have no right to bore you with my jeremiads.'

'Not at all, Sir Seymour. Not at all. You are an old and valued friend.'

'It's good to be appreciated. Doesn't happen often these days. Penelope is not the worst, mind. Bettina's gone mad – quite mad. That's my sister, yes – the "fabled fashionista", heaven preserve us. She lives in Rutland Gate, but she keeps coming over, uninvited, looking like something out of the Chamber of Horrors. Each time she looks *different*, which is jolly disconcerting. Frightens the servants, but does she care? She insists on putting such impossible demands on me – recalling episodes from fifty years ago, things I can't possibly remember having said or done! She enjoys twisting the past and issuing ultimata. She keeps getting something called the "chill". No idea what it is. You've never met her, have you? Pray you never do. It was she who introduced me to Penelope, you see. Probably did it on purpose, out of sheer spite, as an act of revenge. Then there's Nicky.'

'Your son Nicholas?'

'Nicky never forgave me for marrying Penelope. Perhaps he did have a point when he told me I'd live to regret it. That was six years ago. He was quite taken with her himself, mind. I have an idea that she led him on. He's nearly fifty now and hates her –' Sir Seymour broke off. 'Do you think Penelope's got a lover?'

The Master drew back a little. 'I – I couldn't possibly say, Sir Seymour.'

'She is always on the phone, but she stops talking when I happen to enter the room. When I ask her who it was, she says nobody. You can't talk to "nobody", can you?'

'No.'

'Oh, they are all after my money. Nicky can't wait to see me dead and buried. He already envisages himself as the nineteenth baronet. His wife has grandiose plans about renovating Tradescant Hall. Vast wealth is a curse, Master. The title couldn't matter less, but Nicky's set his heart on it. *Sir Nicholas Tradescant, Bart.* He's already got some writing paper with that heading. In gold. Frightfully tasteless.'

'That was naughty of Sir Nicholas –' The Master gave an awkward titter. 'Sorry! Such a silly mistake!'

'One hundred sheets of thick expensive writing paper, waiting in his top desk drawer. Waiting for me to kick the bucket. Don't know why I bothered to have any children. It's not as though I've ever set any value on perpetuation through progeny. Olivia's even worse – that's Nicky's wife. Not much of a marriage, that. I used to feel sorry for him. I am not entirely without a heart, you know. Maybe it is all Olivia's fault. I don't know. Maybe she is the power behind the throne. She's got black eyes, you know. *Come, you spirits, unsex me here.* She's that kind of woman. I am fed up with it all. But I am afraid I must be boring you frightfully, you poor fellow.'

'Not at all,' the Master said.

'Wish I were nobody. Then perhaps Penelope would talk to me. Wish I were a pauper. I do mean that, Master. I want to wake up tomorrow morning and find myself in one of those cardboard boxes under Tower Bridge, or on the river bank, looking at the sunrise, feeling free. Being here is the next best thing. Brought tears to my eyes, seeing the old bookstand and the biscuit tin on the bedside table. When will you have the radiator repainted? I hate that sealing-wax kind of red. None of the other radiators at Mayholme Manor are red, are they?'

'No. I do apologize, Sir Seymour. I promise that by the time you pay us your next visit –'

23

'I don't like the idea of leaving and then coming back and then leaving again. I'd rather stay here all the time. D'you know what? I've got a proposition to put to you. I have made up my mind. I intend to leave *everything* I have to this splendid old institution of yours. What do you say to that?'

'Everything? I am afraid I don't understand.'

'All my earthly riches, Master. In return for the room I occupy each time I come here. How about that? A fair exchange? The room with the lovely view over the bell tower, the maple tree outside the window and the sundial in the centre of the quad. Such peace – waking up to feathered *débats* outside – wondering if it's nightingales or chaffinches – then the early morning walk down to the pond. *I want to move in here permanently.* I want to join the brotherhood. I know I have to be either a widower or a bachelor to qualify, but surely you could stretch the rules the tiniest bit?'

The Master had turned quite pink above his silver beard. 'Goodness me. You want to join the brotherhood. This is quite unexpected. An unexpected pleasure. I believe we could – yes – I'd need to put the matter to the rest of the board first, but I don't think there'd be any serious opposition. You are after all one of our chief benefactors – your generous donations have been greatly appreciated.'

'Don't mention it.'

The Master gave a little cough. 'But there's bound to be opposition of a different kind, Sir Seymour. I mean – your son – your second wife – your sister – they won't be happy about you joining the brotherhood, will they?'

'Of course they won't be happy. My sister regards the brotherhood with contempt. They'll all say I've lost my marbles. They'll try to have me certified and locked away. Nicky will probably call in specialists and employ some gilded legal troupe. But don't you worry, Master. They may try to contest the new will, but they won't succeed. Incidentally, I'm thinking of giving up the title too. That'll be one in the eye for Nicky. Think of all that writing paper going to waste!' He laughed, a slightly manic laugh, the Master thought uneasily.

'You have had a bad day, Sir Seymour. Perhaps things will seem different in the morning, after a good night's sleep.'

'What's the time? Half past nine? Half an hour to go. Oh what difference would it make? I'm going to take that accursed capsule now. Incidentally, who's the fellow in the wheelchair? He seems to be a new brother.'

'That's Dr Fairchild. He arrived last week.'

'Fairchild? Never heard of him. Kept staring at me through his goggles, then whispered something to the steward who was pushing him. Didn't like it, the way they put their heads together.' Sir Seymour took out the silver box from his pocket. The diamond ring on his little finger flashed in the lamplight.

'Actually, Dr Fairchild asked what your room number was.' The Master's eyes were on the ring. Rather an intricate design. It must have cost a pretty penny. An air of exclusivity about it. Exclusivity was something the Master was interested in, nay, aspired to. The Wallis ring, Sir Seymour called it. There seemed to be some strange tale attached to it. Did Sir Seymour mean the Duchess of Windsor? 'I had the idea Dr Fairchild wanted to make friends with you,' he added.

'I don't need any friends. That chap looks older than the Great Wall of China. It's terribly dispiriting for one to mix with people so much older than oneself. One can almost see – how did it go on? *The skull beneath the skin*. What was that joke Mr Lovell made at dinner? Down with Methuselah! Ha-ha. Frightfully funny. Made me laugh. May I have some water?'

'Yes, of course.' The Master rose. He opened the highly polished door of a rather ornate cupboard in the corner. 'Would soda water be all right? Sorry, I think it's my wife,' he said as a ringing sound was heard from his pocket. He produced a mobile phone. '*Do* excuse me. Yes, it's her.' There was a moment's pause. 'Oh, it's only a message.

25

Sorry, Sir Seymour.' The Master poured soda water into a cut-crystal glass. 'Thank God for mobile phones. Marvellous inventions. Would have been completely cut off without them.'

'I've got one in my case upstairs, but I never answer it. Twenty-five minutes won't make much difference, I don't think.' Sir Seymour held the blue-and-red capsule between his thumb and forefinger. He grimaced childishly. 'I won't die, will I?'

'Of course not.' The Master smiled as he watched Sir Seymour place the capsule in the middle of his tongue. Red healthy tongue, remarkable in one of his age. 'Twenty-five minutes won't make the slightest difference,' he added reassuringly.

'Famous last words!' Sir Seymour laughed.

He raised the glass to his lips.

5

Night and Silence

Major Payne waved the printout at Antonia. 'Here it is. I found it. May*holme* Manor, Dulwich. It's the only one that fits the bill. A retreat for unmarried gentlemen and widowers of noble birth who pass the autumn and winter days of their lives in dignified and comfortable routine, "according to the tradition of the house". It's got a Master all right – one Wilfred Cowley-Cooper. The place was once known as "Dutton's Retreat". Quite an interesting history. There's a picture – want to see it?'

The picture showed a placidly beautiful house set in what appeared to be a small park. The photograph had been taken at night. All the windows sparkled like jewels. Like one of those enchanted houses in fairy tales, Antonia thought. There was always some lurking menace in houses like that. 'It looks at once haunted and haunting,' she said. 'Or is that the effect of the pale moon? What is it? Elizabethan?'

'Yes. Built 1632 for the Earl of Sussex, on the site of a Carthusian monastery established in 1380. The monks all wore orange habits with hoods. The will of the founder, Digby Dutton, provided for a hospital for – "such as have been servants to the King's Majesty, who have been misfortunate enough to find themselves in a state of extreme penury or reached a decrepit old age" ...'

'An old gents' home ...'

'Of a particularly exclusive kind.'

'Golden bedpans and walking-frames encrusted with diamonds and rubies?'

'All male staff. Stewards. The residents, either widowers or bachelors, are known as the "brotherhood". When you join, you automatically become a "brother". There is an oath each new brother has to take, that's part of the tradition. It seems they make a huge thing of it. At the moment there are twenty-two brothers living at Mayholme Manor.'

'So that's where your old boy was going.'

'Yes. I can reveal now that his name is Sir Seymour Tradescant, eighteenth baronet. A family of great antiquity and distinction. The Tradescants can be traced back to a thirteenth-century Knight Templar. At one time their family homes included Buckingham House, which changed its name to "Palace" only after it was sold to George III.'

'As grand as that?'

'Sir John Tradescant, Sir Seymour's father, was in the diplomatic corps. In 1946 he was a member of the British team sent to Nuremberg for the trials. They had to ensure things were done properly. Sir Seymour didn't follow any particular career. He chose to play the old-fashioned squire. I thought he looked the part – put me in mind of those not terribly subtle caricatures that were so popular in the '30s.'

Antonia smiled. 'Pendulous cheeks, port-wine complexion, knickerbockers, a tortoiseshell-rimmed eyeglass?'

'Pendulous cheeks and port-wine complexion, but no eyeglass. He wore a blazer.' Payne looked down at the second sheet of printed paper. 'He was born in 1938, which makes him sixty-nine. Married twice, 1956, Lady Frances Talbot (1939–1991), 2002, Penelope St Loup – no age given.'

'*Penelope.*'

'Our fair poisoner, yes. There can't be a mistake. That's the one. We *are* on the right track. Addresses: Half Moon Street, Mayfair and Tradescant Hall, Shropshire. Clubs: Brooks's –'

'If you meant to poison somebody with a single capsule,

you would want to make sure it contained something pretty lethal and fast-acting like cyanide. Death would take place in less than a minute,' Antonia said thoughtfully. 'But, assuming that that indeed was the case, how *could* she have hoped to get away with it?'

'Um. Perhaps she felt certain his death would be taken for suicide? Sir Seymour's mien struck me as a melange of moroseness-cum-melancholy. I would never have described him as a "bouncing baronet". *Did* the type ever exist? Perhaps Sir Seymour does suffer from some depressive illness? Maybe he has already displayed suicidal tendencies and has tried to kill himself? That might have given her the idea.'

'It's possible . . .'

'What would have happened if the substitution hadn't been observed by Jesty? Sir Seymour suddenly keels over and dies halfway through dinner at Mayholme Manor. Or after dinner, as the stewards are handing round the brandy, the liqueurs, the *halva* and the Turkish coffee. So they'll think it's suicide, or else suspicion will fall on Sir Seymour's dinner companions and on the stewards.'

'Or on the Master? For some reason I want the Master to suffer,' said Antonia.

'So do I, isn't that interesting? I want him to squirm. I do believe we share a strong anti-authoritarian streak. If the police did manage to trace the poison capsule back to Half Moon Street,' Payne went on, 'they would probably find a household teeming with suspects – that's what Penelope might be banking on. Sir Seymour may be one of those highly murderable baronets one used to find in detective stories of the well-bred "English" kind. I am sure you could come up with some highly original title?'

'*Death of a Baronet?*'

'I came across a Bettina Tradescant, style editor of a small, rather smart magazine called *Dazzle*. There is a picture of her on the internet, which shows her wearing what looks like a dead pheasant on her head and purple lipstick. I wonder if she is a relative. She looks sinister, in an Edith

Sitwell kind of way, with a dash of the late Isabella Blow thrown in.'

'Why did Penelope swap the capsules at Claridge's? Such a public place. Surely she must have had the opportunity to do it at home? Unless she had absolutely no access to her husband's room. Or else it was a last-minute decision,' Antonia mused. 'Perhaps something happened – some kind of emergency that necessitated Sir Seymour's death? Can you think of a good reason why she should wish him dead?'

'Well, she is young and beautiful while he is an unattractive old thing. He is terribly rich. When he snuffs it, she bags all the dosh – and she continues calling herself Lady Tradescant. I believe titles still matter to some people.' Payne glanced at his watch. 'Do let me try to phone Mayholme Manor and see if I could warn Sir Seymour against swallowing the lethal capsule, if he hasn't already done so, that is. I don't mind making a fool of myself. Better safe than sorry.'

'You don't think you should inform the police?'

'No. Not yet. If it turned out to be a mare's nest, as it well might, I'd be in trouble. Lady Tradescant could take me to court, you know. I could be charged with intrusion into privacy, libel and God knows what else.'

'We have this unfortunate thing about uncovering intrigue.' Antonia sighed. 'We aren't really suited to frequent what is known as "normal society".'

'Jolly well put. We despise normal society. We cock a snook at it.'

'No, we don't. Not really.'

'We excel ourselves in rather bizarre imaginings,' said Pyane. 'Bizarre imaginings have become an integral part of our daily existence. Most of our best friends suspect us of snooping on them.'

'We haven't got any best friends, Hugh.'

'Well, we've got each other.' Major Payne kissed her. 'I wonder what Jesty's doing.'

'Do you suppose he is up to something?'

'I rather think he might be. He isn't the type to let go, or so everybody says.' Payne walked across to the telephone and lifted the receiver, while consulting the sheet in his hand.

Antonia's heart started beating faster. She was aware of a current of suspense generating itself in the room . . .

'There are two numbers given on the Mayholme Manor website – a switchboard and the Master's. This is the switchboard now.' Payne shook his head. 'Nobody answers . . . No signal, actually . . . How curious . . . Let me try again . . . No, nothing . . . Dead silence.'

'Try the Master.'

There was a pause. 'How odd – again, no signal.'

'No signal?'

'No. Both lines are dead.' Major Payne put down the receiver. 'Well, that's that. I am sure there is a perfectly innocent reason for it. I'll try again tomorrow morning.'

'Tomorrow might be too late.' Antonia bit her lip. 'Sorry, I didn't mean to say that.'

'To imagine the worst is somehow to guard against it really happening,' Payne said sententiously. 'Things are hardly ever as bad as you think they will be but often very bad when you anticipate nothing much. Haven't you noticed?'

6

Blackmail

Her phone rang at ten minutes to midnight.

Putting down her glass of whisky, she picked up the receiver.

'Lady Tradescant?'

'Speaking.'

'I sincerely hope you will allow me to call you "Penelope"?'

'Who is that?'

'An admirer. My name would mean nothing to you. You don't know me, though our eyes did meet today, for a split second.'

'I am afraid I don't know what you are talking about.'

'I am sure you do. You have a lovely voice. I haven't been able to get you out of my mind, you know.'

'How do you know my name?'

'I heard your husband address you. Earlier today. This afternoon, to be precise. At Claridge's.'

He heard her draw in her breath sharply. The girlie was losing her poise, eh? 'You have nothing to fear from me,' he said slowly.

'I don't know what you mean. How did you find my phone number?'

'Where there's a will, there's a way.'

'How did you know that that was my husband?'

Captain Jesty smiled. He had started enjoying his power

over her. It acted as an aphrodisiac. *Not* that he needed an aphrodisiac. He reached out for the bottle and poured himself another glass of champagne.

'Questions, questions. How did I know? Let me see. Well, I made some inquiries. I have my spies at Claridge's. I hope you won't think it boastful of me, but I enjoy a certain popularity, mainly thanks to the generous baksheesh and racing tips I bestow on some of the waiters. It was one of them who carried out some checks for me. A most enterprising little chap. You have a Claridge's account, correct? You have provided an address and a phone number. A highly desirable address, I must say. You enjoy life among the fleshpots? Hello? Are you still there?'

'I am still here,' she said.

'You and your husband – who is thirty-six years your senior – have been to Claridge's for tea and dinner a number of times. You are both well known to the staff and, as it transpires, the object of some wide-eyed fascination. People love outrageous age disparities between spouses, since it is invariably linked to big money. Look at the unfortunate Anna Nicole Smith. What else do I know?' Jesty sipped champagne. 'You are a former *Harper's* model. Your origins are veiled in mystery. You appear to have been to a decent school, but you have always been something of a wild girl. You get bored easily. You have lived in sin with a racing driver, an actor and a footballer – before you bagged the eighteenth baronet.'

'The waiters couldn't have told you all that.'

'No, of course not. The waiters, as you so prosaically put it, have their limitations. But they provided me with leads – started me off on my quest. I did my own research after I got back home. These days there is very little one cannot find.'

'The internet,' she said after a pause.

'Your maiden name is St Loup – rather Proustian, what? You have some French blood, apparently. Unless you made it all up – to impress the eighteenth baronet? Penelope St Loup – dashed euphonic – dashed memorable. Pictures of you going back to your modelling days are available on the net. In all of them, without exception, you look stunning. As a matter of fact,' Jesty went on, 'I am looking at one of your pictures at this very moment. I downloaded it, printed it and I intend to have it pinned above my pillow tonight. If you only knew what I'd like to –'

Penelope interrupted. 'Which of the two are you? The fair-haired one or the one with the moustache?'

'Now you are talking. I rather like your matter-of-fact tone. I am the one with the moustache. The dashing one.' Jesty frowned. 'Damned unfortunate that the fair-haired one – I mean, that particular brother officer of mine – turned up when he did. The chap's a major pain.' He laughed at his joke. 'You didn't get that, did you? No, you couldn't have.'

'I didn't get what?'

'Never mind. Even more unfortunate that I told him what I saw you do. Damn. Should have kept my mouth shut.'

'What exactly did you see me do?'

Jesty's eyes opened wide. 'Swap the capsules, of course. What else? Poison for medicine, correct?'

'Aren't you being a little presumptuous?'

'I don't think so. What else could it have been? Powdered monkey glands? Bicarbonate of soda? You wouldn't still be talking to me if you weren't a little afraid of me. You'd have rung off by now. You'd have threatened me with the police. Or maybe you have started playing some game of your own? Well, I like games.'

She said, 'You wouldn't believe me if I told you you'd got the wrong end of the stick altogether?'

'I wouldn't. You looked guilty as hell. But I would very much like to hear your version of events. You have such a lovely voice. I have fallen for you in a bloody big way. I want us to meet. Tonight, if possible? I am not famous for my patience.'

'N-not tonight.'

Jesty smiled again. The girlie was weakening. 'Perhaps

not. I suppose you are expecting to hear the terrible news any moment? Your husband is dead, must be. Unless he forgot to take the capsule? *That* would be a bore, wouldn't it? You must be on tenterhooks. You poor girl. I will take good care of you, I promise. Tomorrow then, it's *got* to be tomorrow. We could have lunch somewhere smart. I am mad about you.' He poured more champagne into his glass. 'Don't tell me you would rather wait till after your husband's funeral.'

7

Beneath a Waning Moon

Quarter past midnight. Somebody walking on my grave, Bettina Tradescant thought. She looked up from her computer screen. Something, she knew, was about to happen – or had already happened.

Bettina inserted a cigarette into a short jet-black holder. She lit the cigarette. She wore a perfectly pressed white shirt buttoned to the top, collar studs and black trousers with a knife-edge crease. About ten minutes earlier she had worn a jacket with a fur-trimmed collar, which seemed to raise her shoulders, and a skirt that reached below the calf and created the effect of elegant but painful attenuation. Since coming back home, she had already worn five different outfits, among them a drum majorette ensemble in white and gold and a silver off-the-shoulder evening dress. At one point she had put on a pale blue toque with a bunch of pink and yellow primulas. She was a compulsive dresser and restless experimenter, forever searching for the right sartorial coup. She had once had a real obsession with all things feathery; no less a man than designer Valentino had told her that he could find her in London by just following the trail of feathers. She found the past a never-ending source of inspiration. At the moment she sported an Edwardian coiffure: hair piled high on her head to form a bird's nest – that was a wig, one of ten. Not even her bitterest enemy – she had a real knack for making enemies – would have dared call her a 'clichéd fashionista'.

Bettina suffered from insomnia. She called it her *tango nocturne*. She couldn't remember when it was the last time she had managed to have a proper snooze. There were people who went off the moment their heads hit the pillow. How she envied them. Her nerves were not in a good state. Her thoughts kept turning to her brother. It always happened at this time of night. Random memories as usual. Seymour teasing her mercilessly when they were children, calling her silly names – Seymour pushing her into the pond at Tradescant Hall – Seymour dressing up as her, doing a perfect imitation of her as a party piece, making their parents' guests scream with laughter while she had sat crying in her room.

(She would love to be able to dress up as Seymour – but that would mean she'd have to shave all her hair – Seymour was getting to be as bald as a coot!)

Seymour had always treated her with senseless malignancy. He'd always managed to reduce her to cowering and sullen states. Always, always, always.

Seymour was very much like the woods in *Titus Andronicus* – ruthless, dreadful, deaf and dull. Well, if he hadn't been such a colossal scrooge, if he had given her the money she needed so badly, she might have been able to forgive and forget. What Bettina wanted more than anything in the world was enough capital for her to start her own fashion magazine. Seymour could well afford it. He had after all received the bulk of their late father's estate and his was a vast wealth. More than four thousand acres of Shropshire. He didn't seem to be doing anything with it, apart from making donations to his 'retreat'. It wasn't as though he was pampering poor Penelope . . .

Bettina looked down at the ring on her fourth finger and sighed. If *only* it were the authentic one and not a mere copy. She was mad about jewellery – though not as mad as Papa had been. She gave a twisted smile. Goodness – those photos of Papa! Mama had destroyed most of them. Papa had had quite a thing about jewellery. A veritable fetish. Papa could have given the ring to her but he hadn't – he'd given it to Seymour – *like everything else.*

Bettina sighed. 'My darling Wallis,' she said and kissed the ring. 'You knew how to do things.' But of course the ring was not the real Wallis. She sighed again.

Bettina glanced up at the computer screen, at what she had written:

Greys, pinks and lace are set to dominate women's wardrobes this season. We may even see the retro trends of the 1930s and 1940s. Buttoned skirts and exaggerated silhouettes will make a comeback. Minimal to smaller prints will be in vogue and a lot of geometry. Yellow gold and diamonds will continue to domin-ate . . . Long hair with cascading waves and soft curls . . . The Veronica Lake look . . .

Bettina stubbed out the cigarette. She couldn't concen-trate. That morning, at some unearthly hour, an anonym-ous voice on the phone had told her she was no longer a person, she was a *concept*, which, unless she'd dreamt it, had been rather flattering. (Her reading Bernard-Henri Lévy might have had something to do with it.) Then Penelope had rung to say Mowbray had pitched herself from the top of their house and the police were coming. Bettina had been in a meeting, so she hadn't been able to ask any questions. Penelope had sounded extremely upset. The poor sweet girl. What she had had to put up with! Being married to Seymour must be the ultimate nightmare. It was a good thing Penelope had – distractions. The idea of a cuckolded Seymour cheered Bettina up. She had tried to ring Penelope later on, but there had been no answer. Perhaps Penelope was with somebody . . .

She yawned and, as she did so, happened to glance back at the computer screen. She saw Seymour's face staring back at her, the mouth extended prodigiously in an agon-ized scream. Seymour appeared in great pain.

Bettina leant back in her chair and sat very still. People who didn't understand that sort of thing would have blamed her imagination – they might even say she was slightly mad. Some fools, she felt sure, might even have argued that it was her own face she had seen – wasn't a yawn very much like a silent sort of scream?

Well, her brother's toucan beak of a nose was very much like hers and they had generally similar casts of features. Not so surprising given that they were fraternal twins. And as it often happened with twins, there existed between them a powerful psychic link, which, since it always made her shiver first, Bettina had come to call the 'chill'. Only Bettina took the chill seriously. Her brother did seem aware of *something*, but he tended to attribute it dismissively to indigestion. She could have done without the psychic link – life was complicated enough as it was – but there was nothing she could do about it.

Their faces were far from prepossessing, though Bettina had always managed to render her ugliness as strikingly picturesque as possible. She pinched the bags under her eyes, pulled a droll grimace, then tugged at her right cheek. She might have plastic surgery when she turned seventy, which was in November. Plastic surgery would destroy the likeness once and for all. It would also, she hoped, make her appear twenty years younger.

Twenty-five to one. Bettina shivered. She invariably felt the chill each time something bad befell her brother – it had happened not so long ago, on the afternoon he had been rushed to hospital with his foot infection. The initial prognosis had been bad. Her brother's condition had been described as 'serious'. She had really hoped and prayed then he might die of blood poisoning.

She clutched at her bosom. She gasped. The chill had cut through her, worse than ever before! Seymour, she felt sure, was either gravely ill, was breathing his last, or indeed was already dead.

'Arise, Sir Nicholas,' said the blonde girl and she laid her hairbrush with great gravity upon his left shoulder.

'It is "Sir Tradescant", actually,' the dark girl corrected her. She put her arm around Nicholas Tradescant's neck.

'It's Sir Nicholas!'

'No, it's Sir Tradescant!' The dark girl kissed him. 'Isn't that right, Nicky?'

'Wait a sec. Don't tell her, Nicky. Listen to this. *Let Nicky marry whoever's got it right.* How about it? Well?' They both turned eagerly towards him.

'It's Sir Nicholas,' he said a little wearily. 'Or rather would be. Heaven knows if I'd live to see the day.'

'Of course you would, my darling.' The dark girl kissed him again.

'My father seems determined to live for ever.'

'No one can live for ever. It's not as though your father is a vampire, is it? He is an old man.'

'Not that old.'

'Perhaps we could bump him off for you? We could, couldn't we?' The dark girl addressed the blonde one. They giggled.

'Think of the headlines,' the blonde girl said. '*Homicidal Hookers.*'

'Don't say "hookers" – *so* common. There won't be any headlines. We'll be so clever about it, we'll never get caught!'

'Sir *Nicholas.* I was right! I know all about the gentry.' The blonde girl nodded. 'I can even speak like them.'

'No, you can't,' the dark girl said. 'You only *think* you can.'

'I would make a much better Lady Tradescant than *you.*'

'No, you wouldn't.'

'*Girls,*' Nicholas Tradescant said in a warning voice.

'Are you going to marry her now, Nicky?'

'Of course he will marry me. Everybody knows that gentlemen prefer blondes.'

'But marry brunettes! There's a book about it, so there.'

Nicholas Tradescant gave a sigh. 'Actually, I am already married, you know that perfectly well.'

40

'Yes, but you said you felt like divorcing your wife. The 'orrible Olivia. I can't believe you haven't divorced her yet. I really can't.'

'It's not as easy as you might think,' he murmured.

'Why not?'

The blonde girl said, 'She's been nagging at you, making you miserable about all sorts of things. She's already ordered writing paper with *Sir Nicholas* at the top, hasn't she? You told us about it last time. She's so desperate to become "Lady Tradescant". She's been making you dine with people you don't like. Lords and ladies and barons and dukes.'

'With the *gentry*,' the dark girl said. She gave a dreamy sigh.

'The gentry are dull, aren't they?'

He nodded. 'I am afraid they are, rather. Where we live at least.'

'The *gentry*,' the dark girl repeated wistfully. 'You live with the gentry. I'd love to live with the gentry. I wouldn't mind them being dull.'

'Nicky can't stand the gentry. That's why you are with us now, aren't you, Nicky? We give you a good time.' The blonde girl cast an anxious glance at him. 'We give you a good time, don't we, Nicky?'

'You certainly do.'

'We are extremely expensive, though. Aren't we?'

'It doesn't matter,' he said.

'We know how to give a gent a good time,' the dark girl said gravely.

'Don't be coarse. Nicky is the only real gent we see. All the others are rich businessmen and jumped-up knights and men who married money.'

'Businessmen,' the dark girl said with a shiver. 'No class.'

'They order pizzas by phone and take their laptops to bed with them!' The blonde girl sounded outraged.

'What did you tell Olivia? Where does she think you are now? At your club in London?'

'Yes.' He looked at his watch. Good God, half past midnight already?

Both girls giggled, then the blonde asked: 'What if she phoned the club? What if she asked to speak to you? Won't you be in trouble?'

'They know exactly what to tell her if she does phone. They've got instructions. Listen, girls, on no account must you ring my home number again, promise?'

'Promise. Cross my heart and hope to die. I only did it once,' the dark girl said. 'I was missing you.'

'She always does things without thinking – always – and they say it's blondes who are dumb,' the blonde girl said.

'Was Olivia 'orrible to you, Nicky?'

'Well, she said nothing, but she just *looked* at me.'

'Poor Nicky! I am so sorry for getting you into trouble!'

The blonde girl asked after a pause, 'Which one of us do you like better, Nicky?'

'I like you equally well,' Nicholas Tradescant said truthfully.

'I don't think that's possible!'

Nicholas Tradescant held up his forefinger. 'Comparisons are odious. We agreed we wouldn't have that sort of talk, didn't we?'

'Let's loosen up,' the dark girl said. 'Let's all have a drink.'

She went to the sideboard and started examining the array of drinks. They were at a rather exclusive moat hotel in Surrey. They had been there on three previous occasions, so they felt quite at home. A minute later the blonde girl was distributing drinks.

There was a pause as they drank. They sat on the bed, the two girls on either side of him. 'I bet Nicky will forget all about us once his dad dies and he gets the title,' the dark girl said with a sigh.

'Will you, Nicky?'

'No, of course not.' Warmed by the drink, he smiled. 'I might even marry the two of you.'

'You would start one of those – what do you call them? Harems? Sheikhs have them.'

'Yes. You will be my two-girl harem. But you must promise not to fight,' he said, falling into the spirit of the thing. 'If you fight, I'll kick you out.'

'We can't do that sort of thing in England, can we? We'll need to become Muslims first.'

'Not necessarily,' the blonde girl said. 'We could only live together. Like Hugh Hefner. Hugh Hefner lives with *three* girlfriends, I read in a mag.'

Nicholas frowned. 'Is that the *Playboy* chap?'

'Actually, there's an English lord – a viscount – who does that too,' the dark girl said. 'What was his name now? There was a programme on the telly about it once. He's got *wifelets*. Lots of wifelets. All the walls at his country estate are covered in dirty pictures. He's got a beard and wears fancy waistcoats.'

'Weymouth.' Nicholas sipped more whisky.

'We could be Nicky's wifelets!' The blonde girl clapped her hands.

'We were with an Arab sheikh once. Oh, it was dreadful, wasn't it?'

'It was dreadful,' the blonde girl agreed. 'No class. Never again.'

Never again, Olivia Tradescant thought. Never again shall I humiliate myself ringing up White's and asking to speak to him. The cheating bastard. Did he really imagine he had managed to deceive her? She knew very well the explanation she had been given as to why Nicholas couldn't come to the phone was a fabrication. Did he bribe people to tell her tales? How sordid. Stooping so low. He claimed he had broken his mobile and was still waiting for a replacement. That was a lie, of course. Did he think she was a fool?

Where *was* he? Who was he with? Well, she didn't want to know, though she could very well guess. That phone call. A young person's voice asking rather perkily to speak to 'Nicky'. An extremely common voice. The exchange had given Olivia such a frightful headache, she'd had to spend two hours lying down in her bedroom. Some girl. At least it hadn't been a *boy*. Thank God for small mercies. Olivia gave a mirthless laugh. The next moment her eyes filled with tears. She pressed her handkerchief against her lips.

Olivia was sitting in bed, a book across her lap. It was the latest P.D. James; however, she hadn't read a single sentence since she had opened it. She felt exhausted but sleep was out of the question. Perhaps if she were to start reading, she might be able to go to sleep? That was the effect P.D. James often had on her.

Olivia was at the end of her tether. Nicholas was becoming quite impossible. He didn't even pretend to like her. He treated her abysmally. What was it he said about the garden party at Fane Park, which she had actually quite enjoyed? *Two ghastly hours of sheer banality, during which I heard not one single remark worthy of remembrance.* Olivia felt certain he said these things on purpose, to upset her. She pressed her handkerchief against her lips once more. If perhaps they had had children, things might have been different?

Nicholas found himself at a loose end too often, that was the trouble. His life lacked purpose and direction. Now, if they were in the country *permanently*, if they lived at Tradescant Hall and Nicholas had a position to maintain, things might be different. *Yes.* It would be an entirely different kettle of fish. Nicholas would be kept busy. He wouldn't like it, but he would soon enough accept his various responsibilities.

Nicholas had a sense of duty, she must give him that. He wouldn't be able to keep rushing to London all the time, no matter what delights awaited him there. (Olivia's Roman nose wrinkled fastidiously.) Besides, he would soon be fifty. One didn't expect the calls of the flesh to continue for much longer, though of course there was no guarantee – men were different from women in that respect – look at her father-in-law, making a fool of himself in his sixties marrying that girl! Still, she felt confident that once her husband became 'Sir Nicholas Tradescant', things would change, gradually, if not overnight . . . When would that be, though?

Olivia looked at the clock as though in anticipation of an answer. Twenty to one. Divorce was not something she was prepared to consider. No, divorce was most certainly *not* on her agenda. But her father-in-law might live to be a hundred. Tradescants were notoriously long-lived. I wish he were dead, she thought. Oddly enough, it was her father-in-law's housekeeper who had died that morning. Mrs Melton – some such name. (Olivia could never remember the names of servants.) The woman seemed to have killed herself. Mrs Mowbray, that was it. Her father-in-law had made a complete recovery, or so she'd been given to understand . . . He would never kill himself . . . Never . . . Could he perhaps be . . . *assisted*? A death could be made to look like suicide . . .

Olivia Tradescant must have dozed off because the next moment she heard herself say, 'It wouldn't really matter. He never seems frightfully happy, so it would be an act of kindness, helping him out of his misery.'

She appeared to be talking to an accomplice of some sort, a shadowy figure whose face she couldn't see.

8

The Rendezvous

The girlie had said yes in the end, as he had been sure she would. She didn't want trouble. Of course she didn't. She knew perfectly well which side of her bread was buttered. She was no fool. She knew what would happen if she tried to be difficult, if she refused to meet him. She knew that all he needed to do was pick up the phone and ring Scotland Yard. The poisoning of Sir Seymour Tradescant, with his great wealth and links to royalty, would be front-page news and the police would certainly listen to what he had so say. She was well aware that he could provide the police with the kind of detail that would leave little doubt that he was a plausible eyewitness.

He could tell the police the exact time Penelope and the pantaloon – Sir Seymour – had been at Claridge's. He could describe the silver box. He could tell them about the reference to Maybrick Manor – or something very similar – and to the 'Master' – about the request for a cab too. When the police did check with Claridge's, his story would be corroborated by the waiters and the maître d' . . . Payne too would be able to testify to the terrified expression on Penelope's face . . . She looks a picture of guilt, Payne had said . . . Payne looked and sounded trustworthy . . . Payne would make a perfect witness . . . *Yes.*

No, the girlie couldn't risk it.

Jesty went on examining his reflection in the mirror. He

opened his eyes wide, then narrowed them. He bared his teeth in a wolfish smile. He gave himself a wink. He looked good, but then he always looked good. He smelled good too. This new aftershave was quite something. He regarded his moustache critically. Not exactly what he expected – well, not yet – he needed to be patient. Moustaches were funny things. Must phone Xandra, he suddenly remembered. Must tell her I couldn't see her today. Couldn't see her ever again, perhaps. She would be terribly disappointed of course – nay, inconsolable. He smiled. He enjoyed being pined after. He adored being adored. He rather liked the idea of breaking hearts too.

The death of Sir Seymour Tradescant was yet to be announced. Jesty had got up early and bought all the morning papers, starting with the tabloids; he had also glanced at the news online, but there was nothing about it. The only deaths the *Mirror* announced were a tragic accident (family in Fife perishing in fire) and a suspected suicide (woman chucking herself from top of house in Mayfair). Nothing on the box or the radio either.

Curious. Perhaps it was too soon? Perhaps the Tradescant family were managing to keep Sir Seymour's unnatural end out of the news. If you had money and influence you could do that sort of thing, he imagined, though they couldn't conceal the death *indefinitely*. Could the police have decided not to release any information while they were conducting their investigation? Maybe it would be in the later edition of the *Evening Standard.*

What was it the girlie had said? Something about him 'getting the wrong end of the stick'? What the devil did she mean by that? She was clearly trying to wriggle out of it. The wrong end of the stick my foot, Jesty thought. Could his eyes have deceived him? No. Of course not. Out of the question. The girlie swapped the capsules all right. What else if not poison could there have been inside the capsule? The fact that she had agreed to a rendezvous was as good an admission of guilt as any.

He could have saved the pantaloon's life, he supposed. He could have dashed out – caught up with them before they reached the exit – tapped the pantaloon on the shoulder and advised him not to take the capsule if he wished to remain in good health – *flush it down the loo, old boy, or better, have it analysed by one of those toxicologist fellows.*

Why hadn't he done it? Why hadn't he run after the pantaloon? Had he feared making a fool of himself? No, that was not the reason. He hadn't warned the pantaloon because – if he had to be perfectly honest – because he'd *wanted* the pantaloon to swallow the poison and die . . . Yes . . . He'd wished the pantaloon poisoned, so that he, Jesty, could have the girlie to himself, at his mercy. To do with her as he jolly well pleased. He'd envisaged establishing some sort of a hold over her. How curious. Jesty frowned. Did that mean then that he'd known, instinctively known, even at that early stage that the pantaloon was the girlie's aged husband? Yes. He seemed to have a sixth sense about that sort of thing.

Jesty's hand went up to his moustache. He had made love to all sorts of women – from barmaids to baronesses – but never before to a poisoner. Or if he had, he wasn't aware of the fact. The idea of making love to a poisoner was oddly titillating. He licked his lips. Was the girlie likely to try the same trick on him? Slip something into his drink – attempt to eliminate the witness, eh? That was said to have been Lucrezia Borgia's favourite party trick. Jesty smiled. Could he possibly be in *danger*? Well, he was perfectly capable of taking care of himself.

He would watch her like the proverbial hawk.

Io son colei che ognuno al mondo brama . . .
The line popped into his head the moment he set eyes on her across the dining hall. He had little Italian but he knew how it translated. 'I am she whom everyone in the world longs for.' That, as it happened, had been the inscription below an etching he had seen once during a

holiday in Venice, inside some cathedral or other. What was the etching called? *An Allegory of Fame.* Something on those lines.

'The lady at the corner table is expecting me. I booked the table this morning,' he told the waiter, his eyes on Penelope Tradescant.

'What name?'

'Jesty.'

'Captain Jesty? For one o'clock? Of course. This way, sir.'

With its grand sweeping curving staircase and illumin-ated skylight running the complete length of the restaur-ant, Quaglino's had an air of romance about it, also of the theatre. Appropriate on both counts, Jesty thought. He had no doubt that the girlie was a good actress.

The etching he had seen in Venice showed an extremely enticing woman, a proper tigress, who, he assumed, was Fame, flanked by two other figures: an insipid-looking angel, blowing a trumpet and holding a wreath while expertly standing on a sphere, and what looked like a lascivious satyr who was stretching his greedy paws out towards Fame's breasts. Oddly enough Fame was not gaz-ing at the angel, the representation of all that was good and pure and noble and so on, as one might have expected her to, but towards the satyr, the symbol of evil. Was it poss-ible that Fame was enamoured of the satyr? Jesty felt encouraged, thinking about it.

Penelope Tradescant's light brown hair fell in a gleam-ing wave down to her shoulders, her eyes were cosmetic-ally enlarged and darkened, her Chanel suit was a sharp, animated green, the lapels a striking deep kind of red that brought to mind morello cherries, her perfectly shaped mouth a lighter shade of the same colour. The faintly flushed skin of her face wasn't just peachy, it looked softer than velvet. Jesty was sure it would feel soft to the touch too. He had been with some very beautiful women in his time, but nothing like this one. What would it be like to run one's forefinger down her cheek and trace her lips?

She had clearly taken the trouble. That was very interesting. She hadn't been exactly forthcoming on the phone, so why had she taken the trouble now? Well, wishful thinking aside, it seemed she was prepared to play ball. She *wanted* him to fancy her. Or, rather, she meant him to fancy her even more. She had made herself irresistibly attractive. She was trying to mollify him. *Whatever you say – anything – please, don't tell the police –*

She was ready to give herself to him.

'Lady Tradescant,' he said as he stood stiffly beside the table.

Damn. He had meant to address her less formally, as 'Penelope'. Too late now.

'Captain Jesty.'

'Hope you haven't been waiting long?' His voice, he noticed with astonishment, sounded different, not like his voice at all. His throat felt extremely dry. How ridiculous his name sounded on her lips – why hadn't he noticed it before?

'Not at all. Five minutes at the most. I like to arrive early. Won't you sit down?'

She looked calm and composed – serene – ever so slightly bored, perhaps. She appeared to be taking control of the situation. He had envisaged her looking tense, nervous, on edge. He hadn't expected her to sit smiling graciously at him. He had imagined she'd be casting furtive glances around, that she'd be worried lest she be seen by someone who knew her or her husband, but no – her eyes met his levelly. Rum, to say the least. He was not sure he liked it.

It didn't seem as though she had been called to identify her dead husband's body. She most certainly did not look as though she had been up since the small hours of the morning, paying visits to the mortuary, calling her solicitor, answering questions from the police. She didn't have a recently widowed air about her. Not a scrap of black on her. Had she used some untraceable poison? Did such poisons exist? Or maybe Sir Seymour's death hadn't been discovered yet? Jesty glanced at his watch. There was also the possibility that the bloody pantaloon had forgotten to take the capsule. Which meant he was still alive. What was she doing here then, if that indeed were the case?

He sat down. He was aware of his heart racing. She seemed to expect him to start the ball rolling, but he felt tongue-tied. That was unlike him. He had always been at ease with the fair sex, man of the world par excellence, it didn't matter whether he was in the company of countesses or call-girls, he'd had them all, he never lost his poise –

'Lovely colour,' he heard himself say. 'I mean your lapels. Damned attractive. A curious shade of red. Not exactly red, is it?' At once he felt like kicking himself. Man of the world? Gabbling like some gauche schoolboy!

'It's called "magenta". Did you know that Napoleon III invented the colour magenta from the mixture of mud and blood on the battlefield of that name?' She smiled. 'As a military man, you must be familiar with the battle of Magenta?'

'Magenta. Yes. To be sure.' Jesty had only the vaguest recollection of having read about the battle at Magenta. 'Blood and mud, did you say?'

'Blood and mud. You wouldn't think it, would you? It is hard to associate a smooth rich colour like this with filth and violence.' She stroked her lapels with her hand.

He swallowed. Such a lovely hand, like everything else about her. Filth and violence. The last thing one would have associated with her. She was perfection personified. She was a goddess. How could he have ever thought of her as a 'girlie'? His eyes remained fixed on her lips – strayed down to her hands – then back to her lips. He wondered if he was falling in love with her . . .

'Are you ready to order? Madam? Sir?' The waiter was standing beside their table, very correct, bending slightly from the waist.

'Yes, of course. What would you like to have?' Jesty asked.

'They have king prawns *al forno*,' he heard her murmur over the menu.

Later Jesty was to tell Payne that he had absolutely no recollection of what they had had to eat or drink. He had chosen something with lots of vodka in it for himself, to give himself courage, that much he remembered. He'd hardly eaten anything, in fact. It had never happened to him before, that sort of thing. He believed he was in love with her, yes. Head over heels.

Absurd, he thought defiantly. Tommy rot. Absolute rubbish. He'd never been in love, never. Not even in his adolescence. He had been tormented by desire, lust he was jolly well familiar with, but what he felt now was – well, it was something completely different, dammit. A fluttering in his stomach – a great tension in his chest – the ridiculous urge to prostrate himself at her feet – *tendresse*. Was that what *tendresse* felt like? So far he'd only heard such sensations described; he'd never experienced them at first hand. He'd always despised chaps who went on about being head over heels in love with some girlie.

All I want is to get her between the sheets, Jesty reminded himself.

No – not true – he wanted more than that. *Much* more. I want to spend the rest of my life with her, he thought, appalled.

Jesty was experiencing an odd sense of dislocation. It felt as though there were two people inside him. Him – and, well, bloody *not*-him. If such a thing were possible. She's bewitched me, he thought in a sudden panic. I am under Penelope's spell. I am her slave for life. He made a desperate effort to pull himself together.

'Such a warm day,' Penelope Tradescant said. 'Much warmer than yesterday, wouldn't you say?'

'Yes. You are absolutely right.'

'Have you come a long way, Captain Jesty?'

'Albany.'

'That's not too far.'

'Not too far, no.'

'Albany or *the* Albany?'

'Both are permissible. I prefer Albany. The Albany sounds too much like a public house.'

'It does. How funny. You'll never believe this, but I have taken quite a fancy to the waiters. Look at them! Sombre, attentive and perfectly charming.' She smiled. 'Like – like those Florentines Dante meets in Purgatory.'

Her expression, he imagined, was ironic but not unfriendly. Once more he glanced down at her hand. He wanted to reach out and take hold of it in his but didn't dare. She was looking at him in a quizzical manner now. He had the idea she was assessing him – appraising him. He was put in mind of those princesses in fairy tales who set their suitor some impossible task. I'd do anything for her, he thought. *Anything.*

'Have you been to Italy, Captain Jesty?'

'I have. To Rome and to Venice. Also to Tuscany. A bloody marvellous place, Tuscany.'

'We have a villa in the South of France but I try to go to Italy whenever I can.'

'Do you? Italy is jolly amazing.'

'I agree.' She nodded.

'All those cathedrals. All those wines. And of course the weather. All bloody marvellous.'

Small talk, he thought incredulously. We are making small talk. Albany, the Albany, cathedrals, the weather –

It was all wrong. He'd allowed her to get the upper hand. He'd forgotten that it was he who held the trump card. He needed to take decisive action, dammit. He had always prided himself on being a man of action. Would be madness to waste any more time. He was a soldier, dammit.

He cleared his throat.

9

The Turn of the Screw

'You ...'

'Yes, Captain Jesty?'

'You mustn't be afraid of me,' he said in a low voice. That was not what he intended to say, but the idea that she might be afraid of him was unbearable. He was anxious to reassure her.

'I am not afraid of you. Whatever gave you the idea?'

'You know perfectly well what.'

'I believe there has been a misunderstanding –'

'I want you to know that your secret is safe with me.'

'What secret?'

'The capsule, dammit. The little box. At Claridge's. You poisoned your husband,' he blurted out.

There was a pause. Her expression did not change.

'You believe I poisoned my husband.' Her voice was oddly uninflected. She had leant slightly forward and at the same time put her hands on her lap. Out of my reach, he thought with a pang, also out of my sight. This saddened him – it saddened him so much, he felt the sudden urge to blub. Then he felt annoyed, with himself, as well as with her. He felt blood rushing into his face. He pursed his lips.

'I am convinced of it,' he said.

'Well, you are very much mistaken. I am afraid you've got the wrong end of the stick altogether,' she said briskly. 'My husband is alive. He is fine. You could go and check, if you like. I could give you the address.'

'You mean he didn't take the capsule?' Damn, he thought.

'As a matter of fact he did take the capsule. Last night, after dinner. I specifically asked him about it.' She gave a little smile. 'Seymour can be a bit absent-minded, it's his age, I suppose, but it was important that he complete the course. That was what the doctor said.'

'What course?'

'Antibiotics. The capsules contained an antibiotic. There are no more capsules now. He took them for his big toe.' She was speaking slowly now, as though to a child. 'Seymour's had a bad infection, but he has managed to recover. He is no longer in pain. He is enjoying his stay at Mayholme Manor immensely. He said so.'

'Mayholme Manor,' Jesty echoed.

'Yes. Also known as Dutton's Retreat. Place in Dulwich. I personally think it is the spookiest of places, but that's neither here nor there.' She smiled again. 'I spoke to Seymour on the phone just before I came here. He's had a good English breakfast and been for a walk. He still uses his stick, but he said he could have done without it. He was looking forward to a game of chess with the Master. He believes the antibiotics have done the trick, that was how he put it. You don't seem to believe me?'

'You swapped the capsules,' he said stubbornly. 'I saw you do it. You did it the moment your husband's back was turned. You glanced round first. You did it fast. You opened the silver box which your husband had left on the table, then you took a capsule from your bag. You looked furtive as hell.'

'Why were you spying on me?'

'When you realized I had seen you,' he went on, 'you panicked. You looked terrified. Your face was a picture of guilt.'

'You don't think you might have imagined things?'

He felt anger surge through him. Good! That was a damned sight healthier than moping over her. 'Payne saw you too,' he said.

'Payne? Oh yes. Your fellow soldier. He also saw me exchange the capsules?'

'No. *No*. He turned up a couple of minutes later. After you had done the substitution. I told him about it. But he saw the guilty expression on your face all right.'

'Both of you had been to a regimental reunion,' she said. 'It was a regimental reunion, wasn't it? That was what one of the waiters told us. You were making such a dreadful noise that I asked what was going on. You all seemed to have had a little bit too much to drink, correct?'

'What are you driving at?'

'You were a little the worse for wear. The evidence of your eyes was perhaps not particularly reliable? It's a well-known fact that –'

'What absolute rot! Neither of us was drunk. Are you suggesting we had some kind of hallucination? The two of us? *At the same time?*'

'Mass hallucinations happen more often than people imagine.'

This infuriated him. By now they should have been on first-name terms, he thought bitterly – he should have been holding her hand and making arrangements for later on!

'I could get you into trouble if I chose and you know it perfectly well.' Jesty spoke through gritted teeth. He tried hard not to raise his voice. 'I could destroy you. All right. Say, your husband didn't take the poison, for whatever reason. I could still tell him exactly what I saw.'

'Seymour wouldn't believe you.'

'If you'd been innocent, you wouldn't have agreed to meet me. It makes no sense. Why did you agree to meet me?'

'I believe in clearing up misunderstandings.'

'There's been no misunderstanding.'

She bowed her head. Several moments passed. He wondered what she would come up with now. Would she get up and leave without another word? Had he blown his chances with her? What should he do next, if that did happen? Great heaviness descended upon him. He couldn't really see himself making his way to the police station and reporting the capsule-swapping incident at Claridge's. They would make him write it all down, which would be a bore. They would ask him all sorts of questions. *And what exactly were you doing behind the potted palm, Captain Jesty?* He knew he didn't invite immediate trust –

He started up. Penelope Tradescant was speaking.

'Very well. I see you are a determined man, Captain Jesty, so I will tell you the truth. I'll tell you the whole truth. I don't think I have any other option. I am afraid you misread the situation completely. No, listen, *please*. I don't blame you. It is rather a complicated story. I hope you understand. Some of it is quite distressing. There are other people involved.' She gave a weary sigh. 'I was rather hoping I wouldn't have to tell anyone about it.'

'You admit that you swapped the capsules?' He picked up his glass. The tide had turned! He resisted stroking his moustache.

'I swapped the capsules, yes. There were two of them. One capsule contained the antibiotic Seymour had been prescribed for his infected toe. The other capsule contained deadly poison. Yes. You were right. I did exchange them. But – it was the other way round.'

There was a pause.

'The other way round?' Jesty stared at her. 'What the hell do you mean?'

'*The poison capsule was already in the box.* The capsule with the antibiotic was in my bag. Outwardly the two capsules were identical.' Her eyes, he noticed, were very bright now. 'I managed to replace the poison capsule with the antibiotic. I had been waiting for an opportunity to do so. I had been worried silly about it. I had started panicking. I knew Seymour was going to take the poison capsule later on, you see. After dinner that night. I knew my husband would die moments after he swallowed it.'

Jesty frowned. 'You aren't suggesting he intended to commit suicide?'

'No. Seymour had no idea the capsule contained poison. He didn't know that someone was trying to kill him.'

'Are you saying it wasn't you who filled the capsule with poison, if that was the way the damned thing was done?'

'Of course it wasn't me!' Penelope Tradescant spoke with great vehemence. It crossed his mind she might be telling the truth after all.

'Did you know what the poison was?'

'It was nicotine.'

'You didn't want your husband to swallow it?'

'I didn't. I didn't want Seymour to die.'

'You wanted him to live?'

'I wanted him to live,' she said patiently. 'That's why I exchanged the capsules.'

'Wouldn't it have been easier if you'd told him about it? Warned him against swallowing the capsule?'

'That seems the logical thing to have done, doesn't it? Well, I didn't tell Seymour because I didn't want him to know that someone was trying to kill him. I didn't want to have to explain. I was afraid of complications. There were certain factors –' She broke off. 'I am a coward. Seymour is an extremely difficult man. There would have been all kinds of complications, believe me. I thought I'd do the exchange quietly and then – then all would be well. That's God's truth.' Penelope Tradescant's eyes met his steadily. 'It was most unfortunate that you saw me.'

There was another pause.

'Do you know who the person is? I mean the person who tried to poison your husband?'

He went on watching her carefully. Damned odd, the whole bloody thing. She sounded as though she were telling the truth, but of course he couldn't be certain. It might be just acting. She might be a bloody good actress. Beautiful women usually were. It occurred to him that she might have started playing some game with him.

'I know who it is. Yes. I saw her switch round the capsules. She had no idea I'd seen her.'

'*She?* It was a woman?'

'I see I'll have to tell you the whole story . . .'

10

From the Life of the Detectives

It was later that afternoon.

Major Payne turned off the TV set. 'Nothing on the news. We are still facing what could be best described as the menace of the unknown. Oh well, I don't know.'

'Did you try phoning Mayholme Manor again?' Antonia asked absently. She sat on the sofa with a sheaf of papers on her lap, a pen in her hand.

'Yes. I've tried four times now. No signal. Dead silence with a hollow ring to it. There seems to be some major fault. I may be imagining the hollow ring, actually. Unless it is all part of the conspiracy. I could go to Mayholme Manor and check in person, I suppose. Or would that be overdoing things a bit? You don't fancy a drive to Dulwich?' Payne glanced at the open window. 'It's a jolly lovely day. The longest day in the year.'

'Is it?'

'Summer solstice. The twenty-second of June.'

'Of course. Sorry, Hugh, but I can't go anywhere. I *must* finish these proofs.'

'Are they teeming with silly mistakes and annoying misprints?'

'Not at all. It's me. I keep changing my mind about things I have written. I hate a great deal of what I have written and want to make changes. I know my copy editor will detest me.'

'Nobody can detest you.'

'She will.'

'You are being neurotic.'

'Maybe.'

'I have read your latest book twice, at your request. There's absolutely nothing wrong with it. Not a thing. Quite the reverse.'

'You are too kind. You are always too kind when it comes to my writing.'

'I am not too kind. As you know perfectly well, I am exceedingly critical of the detective stories I read.'

'Of other people's detective stories, yes. You have a blind spot when it comes to mine.'

'Not true. Literary taste is literary taste. Not the kind of thing one compromises with. Anyhow, your copy editor didn't think there was anything wrong with your novel either, so that proves it's all in your head.'

'She is just being professional. I suspect she despises it secretly.'

'Rubbish. Or, as Major-General Knatchbull likes to say, fearful piffle.'

'She is quite formidable. She has very high literary standards. You'd like her.'

'Would I?'

'You like clever women. We really should have her over to dinner sometime. The only chink in her armour seems to be a contained passion for horoscopes.'

'Perhaps she tells fortunes as a sideline. To supplement her income.' Payne picked up the pot. 'Would you like some more coffee?'

'No, thank you.'

'Is it true what they say, that if you put enough effort into making sure the story's beginning and ending are right, the characters can be relied on to take care of the middle?'

'It doesn't quite work that way for me.' Antonia ran her fingers through her hair. 'The middle of the kind of detective story I write is always the trickiest part.'

'How to continue causing the reader to turn the pages, eh?'

'That indeed is the question. I begin to panic at around Chapter 10. As you know, I try to delay the murder for as long as I possibly can. My principle is, if one gets the suspense right, then the middle of the story will be right too.'

'There are readers, apparently, who read Chapter 1 and then they read the denouement, then they go back to Chapter 2 and carry on from there. This is the result of a survey,' Payne explained. He put down his coffee cup. 'I've never been able to understand it. Strikes me as rather an idiotic thing to do.'

'They want to see how everything fits in. They want to catch the author out.' Antonia spoke angrily. 'That is their sole intention.'

'Then they write tedious letters and complain?'

'Gloat, rather.'

'My poor darling.' Payne gave her a kiss, then glanced at the clock and back at the window. Their garden was bathed in brilliant sunshine. He liked the look of the lilies and fuchsias in the new pots. Their gardener had done a first-class job. Shame the chap hated Antonia's cat. Payne had observed him mouth an unprintable word at Dupin once. Why did there always have to be a fly in the ointment? Where *was* Dupin? Payne hadn't seen the beast since last night.

He rose. It would take him less than an hour to get to Dulwich, forty-five minutes perhaps, depending on the traffic. 'I suppose I could go by myself. What do you say?'

'I don't see why not. You don't really need me. You are a big boy now. You will tell me all about it when you come back. Actually, we might have been looking at the case the wrong way up.'

'You think we are doing Lady Tradescant an injustice?'

'Penelope Tradescant may not really be evil wickedness personified,' said Antonia. 'Rather, she might have acted as her husband's guardian angel.'

'She might have lived up to her name, eh? Penelope – the epitome of conjugal loyalty? Odysseus, don't you know. What exactly do you mean by the "wrong way up"? No – don't tell me.' Payne stroked his jaw with his fore-finger. 'Penelope knows the capsule in the snuff-box contains poison, so she takes it out and replaces it with a harmless one. Say, one of those vitamin supplements my aunt raves about. Is that it? Why did she look guilty then?'

'Did she really look guilty?'

'I thought so. That was when she realized we had been watching her ... It might have been mere dismay, I suppose. She might have been worried about us misinterpreting her action?'

'Which you did! *Yes*. Lady Tradescant doesn't want her husband to die, but nor does she want him to know about the attempt on his life, so she tells him nothing about it ... She *knows* the person who performed the first switching around of the capsules ... It's someone she is averse to getting into trouble ... Who is he? We assume it's a "he", don't we?'

'We assume no such thing. Just because she is an attractive girl, it doesn't follow that she's got a lethal lover. What kind of man would have access to Sir Seymour's medicine cabinet anyway? Sir Seymour's valet?'

'Do baronets still have valets?'

'They most certainly do.'

'You sound positive.'

'You seem to be forgetting some of my best friends are baronets.'

'What if you found that Sir Seymour was dead, but the doctor insisted that he had died of natural causes? What if no positive proof of foul play ever came to light? Oh well.' Antonia picked up her book proofs once more. 'In the end it is the mystery that counts and not the explanation.'

'Is the pretty lady a poisoner, or isn't she? Will we ever know? It's a bit like *My Cousin Rachel* ...'

'Oh, don't let's be bookish and clever, Hugh. Life is not a bit like mystery fiction.'

'With us it always is somehow. Haven't you noticed? Happens all the time. Sometimes I think we should be in a book ourselves . . . Where *did* I leave the damned car keys?'

'Is Lady Tradescant really attractive?'

'Her charms deserve to be dithyrambically extolled. Just to look at her mouth makes one think of great poetry and wide seas . . . Hope you aren't jealous.'

'Not a bit.' Antonia tapped her teeth with her pen. 'Sir Seymour might have forgotten to take the capsule. If you do get to speak to him and he's still in possession of it, will you ask him to hand it over for inspection?'

'I most certainly will. Otherwise my journey would have been a waste of time. My mission would have been fruitless or bootless. He's bound to think me mad. On the other hand he may be perfectly friendly and cooperative. I glanced at my family tree earlier on and discovered that a Payne had married a Tradescant girl back in 1750.'

'That should break the ice. Aren't you going to change?'

'You think I should?'

'Why don't you put on your uniform?'

'That would make me appear wildly eccentric. I shall wear a dark double-breasted suit with a discreet stripe and a bowler, perhaps?'

'A bowler would be equally eccentric,' said Antonia. 'Though perhaps they wouldn't think so at the place where you are going.'

11

Manoir de mes rêves

It clouded over as he drove along the narrow road, which, if his antiquated map spread out on the seat beside him was to be believed, led to Mayholme Manor. He had got the address from the Mayholme Manor website. How easy everything was nowadays. All one needed to do was to turn on the computer. They had been buying books and CDs and DVDs on Amazon and only the other day a Mark & Spencer van had delivered their shopping to their front door. His aunt, it seemed, had discovered the delights of Amazon too. Her butler had helped her set up her computer and now she spent hours on end in front of it, she informed him. She had phoned over the weekend to say she had managed to find a copy of a book her Scottish governess had read to her back in 1933 – long out of print. She had bought it from a private seller for the curious sum of sixteen pence.

He wasn't going to drive into a storm, was he? Everything turning the colour of gun metal. A sinister Valkyrie sky. He should be listening to Wagner, not to Django Reinhardt. What was the name of the piece that was playing? *Manoir de mes rêves.* The manor of my dreams? He hadn't quite decided on his line. Was he a friend of Sir Seymour's, come to say hello? Or was he looking for a suitable retreat for his decrepit old uncle? Or was he, perhaps, writing a book about Mayholme Manor and its history? Mayholme Manor had been a monastery once.

There it was. Massive iron railings with rusticated corner piers topped by eagles – most certainly not Elizabethan – more of an eighteenth-century addition – 'Mayholme Manor' in big block letters at the top. Squat gate-piers. Sentry boxes. Would there be French horns for visitors who wanted to announce their arrival? Would the porter be clad in a monk's habit?

But no porter was in evidence. The place seemed deserted. The gates gaped open and, after a pause, he drove through. So anyone could enter and exit undeterred . . .

Payne was driving very slowly now. He saw a moss-grown pyramidal structure on his right. It had an ancient and abandoned air about it – a Victorian ice-house? On his left he caught sight of a Chinese-style pavilion. It sported trelliswork, umbrella'd sages, dragons and bells and, in his humble opinion, seemed better suited to adorn the shores of a Soochow lake. There should be a ditty about it, Payne thought idly. *Dastardly Rhoda rents a pagoda.*

The parking. A couple of cars were already there. No police cars and no ambulance either. All seemed to be well. Perhaps, after all, Sir Seymour hadn't died in suspicious circumstances. Payne parked his car beside a battered two-seater the colour of what he believed to be a cedar rose.

Placing the bowler firmly on his head, he made for the main entrance. The manor of my dreams, eh? An exuberant Elizabethan frontispiece. 1570s, at a guess. A bit like old Somerset House in London. A screen of ivy, through which, on a bright day, the sun rays would come in fancy patterns, he imagined – a sight that would no doubt please the more aesthetically inclined residents, or 'brothers', as they seemed to style themselves. As he went up the flight of steps to the front door, he heard rapid footfalls and laboured breathing. The next moment the door was flung open and nearly hit him in the face.

A woman emerged.

She wore a velvet golf suit in a rusty colour, the trousers exaggeratedly baggy, and a silk shirt of a striking shade of reptilian green. Her hair was short, bobbed and jet-black – it brought to mind silent film actress Louise Brooks. The woman's face was dead-white with make-up, so her age was difficult to guess. Far from young – and ugly as sin. The black hair was too glossy and too perfectly shaped to be real. A wig?

'Really!' The woman glared at Payne.

'So sorry,' he murmured, taking off his bowler, though it was she who should have apologized. Her right hand was in a velvet glove embroidered with rosebuds. Cedar roses. Her other hand was bare. She was wearing a ring that appeared to be loose, Payne noticed. She held on to it with her gloved hand.

Something of the bloodhound about her features ... Pendulous cheeks ... She reminded Payne of somebody.

For a moment her eyes rested speculatively on his bowler, then she pushed past him and stumbled down the steps. She's the owner of the two-seater, he suddenly thought. The next moment several things clicked into place –

'Miss Tradescant?' Payne called out. 'It is Miss Bettina Tradescant, isn't it?'

She swung round. 'Can't stop. Got to dash.' She spoke in a hoarse contralto voice.

'My name is Payne. I am – um – a friend of your brother's.'

'A friend of Seymour's?' She stopped short, an incredulous expression on her face.

'I don't think we have met before –'

'Did you say "Payne"?'

'Yes. Major Payne. I believe we are distantly related.'

She took a step towards him. 'Belinda de Broke married a Jack Payne. You are not –?'

'That's my mama,' Payne said with a smile.

'You are Belinda's boy? How lovely. I knew your mama.' Her features softened. 'Not terribly well, but I remember her. She had *glamour*. Glamour is terribly important, don't you think?'

'Absolutely. Your brother is still here, isn't he?'

'You want to see Seymour?' Her hand gripped her loose ring. 'I am afraid you can't.'

'Why not?'

She licked her lips. Her tongue was very pale. 'Nobody is allowed to go anywhere near Seymour's room. He is unwell, or so it is claimed. It's all very hush-hush. He has issued a strict injunction *not* to be disturbed. That's what the bearded fool told me. Complete rot. Chap known as "the Master". I personally think that Seymour is dead.'

'Why is that?' Payne asked lightly.

'That's the reason I came, actually. To check. I find I am frequently misunderstood. Most people are fools, have you noticed? I haven't been able to get down to *any* work today. That's the effect the chill has on me.'

'The chill?' I am in the presence of an eccentric, he thought.

'Nag, nag, nag. *Here.*' She touched her bosom. 'As though I've swallowed an ice-cube that's refusing to melt. Though it starts *here.*' She now touched the back of her head. 'It's been like that ever since I was a girl. The bane of my life. Each time Seymour had a nosebleed, I had one too. Frightful bore. Funnily enough, it never happened the other way round, if you know what I mean, so people used to suspect me of fibbing.'

'Is that the twin thing? You and your brother are twins, of course.'

'I am *so* glad you understand. Your mother was always kind to me. Once I threw myself down the big staircase at Tradescant Hall. I did it quite on purpose. I must have been about thirteen. That's the age a girl becomes a woman.' Bettina sniffed. 'I was so innocent, so trusting, so full of hope. I was blue all over. I wanted to see if Seymour would get mysterious bruises, the way the cognoscenti claim, but he didn't. Oh, never mind. Fussing like an old hen, *so* annoying. Cluck-cluck-cluck. I mean the Master. Have you ever met the Master of Mayholme Manor?'

'No. I haven't had the pleasure.'

'Pleasure doesn't come into it. I am afraid I lost my temper with him. Gloriously garbed, I must say. Looks like somebody who attended the Paris conference in 1918. I can forgive a true original almost *anything*.' Her restless eyes fixed on the bowler in Payne's hands. 'No, not black. Please, *not* black. You will look good in a *grey* bowler. Have you ever worn a *grey* bowler?'

'I have. Ages ago. Which one is Sir Seymour's room?'

'No idea. If I were you I'd go away. You'd be wasting your time. *Abandon hope all ye –*' She broke off. 'Terrible place. Gives me the creeps. Heaven knows what Seymour saw in it. The only thing I liked was the radiator. *Sealing-wax red*. It's got hold of my imagination. Oh – and the orange habits. Glorious gorgeous orange!' Bettina Tradescant sang out as she walked briskly in the direction of the car park.

Payne entered the flagstoned hall. It felt so chilly that he shivered. There was a musty monastic smell too. One almost expected to see coffers containing old bones. What was wrong with Sir Seymour? Was he really dead? Bettina seemed to think so. Bettina had spoken of her brother *in the past tense*. Twins, eh? As a matter of fact, Bettina Tradescant looked like Sir Seymour in drag. What if –? No – too fanciful for words! He should be ashamed of himself.

The hall was bare apart from a console table made of black marble and what looked like a font. A tall obelisk-like vase containing mauve gladioli stood on the console table. The windows were narrow and had a sucked-in, religious kind of shape, imparting to the whole area the appearance of a Victorian church.

One whole wall was taken up by an ancient frieze showing monks wearing orange habits. The monks were kneeling and they all had ecstatic expressions on their faces. They were holding their hands up in adulation of what looked like a spaceship descending from the sky. The spaceship was bubble-shaped and transparent and inside it stood a figure. Payne stared. Good lord. The chap, if a chap indeed was what he was, had no head. Can't be a spaceship – some aura-like thing, surely? Perhaps there had been a head once but it had been erased by Time?

That old fraud Erich von Däniken would be interested in seeing this, Payne decided. Von Däniken's book – an international bestseller in the '70s, if he remembered correctly – made the claim that Greek gods were in fact extraterrestrial beings who had arrived on the planet Earth thousands of years ago. Von Däniken had referred to the writings of the ancients, including Aristotle, to prove that gods interbred with humans, performed genetic experiments, and bred 'mythical' creatures, such as centaurs and Cyclops. The oracular site of Delphi was apparently an aircraft refuelling station. Jason's pursuit of the golden fleece was in fact a search for an essential aircraft component.

Payne's thoughts turned once more to Bettina Tradescant's strange goat's eyes, suffering lips and female-impersonator's voice. Bettina claimed to possess the telepathic twin thing. One twin always knows when something awful happens to the other . . . Parapsychology . . . Was it all nonsense?

Father Ronald Knox had decreed against twins in his famous decalogue for detective story writing. Rule number ten – *Twins and doubles must not appear unless we have been duly prepared for them*. Bettina's relevance to the plot might not go beyond providing the usual exotic obfuscation. Well, this was *not* a detective story and if there was a twin sister, there was a twin sister, and absolutely nothing could be done about it.

'May I help you, sir?'

Payne turned round. A man in a monk's habit. Early forties, short cropped hair, perfectly ordinary features. One of the stewards. So they did wear monks' habits!

'Oh, hello. I am a friend of Sir Seymour Tradescant's. Would you be kind enough to direct me to his room?'

'You will need to talk to the Master first, sir. Would you like me to escort you to the Master's study?'

'Is Sir Seymour ill?' Payne asked as he followed the steward up a flight of flagstoned steps.

'Sir Seymour hasn't been feeling very well.'

Did that mean Sir Seymour had been poisoned after all? Sometimes people didn't die, only became ill . . .

Payne noticed that the hood hanging on the back of the steward's habit was rather large, twice the size of the chap's head. 'Do you ever put your hood up? If you don't mind me asking.'

'We rarely put our hoods up outdoors, sir, and *never* indoors,' the steward explained. 'It would be against the regulations.' His otherwise neutral tone held a touch of asperity.

12

The Bafflement of the Elusive Baronet

'How very interesting. Most gratifying too, of course – though, if you don't mind me saying so, Major Stratton, I am a little puzzled. Major *Payne*. So sorry. Ha-ha. We used to get regular visits from a Major Stratton at one time. A most remarkable fellow. There have already been *two* histories of Mayholme Manor. I've got them both . . .' The Master waved his hand towards the carved and highly coloured group of heavy panels, vaguely Burmese in style, which, Payne imagined, concealed bookshelves filled with vellum-bound volumes. Earlier on the Master had referred to this massive freak of fancy as his *petit cosy-corner chinois*.

'I am certainly familiar with the previous two books.' Payne executed a stiff nod. Before setting off that afternoon he had done some research on the net. 'One by Lofthouse, the other by Smithers. Both privately published.'

'Magnificent editions. Gold-embossed. Lavishly illustrated. A joy to handle.'

'But not to read?' Payne was sitting on what he believed to be a sham Louis XVI canapé in grey painted wood.

'To read too! Oh. Ha-ha. You have reservations about Lofthouse and Smithers?'

'*Tout au contraire*. I regard those two books as absolute triumphs of the embalmer's art.'

'I fear the weather is letting us down, wouldn't you say?'

'Most decidedly.'

'I fear there will be a storm. Coffee. Let's have coffee, shall we?' The Master rose. 'I do hope you will find my coffee no worse than modestly meritorious.'

The Master's study had tall windows, improbably draped with enormous velvet curtains, abundantly tasselled and overlooking the smoothest shaven lawn imaginable. Payne's eyes lingered on its razor-trimmed edges enviously. A showcase lawn. Where did the money come from? Donations from grateful brothers?

A gigantic clock made of dark ebony stood in one corner, its pendulum swinging to and fro with a dull, heavy, monotonous sound. There was also a Regency armoire, which Payne suspected was only the façade for a well-stocked bar.

The Master poured coffee out of a silver Queen Anne pot. He handed the cup over to his visitor with a ceremonious gesture, then he poured a second one for himself.

'Sugar? No?'

The Master was dressed in a charcoal-grey frock coat and wore a waistcoat the colour of port wine and a cravat striped red and black. His silver beard ended in a sharp point. His gestures could only be described as 'courtly'. He looks and sounds as sham as the canapé on which I am sitting, Payne thought. Very much like a character actor playing a part. Modestly meritorious indeed. How long did the fellow take to groom his beard each morning?

'I always imagined our establishment was of a somewhat esoteric interest,' the Master went on. 'That's why I can't help being a little surprised. Do you believe you will have anything new to say?'

'As a matter of fact, I have made a couple of rather curious discoveries. The original name of the frieze in the hall downstairs, for example.' Until quarter of an hour ago Payne had had no idea such a frieze existed.

'It's already got a name.' An impatient note crept into the Master's voice. '*The Vision of St Adolphus.*'

'That name was given much later. At least a hundred years later. Initially the frieze was called *The Dreadful*

Holiness of the Groaning Bubble.' Payne had been a little
unsettled by the mad-eyed monks and the headless figure
and this now was his revenge. *Reductio ad absurdum.* Make
the bloody thing appear as silly as possible. Burst the
bloody bubble. 'I came across it in a thirteenth-century
document. Fascinating stuff. Made my hair stand on end.
You had no idea?'

'No. The groaning bubble? Why groaning?'

'It's a literal translation from Latin.' Payne took a sip of
coffee.

'Bartholomew Lofthouse makes no mention of an earlier
name.'

'I am afraid Lofthouse is not exactly the most reliable of
chroniclers. You only need to look at his other books.'

'I thought his history of Dutton's Retreat was the only
book Lofthouse ever wrote.'

'There are *two others.* Lofthouse wrote them under a
pseudonym. Not surprising, since they are both on rather
controversial – some would say "unsavoury" – subjects.'

'Really? I would never have thought it of Lofthouse.' The
Master's fingers absently stroked the ornate lid of the little
silver box on the desk before him. 'Have *you* written any
other books, Major . . . Payne?' A note of doubt seemed to
have crept into the Master's voice.

'Isn't that Sir Seymour's snuff-box?' Payne wasn't sure it
was the box he had seen at Claridge's, but decided to take
a gamble. High time the conversation turned to Sir
Seymour.

'Yes, it is his box. He left it behind last night, after taking his medicine. Must give it back to him. But how did
you know? Oh, sorry. You are a friend of Sir Seymour's,
aren't you? Travis said something about you wanting to see
him. I thought at first that was the reason for your visit.'

'Partly the reason.' So Sir Seymour had taken the capsule! Payne felt an ice-cold thread run down his spine. 'I
am a friend of Sir Seymour's son's, actually,' he improvised. What was the son's name now? 'Um. Tradescant was

a bit concerned about his father's health and asked me to look him up.'

Good thing he belonged to the officer class where calling one's friend by his surname was still very much the done thing. He wouldn't have been able to get away with it if he had been an accountant, say, or a state school teacher.

'The family are all rather worried about Sir Seymour's health,' Payne went on. 'You have met Lady Tradescant, of course?'

'I have. Lady Tradescant came with Sir Seymour yesterday, which was an exceedingly pleasant surprise. She didn't stay long. I found her most charming. A most *sympathetic* kind of person,' the Master said firmly.

'What was the capsule for? Tradescant told me but I've forgotten. Was it ulcer? Diabetes?'

'No, no. Sir Seymour has had an infection.' The Master cleared his throat delicately. 'His big toe. He has been taking antibiotics.'

'Antibiotics. Of course. Every eight hours?'

'Every six hours, I believe. He took the last capsule yesterday evening.'

'And he is – fine?'

'I am happy to report that Sir Seymour is no longer in pain.'

'That's splendid news. Though isn't that what they say when someone dies?'

'Sir Seymour is not dead.'

'Tradescant will be so pleased. But then why is Sir Seymour being kept behind such an impenetrable *cordon sanitaire*?'

'Goodness, Major Payne, whatever gave you that idea?'

'Sir Seymour seems to be quite inaccessible. His sister was not allowed to see him. Your steward was jolly evasive. He wouldn't divulge Sir Seymour's room number. One could be excused for thinking Sir Seymour's got the plague or cholera or maybe one of those deadly flesh-eating bugs.'

'No, nothing as serious as that. Flesh-eating bugs! Ha-ha.

You seem to be letting your writer's imagination get the better of you. More coffee?'

'No, thank you.'

'I think I will treat myself to another cup. I must admit I am fatally drawn to stimulants.' The Master picked up the coffee pot. He held his little finger elegantly crooked. He hummed a tune under his breath.

Was the old fraud playing for time? Payne was suddenly assailed with sinister thoughts. *He is no longer in pain.*

'Have you seen Seymour since last night?' Payne asked.

'I have. I saw him at about nine this morning. One of the stewards had reported that Sir Seymour was a bit under the weather. Well, he didn't look particularly bobbish and he complained of a headache and blurred vision. I called Dr Henley – that's our resident doctor,' the Master explained. 'Dr Henley diagnosed high blood pressure and he gave Sir Seymour an injection. Sir Seymour felt better almost at once, but he asked not to be disturbed. He hadn't had a good night, it seems, so he needed to rest. He said he proposed to spend the day in bed, reading a detective story. He ordered a full English breakfast, which I thought a very good sign.'

'He refused to see his sister. Bettina seemed put out.'

'Sir Seymour did not refuse to see his sister. Sir Seymour doesn't know his sister was here. It was I who made the decision. Miss Tradescant is a splendid woman, absolutely splendid, but I am afraid sometimes she is – how shall I put it?'

'A trifle impetuous? Lacking in wisdom?'

'I honestly feared Miss Tradescant might say something that would send her brother's blood pressure soaring and bring on a seizure. So I said no. I couldn't risk it. Miss Tradescant, you are probably aware, is given to entertaining some highly unorthodox ideas.'

'She is convinced that her brother is dead.'

The Master stroked his beard. 'So she is. I am aware of the fact. Miss Tradescant was in what could only be described as an "occult mood". She insisted her brother was dead and I said he wasn't, and she said she was sure he was. She then accused me of lying and asked me to show her Sir Seymour's body at once. She said she would call the police and, for some reason, the fire brigade. She had worked herself up into quite a lather. I remained adamant. I couldn't possibly let her upset Sir Seymour.'

'I see. Incidentally, is your phone out of order? I tried to ring you several times last night and again today, but there was no signal.'

'The phone? Oh dear, yes! I am so sorry. We've had some major fault. All the lines were down for quite a bit, but, thank God, they've been fixed now.'

'Well, I should very much like to look around, if I may,' Payne said. 'I'd like to soak in the atmosphere.'

'Yes, of course. I will ask one of the stewards to be your guide. Make sure you visit our chapel. It is quite remarkable. Rich in interesting historical associations,' the Master went on. 'Baden-Powell prayed there once, back in 1899, two months before the Battle of Mafeking, and then Queen Mary in 1941, on the eve of the Battle of Britain. Profumo also came to pray at the chapel in the spring of 1963.'

'What did *he* hope to win? Christine Keeler?'

'As it happens, Mr Lovell, our librarian, often includes these three in the quiz we do around Christmas. *Who is the odd man out and why? Profumo, Queen Mary or Baden-Powell?*'

'I would say Profumo, since he was the only one who, in a manner of speaking, lost his battle?'

'It isn't a battle question. Ha-ha. The correct answer is Queen Mary, since she is the only one of the three who is not a man. Mr Lovell can be very naughty. He is extremely popular with the brothers. Exceedingly popular. Mr Lovell's *bons mots* are the stuff of legend. I couldn't recommend the chapel more strongly, Major Payne.'

'I should love to see the chapel.' Payne rose. 'I'd also like to say hello to Sir Seymour from his son, if I may?'

'I am afraid Sir Seymour made it absolutely clear he didn't want to be disturbed. Peace is something that is very much taken for granted at Mayholme Manor. Peace and permanency. In fact I can't think of anything else that's been taken for granted more – apart from an unwillingness to eat eels, as Mr Lovell put it. Ha-ha.'

'Ha-ha. Well, Tradescant would be terribly disappointed if I told him I hadn't been able to talk to his father. You see,' Payne improvised, 'he is the kind of chap who would worry and imagine things. You have met him of course?'

'No, I've never had the pleasure.'

'He might even decide that something dreadful has happened to his father and that you are involved in some kind of *suppressio veri*. He then will come himself!'

'You think Nicholas Tradescant may decide to pay his father a visit?'

'I would say it was most likely. His aunt's psychic prevision has had him perturbed.'

'Goodness me. I don't think Sir Seymour will like that at all. There appears to be a certain – um – *froideur* between Sir Seymour and his son.'

'Would you describe relations between Sir Seymour and his son as "strained"? Or worse?'

'No, I wouldn't. We mustn't gossip. *Loose lips sink ships*. That, as it happens, is Mr Lovell's catch-phrase of the moment. Ha-ha. An incorrigible comedian, Mr Lovell. Very well.' The Master rose to his feet with a resigned air. 'I will take you to Sir Seymour's room, but we must be careful *not* to tire him. Such an oppressive day, isn't it? Wonder if there's going to be a storm.'

13

Holy Dread

The ponderous, electric-charged air seemed to grow steadily more weighty as they walked down the corridor. Sir Seymour's room, it transpired, was on the third floor. They went up in an ancient lift that wheezed and creaked horribly. There was a black, incredibly battered-looking armchair in one corner, which might have served as a prop in a Lucien Freud painting. Payne found himself thinking of the particularly silly denouement of a locked-room mystery he'd read not long ago, in which the killer conceals himself inside an armchair.

They met nobody on the way. The place seemed empty. 'The brothers like a bit of a rest before dinner, unless they are watching a film in our *salle de ciné*,' the Master explained with an air of proprietary complacency. 'Extreme horror and tasteful erotica are particular favourites. Not so domestic dramas or anything that smacks of the serious-minded. *Film noir* and sci-fi epics send them to sleep.'

'In thrall to Eros and Thanatos, eh?'

Solid mahogany doors. Numbers. Name plates. One of the doors – number 35 – was open and Payne saw a very old shrunken man in a wheelchair, holding a large magnifying glass and leafing through a book. There was an odd pale greyness about him, as though colour were continually being drained out of him. Payne's eyes went to the portrait on the wall. Was that –?

'Are you comfortable in your new room, Dr Fairchild?' the Master called out.

'Yes. Infinitely better. A vast improvement.' The old man gazed across at them through his thick horn-rimmed glasses. 'I feel reborn. It is a most curious feeling.'

'Were the croissants to your taste this morning?'

'Thank you, yes. Exactly as I like them this time. Not hot but with a memory of heat.'

'Some of the brothers can be a little capricious,' the Master said *sotto voce* as they walked down the corridor. 'I wouldn't use the word "unreasonable", but Dr Fairchild's old room was much larger and it had a better view. It was also on the ground floor, which was much more convenient for his wheelchair, but he kept complaining. He said his old room smelled most disagreeably – of cats, if you please. He insisted on being moved to the third floor.'

'Are there cats at Mayholme Manor?'

'Of course not. Keeping pets is against the rules. Dr Fairchild is ninety-one. Our oldest brother at the moment. People start getting fancies at that age, I suppose. Somewhat ghoulish back history. Nuremberg in 1946. Dr Fairchild had the unenviable task of ascertaining whether the necks of the convicted Nazi elite had been properly snapped. Or so I have been given to understand.'

'I believe Sir Seymour's father was also in Nuremberg at the same time. He was a member of the British team that was sent to make sure things were done properly. It seems more than likely that they met,' Payne said thoughtfully.

'Yes. I wonder if Sir Seymour is aware of the connection . . .'

They had stopped outside number 33.

'We shouldn't be bothering him like this, really,' the Master murmured as he knocked on the door. Since no answer came, he tried the door handle.

The door opened.

'Sir Seymour never locks his door. He sometimes has a pre-parricidal nap. I mean, pre-*prandial*. Ha-ha. I've been steeped in *Oedipus Rex*. Steeped. I belong to a literary circle. Are you familiar with *Oedipus Rex*, Major Stratton?'

'Payne ... *It was my fate to defile my mother's bed.*'

'I've been haunted by the vision of the distraught Sphinx throwing herself off a cliff. I never imagined Sphinxes were *female*. Conjures up a most disturbing image. Thought they were without a gender.'

But Sir Seymour's bed was empty. The bed sheets were crumpled, the pillow bore an indentation where his head had lain and there was a book with a lurid cover on the floor beside the bed. Of Sir Seymour there was no sign. An oak-panelled room, rather Spartan. It reminded Major Payne of the rooms at the Military Club.

'Sir Seymour?' the Master called out. 'Maybe he is having a bath.' He pointed towards the bathroom door indecisively. 'I would hate to disturb him, really.'

Outside it had started raining and they heard the pattering of desultory raindrops on the window panes.

Pre-parricidal. Another Freudian slip? Payne wondered. Were relations between the Tradescants, *père* and *fils*, as bad as that? At some subconscious level the Master seemed to believe that Nicholas Tradescant was capable of killing his father. Too fanciful? Freud was a fraud, according to some. There should be a detective story entitled *The Black Box*. The black box would represent somebody's subconscious, which would be central to the plot, but to throw readers off the scent a lacquered black box should be found lying open beside the dead body. Would Antonia think it a good idea?

'Sir Seymour enjoys taking very hot baths. Dr Henley has warned him against it. Bad for the blood pressure. He's had problems with his blood pressure.' The Master knocked on the bathroom door lightly. 'Sir Seymour? Are you there? He is a bit deaf. Sir Seymour? Dear me. I do hope he hasn't been taken ill. Shall I . . .?'

Sir Seymour wasn't in the bathroom either. The bath was empty and contained nothing but a red rubber duck with a cheerful silly face. They stood staring at the duck. Payne caught sight of their faces in the bathroom mirror and thought they looked rather silly themselves.

'Well, Sir Seymour is clearly somewhere else, which, you will agree, is most reassuring. It shows that he has made a complete recovery,' the Master delivered in clipped tones. 'I expect he has gone for a walk. Sir Seymour loves the gardens. The gardens are absolutely splendid at this time of year.'

'It isn't the best time for a walk.' Payne pointed towards the window where the haphazard raindrops were turning into a steady crashing cascade.

'Perhaps not. Well, Sir Seymour is clearly somewhere else. Um. In the library – or he may be playing billiards. Goodness, what was that?'

They had heard a crack like that made by a bullet.

'A lightning bolt seems to have struck one of your ancient walls, Master. Some may say it is an omen.'

Back in the bedroom, Payne stood looking at a silver dish containing cuff-links that bore the initials ST, a pair of pearl studs, a ring and a number of loose one pound coins. Tips for the stewards?

It was as they were about to walk out of the room that Major Payne noticed the radiator under the window sill. The radiator was pillar-box red – which was also the colour of sealing wax. Who was it who mentioned sealing wax earlier on? No, not the Master. Why did he think that important? The next moment he remembered.

He said, 'Are there any other radiators at Mayholme Manor which are that particular shade of red?'

'No. That is the only one. We are going to have it repainted.' The Master gave a little sigh. 'For some reason Sir Seymour has taken exception to the colour.'

The Captive

Nearly seven o'clock. Captain Jesty parked his car and glanced across at Mayholme Manor. It looked grey and menacing in the twilight, under the sheets of falling rain. He hated ancient buildings. He found them singularly lacking in comfort. This one looked like an ogre's castle. He felt his spirits sinking lower, if that were possible. He should never have come. Of all the pointless journeys! What did it matter if Sir Seymour Tradescant was dead? What did it matter if he was alive? I don't care a hoot if her incredible tale is true or false, Jesty told himself.

Actually, he did care. He needed to find out if she had lied to him. That was why he had driven to Mayholme Manor, though he couldn't bring himself to leave his car now. If the old buffer turned out to have died, Jesty would call the police. He would tell them exactly what he had seen at Claridge's. The capsule-swapping incident. He would get Payne to testify as well. Payne would be a good solid witness. Payne's word would carry weight.

He would make sure the girlie didn't get away. He would make the girlie cry. He would make her suffer. He had the power to ruin her life, he realized. To destroy her. A long jail sentence for the cold-blooded murder of her husband was bound to ravage her beautiful face. Those lovely lips would wither. The eyes would lose their brightness. The clear skin would turn sallow. Nothing would ever be the same again.

He remembered her parting words at Quaglino's. 'Mayholme Manor is where you will find my husband.' She had handed him a slip of paper with the address. She had thanked him for the lunch. She had spoken with exaggerated politeness. He had been aware of a contemptuous glint in her eye.

He had made the mistake of baring his soul to her, of telling her he was mad about her, of promising to dismantle the moon for her, to present her with a star on a silver salver. Never before had he said things like that to a woman. *Only* as a joke. He had told Penelope he couldn't live without her, that he would do anything for her, *anything*, that he wanted to be her slave. Jesty squirmed at the memory. She, on the other hand, informed him she was flying to the South of France that same evening, or early the next day. She intended to stay in France for some time. Perhaps indefinitely, she said.

After she left, he remained seated at the table. He looked across at her coffee cup, at the slight smudge of lipstick on the brim. He reached out and stroked the starched napkin Penelope Tradescant had used. The moment his fingers touched it, he felt a burning sensation. He might have passed his hand through fire. When he examined his fingers later on, he saw red marks across them. The marks were still there. That was how much he loved her.

No, they were not. What absolute rubbish. Jesty flexed his fingers. He was imagining things. He should have his head examined. He should go and get drunk and forget all about her. She was no good. She was trouble. She was the devil. He cursed the moment he'd set eyes on her. He shouldn't have touched her with a barge pole. Let her go to France. Let her stay there indefinitely. That would be fine by him. Out of sight, out of mind. *Je vais te porter disparu.* Yes, quite. *Bon voyage, ma chère.* Goodbye and good riddance.

You'd forget her in no time, the old Captain Jesty went

on whispering in his ear. Console yourself with what you've got. It's only injured pride that's making you react like this. Phone Xandra. Phone Christine. Phone Leonora. Phone Petunia Luscombe-Lunt. Your call would make them happy. They would greet you with open arms. They would take your mind off her.

But the very thought of Christine and Xandra made Jesty squirm. He hadn't seen Petunia for a long time, but till a year ago she had been showering him with gifts – she'd kept ringing him at all times of day and night – asking him to go over – making arrangements for holidays together. Petunia *adored* him. She hadn't minded him calling her 'Pill' – she had taken the nickname as proof of his affection for her. Where *had* Petunia disappeared to? It was unusual for her to be silent for so long –

No, he didn't want Petunia either. He wanted Penelope. *He wanted Penelope.* No one else would do.

Suddenly he had the strong feeling, nay, the absolute certainty, Penelope was sitting beside him in the car . . .

What a perfect profile she had . . . He let his fingers encircle her arm just above the elbow. He increased the pressure gently, then drew her to him. He didn't kiss her at once. He watched her lips part – a sensual ungluing marked by a soft sound. Her lips were supple and pliant and rich in colour. Magenta. Blood and mud. When he eventually kissed her, her body felt as taut as a bowstring to start with, but then she grew weak and curiously fluid in his arms. He heard her soft voice. *Do with me as you please.*

He had no idea how much time had passed. When his eyes opened, he felt dazed and disoriented. A sick feeling in his stomach. He was shivering. The passenger seat was empty and it felt cold to his touch. She had never been there. No, of course not. He had become enthralled with her to the point of allowing any form of rational judgement to abandon him. Penelope was on her way to the South of France.

She was fleeing, moving out of his orbit. He could find her if he put his mind to it, he supposed; it wouldn't be an unsurmountable problem, but what would be the use if she didn't want him?

Outside the sky was still overcast. The rain appeared to have stopped. It was very quiet. Where *was* he? Why was he sitting in his car? What a terrible building. A monastery? A figure appeared. Somebody coming from the direction of the building. Chap in a bowler hat, swinging a rolled-up brolly? Seemed familiar . . .

It wasn't Payne, was it? Good grief. It *was* Payne. Jesty couldn't believe his eyes. Payne again! Payne had the knack of turning up when least expected. Payne had started playing at sleuths. Payne was intent on cracking the conundrum of the contaminated capsule. It was all a game to Payne. Annoying sort of chap, Payne. A damned meddler, in fact. Payne had followed the scent – all the way from Claridge's!

Jesty didn't particularly want to see Payne. He watched him covertly through the car window.

Payne was walking rather slowly. He appeared lost in a brown study. Jesty saw him shake his head. Had Payne unearthed something? Had he perhaps seen Sir Seymour's body?

I need to know, Jesty thought. He remembered where he was and why he had come. Payne had stopped beside a car and was patting his pockets. It was Payne's car, of course. Another minute and he'd be gone. Jesty wound down the car window and called out his name. How odd his voice sounded. Not like his voice at all. Hoarse and feeble.

A minute later Payne was peering down at him. 'My dear fellow. What's happened? You don't look well.'

'I am shot all to hell, Payne,' Captain Jesty managed to say.

'I do believe you are in need of a slug of something chilled and remedial. Let's go and have a drink somewhere. We'll find a pub in Dulwich.'

15

This Sweet Sickness

'You poor fellow,' Payne said some half an hour later. He had heard the first half of Jesty's tale.

They were starting on their second scotch.

'I'd never have imagined I had it in me to act like a besotted idiot, but there you are. And I haven't so much as touched her, that's the amazing thing, Payne. We never even shook hands. Our hands never brushed when I passed her the menu across the table. There was – *nothing*. And look at me! Ridiculous, isn't it?'

'Well, there's never a rational explanation for a thing like that,' Payne said philosophically. He lit his pipe only to be told by a smiling, Polish-sounding waiter with flaxen hair that, unless the gentleman extinguished his pipe at once, he faced a hundred-pound fine.

'This is an outrage,' Payne said.

'I do wish I could forget her.' Jesty covered his face with his hands. 'I don't even dare say her name aloud, it hurts me so.'

'Penelope,' Payne said automatically. 'Sorry, old man. Didn't do it on purpose.'

'It's the kind of name that conjures up the image of some staid matron. Don't you think? I tell myself things like that in the hope it would put me off her. Common sense, what I've got left of it, tells me I will get over her eventually, but at the moment I feel as though it's the end of – of *everything.* The end of the world, as far as I am concerned. Awful rot, I know, but there it is. Is that love, Payne? Great love? Is it? Do tell me.'

'I wouldn't call this "great love", no. I am afraid you are suffering from a serious bout of *amour fou.*'

'I only want her to love me. Is that too much to ask?'

'As a matter of fact it is. One can't really *make* anyone love one.'

'I feel like killing myself. Or killing her.'

'I very much hope you will do neither.'

'I know this will strike you as awfully peculiar, Payne, but I have never been in love. Not even when I was a boy. I've never really cared for any woman. No, honestly. That's God's truth. For my ex-wives least of all. My third wife, I remember, had some jolly biting things to say on the subject of my monstrous ego and my – what was it? – my incapacity for self-knowledge. She used big words like that. Bloody stupid woman. Called me some awful names. Duplicitous scoundrel – suave voluptuary – dangerous sociopath. Bloody awful, isn't it? You don't believe I am any of these things, do you?'

'No, of course not ... "Suave voluptuary" is not that awful, actually.'

'I never loved any of my wives. I was attracted to them. For a while. I desired them. I had fun with them. But then suddenly it was all over. I started hating them. Came to a point when I couldn't stand the sight of them. No one should ever get entangled with a wife.' Jesty took a gulp from his glass. 'Don't tell me you love your wife.'

'As a matter of fact I do. Very much.'

'I can't get Penelope out of my head. I tell myself I hate her, I tell myself I am better off without her, but that's not true. I am only trying to deceive myself. I love her. I *love* her. Can't help myself. I am frightened, Payne. This is so unlike me. Why am I so frightened? Look at me, I'm shaking!'

'Well, a sudden onslaught of self-knowledge is always a little scary. For the first time you have found yourself on *terra incognita*. You are not used to acting out of character and you are out of your depth –'

'I've had an awful lot of affairs as well as flings, you know. Hundreds and hundreds, if not thousands of affairs. Sometimes several affairs on the go. At one time I had a number of commitment rings specially made, all identically inscribed on the inside. "No one but you". I thought that *such* a neat touch.'

'Awfully neat,' Payne agreed. Though the inscription should have read, 'No fool like you', he thought.

'I've had to deal with angry husbands and angry boyfriends and furious fathers and – and absolutely livid girlies – livid because they'd caught me cheating,' Jesty explained. 'Frequently with their best friends. Or with their younger sisters. Or with their mamas. Last year I had an affair with a girlie, with her mama *and* with her maiden aunt as well. Don't know what possessed me. Still, quite a coup. Wouldn't you say?'

'Most decidedly.'

'What I mean, Payne, is that I've been in some jolly tricky situations, the stickiest of wickets, you may say, but I've never once batted an eyelid. Never once. That's what makes this whole thing so bloody extraordinary.'

'Simenon is said to have made love to a thousand women. As it happens, he also wrote nearly as many books.'

'Who the hell is he?'

'A French writer of detective stories. The funny thing is that Maigret is the most faithful of husbands.'

'What I want to know is why it's hit me so hard, this thing. Why do I feel as though it's the end of pretty much everything? Why can't I say, so what – the best of luck to her and good riddance? Why can't I laugh it off?'

'Have your advances never been turned down before?'

'Have I been given the raspberry? Of course I have. Good grief. Millions of times. *It's never affected me.* I may have moped about for a bit, but I've never shed a single tear over a woman. Now I can hardly hold back the waterworks. I feel like howling. *I can't get her out of my head.* It's not me, Payne.' Jesty thumped his chest with his fist. '*It's not me.*'

'Perhaps Lady Tradescant cast some sort of a spell over you?' Payne suppressed a yawn. He was getting a bit bored.

'A spell?' Jesty scowled over his glass. 'The thought did occur to me, actually, so you may be right. I keep getting the oddest ideas. Either that she's here, sitting beside me – her body pressed against mine – or else that she's just gone off temporarily, to powder her nose, but is coming back any moment.'

'Is that why you keep looking at the door?'

'You noticed it? Mad thing to do, isn't it? She looked lovely today. You should have seen her. It's not only that she is attractive. There's something about her. *Something.* Her lips are the colour of filth and blood. I can't explain it, but it's got hold of me, this thing, and won't let go!'

'*La belle dame sans merci,*' Payne murmured.

'Is that the same as *femme fatale*?'

'Worse, I think.'

'Perhaps this is my punishment for the reckless and irresponsible way I've treated so many women?' Jesty shook his head. 'What utter rot I talk.'

'Hasn't the scotch made you feel a little better?'

'Not really. I am sorry to disappoint you, Payne, but I still feel very much the same. Bloody awful.' Jesty's eyes were bloodshot. He looked feverish. 'What I feel is a kind of hunger mixed with agony. Does that make *any* sense? I can't see myself going on living without her. I want her, Payne. *I want her.*'

'You started telling me about the poison capsule. About the explanation Lady Tradescant gave you. She told you you'd got the wrong end of the stick altogether – that it was the other way round?'

For a moment Jesty looked as though he had no idea what Payne was talking about, then he waved his hand dismissively. 'Oh, *that*. Yes. Those were her exact words. Can't say I believe any of it. D'you think I should have?'

'You haven't given me any details yet.'

'It all makes perfect sense, actually. The reckless moment and so on. That's what she called it. The reckless moment. Anyhow. Sir Seymour is not dead, is he? Of course he is not. You'd have told me at once if he was. There would have been police cars and so on.'

'Well, I wasn't able to establish whether Sir Seymour is dead or alive.'

'You mean he *may* be dead?'

'Or he may not be ... Who was it who said he must apologize for being such a long time in dying? Charles the First or Charles the Second? I always forget.'

'What are you talking about, Payne?'

'Is he dead, or isn't he? If he is dead, where is he?'

'You make it sound like some bloody game.'

'The Dying Game?' Payne murmured. 'Do forgive me, Jesty. This is no jesting matter. I am being an ass.'

'Can't you stop speaking in riddles and explain what you mean?'

'Let's swap stories. You go first. Tell me what it was Lady Tradescant did or didn't do, or rather what she *said* she did or didn't do. I'll go second. It would help if we kept events in their chronological order.'

16

The Reckless Moment

'She happened to pass by the open door of Sir Seymour's dressing room at the precise moment the capsules were being switched round. If she had been five minutes late or five minutes early she wouldn't have seen anything. It was fate, she said. The box with the capsules had been inside one of the pockets of Sir Seymour's jacket. Sir Seymour's suit had been laid out on his bed, in readiness for his departure. Sir Seymour was having a bath at the time. Apparently he is fond of hot baths.'

'Lady Tradescant saw the person who swapped the capsules? The poisoner is a member of Sir Seymour's household?'

'She is – or rather was.'

'She? A woman? *Not* Sir Seymour's sister?'

'No. It was one of the staff. Their housekeeper, actually. A Mrs Mowbray. Mrs Mowbray and Sir Seymour had had a row earlier on, sometime after breakfast. Sir Seymour caught her cooking the accounts and he gave her the sack. Told her to pack and clear out of the house. Well, Penelope described Mrs Mowbray as dishonest and devious. Also, as vindictive. There had been problems with her before. What happened that morning was the final straw. Mrs Mowbray was clearly in a deranged state of mind, because after swapping the capsules, she went up to the top floor of the house and chucked herself into the abyss. She was killed outright.'

'Lady Tradescant had no idea Mrs Mowbray intended to kill herself?'

'No. Of course not. It was only when she heard the commotion that she realized what had happened.'

'I believe there was something about it in the paper this morning. House in Mayfair. Suspected suicide. I was looking for news of Sir Seymour's death.'

'I saw it too. Of course I had no idea there was a link between her and the Tradescants.' Jesty took another gulp of whisky. 'Where was I? Oh yes. Mrs Mowbray swapping the capsules. Penelope said she suspected poison at once, though of course she had to be sure, so, after Mrs Mowbray left the dressing room, she walked in and took the snuff-box out of Sir Seymour's pocket. There were two capsules inside the box. She opened each one in turn and she sniffed at the contents. She discovered bona fide antibiotic in one capsule. The other capsule contained nicotine.'

'Nicotine?' Payne glanced at his pipe. If this doesn't put me off smoking, nothing will, he thought.

'Yes. She knew it was nicotine because of the powerful smell of tobacco. She says she has no knowledge of poisons but she knew at once it must be highly poisonous. She knew her husband would die if he swallowed the capsule. She felt excited at the thought. She put the capsule back into the box and the box back into her husband's pocket. It was a snap decision. She said she wanted him to die.'

'She had no misgivings or reservations?'

'No. Penelope described it as her "reckless moment". She'd been wishing her husband dead for months. She hated and despised him. She wanted to be rid of him. She'd never actually considered killing him herself – but she would be damned if she prevented someone else from killing him. That was her chance to be free – as well as fabulously rich. She left the dressing room without looking back. Sir Seymour was still in the bathroom. Outside in the corridor she spotted a capsule on the floor and she picked it up. It was the antibiotic. Mrs Mowbray seemed to have dropped it. Penelope put it in her bag. It was something she did automatically. She didn't want it to be found, she said.'

'What happened next?'

'Well, Mrs Mowbray's body was discovered, the police came along and they questioned everybody in the house. They went to Mrs Mowbray's room. They were looking for a suicide note, it seems. They found a bottle of liquid nicotine in Mrs Mowbray's chest of drawers. They assumed that initially Mrs Mowbray had considered poisoning herself with it. Penelope had no idea such a bottle existed but she said she was rather pleased about the discovery.'

'She realized it was Mrs Mowbray who would be incriminated when it was discovered that Sir Seymour had died as a result of nicotine poisoning?'

'Yes! Penelope said she couldn't believe her luck. Sir Seymour had already told the police that he'd sacked Mowbray. Well, Sir Seymour was on his way to Mayholme Manor but he had been unsettled by Mrs Mowbray's death, so he suggested that they went to Claridge's for coffee. He needed diversion. Penelope didn't want to go, but he insisted that she accompany him. After he had his coffee, Sir Seymour produced the snuff-box and took out one of the two capsules –'

'Lady Tradescant couldn't have known which one.'

'No, Payne. She couldn't have. It was one or the other. The antibiotic or the poison. She watched him swallow the capsule. The next moment it hit her – the enormity of it. She said she started shaking. She hid her hands under the table. She felt sick. She said she felt thoroughly disgusted with herself. She is *not*, she said, a cold-blooded murderess. She hasn't got the mentality. She was in a state of absolute horror. Would he die or wouldn't he? He had started talking about his sister, how Bettina wasn't going to get a penny out of him, how he intended to cut her out of his will and so on. A minute passed. Then another. He seemed to be fine. Eventually he got up and toddled off to the loo. He left the silver box with the remaining capsule on the table. Well, she said she saw her chance then –'

Payne leant forward. 'Her chance for redemption?'

'Yes. How funny. "Redemption" was the very word she used. She took the remaining capsule out of the box and replaced it with the one with the antibiotic. She no longer wanted her husband to die. She wanted him to live! Of course it occurred to her that the nicotine might simply be taking longer to dissolve in his stomach. So her agony continued. She thought how undignified it would be if Sir Seymour collapsed and died in the lavatory at Claridge's, but then – then he reappeared. He seemed all right, not at all ill. She felt enormous relief. She said she nearly kissed him.'

'Apparently she accompanied Sir Seymour to Mayholme Manor . . .'

'She told me she hadn't intended to, but now she wanted to make sure he got to Mayholme Manor without a hitch. She suddenly felt extremely protective of him, she said. She didn't want anything bad to happen to him . . . She said she wouldn't have been able to live with herself if he had died.'

There was a pause.

Payne cleared his throat. 'Well, it's a perfectly plausible story. It explains why she looked guilty when she realized we had seen her, the Lady-of-Shalott expression, pallor and everything.'

'Practically everything. *Yes.*' Captain Jesty gazed at him. 'But you still believe Sir Seymour might be dead?'

'I am sure I am wrong. I have the Master's word that Sir Seymour is alive and well. Sir Seymour ordered a full English breakfast this morning–'

'Penelope mentioned the English breakfast!' Jesty cried. 'She said she phoned Sir Seymour this morning and he told her how much he had enjoyed it. It seems she did tell the truth after all!'

'It seems she did. Unless she and the Master are in cahoots? The Master might be hiding the body –' Payne broke off. 'There I go again! I am worse than Antonia. Sorry, Jesty.'

'Who's Antonia? Your mistress?'

'My wife. What bothers me is that I never managed to see Sir Seymour. I persuaded the Master to take me to his room, room number 33, but Sir Seymour wasn't there. He wasn't in the garden either – nor in the chapel. He wasn't in the library or in the billiards room. We went round looking for him. I insisted, you see. Eventually we got to the *salle de ciné*. A film was in progress and there were at least a dozen old boys watching it. The Master didn't turn on the lights, but he called out and asked if Sir Seymour was among the spectators. Well, Sir Seymour *appeared* to be there –'

'What d'you mean, appeared? He either was there or he wasn't!'

'The Master didn't turn on the lights, so I couldn't see much. We heard *somebody* – an old buffer's voice – rasp out in an irritated manner that he was there. What did we want? Couldn't we bloody well see he was watching a film? Didn't the Master know how annoying it was to be disturbed? At which the Master, in a fluster, apologized and we went out.'

'You think the old buffer who spoke to you in the *salle de ciné* was not Sir Seymour? You think Sir Seymour might have been poisoned after all? You think he died last night and that for some mysterious reason the Master is concealing his death? You suspect some kind of a cover-up?'

'Golly, it sounds even more ridiculous when somebody else says it,' Payne said.

17

Prelude to Murder

A ringing sound came from inside Captain Jesty's pocket.

'Sorry, Payne.' Jesty produced his mobile, looked down at the number and murmured, 'No idea who that is. Hello? It's Jesty speaking. Yes? Who is that?'

The next moment his lips parted and a light sprang up in his eyes. At the same time his face turned paler. He looked incredulous – delighted. '*Pe*—?' He broke off.

Payne leant slightly forward and whispered, 'Is it – *her*?'

How very interesting if it was her. Had she changed her mind? Penelope, the pulchritudinous poisoner by proxy . . .

Only it wasn't her. Jesty shook his head. The light in his eyes died to be replaced by an expression of crushing disappointment.

'Pe*tunia*, my darling – this *is* a surprise! It's been *ages*. I thought you'd forgotten me. No, not feeling awfully chipper at the moment. I am with one of my chums, actually, having a little drinkie,' Jesty croaked. He is making a brave effort to sound breezy, Payne thought. 'No, not a woman, darling – quite the reverse. One of my fellow soldiers. Where have you been, Pill? Oh yes. I do apologize for what happened last time. I was an absolute beast, wasn't I? *Mea culpa*, darling. I stand corrected –'

Jesty was going through the motions, and only a very careful observer would have realized that his heart was not in it.

'So sweet of you, Pill. I would *love* to come and visit you sometime. Towards the end of the week perhaps? *Tonight?* Getting a bit late, isn't it?' Jesty stole a glance at his watch and grimaced at Payne. 'A bit late for fun, don't you think? You need your beauty sleep, darling? Don't you?'

Payne gave a rueful smile. Poor blighter. How often do we get what we really want? Ah, the delusions of love, or what *passes* for love . . .

'As it turned out, it wasn't Penelope but one of the discarded lady friends. Poor chap. He said that for a wild moment he'd imagined it was Penelope. The lady's name was Petunia Luscombe-Lunt. Quite a mouthful. Jesty said he found double-barrelled names something of a turn-off. Same first syllable as in "Penelope". Jesty called that a "particularly cruel joke". He kept addressing her as "Pill".'

'Not terribly flattering,' observed Antonia.

'Pill apparently likes being addressed as "Pill". She regards it as proof of affection, or so Jesty told me. Pill is an unhappily married woman of a certain age. She has been separated from her husband for some time. She has a smart flat in South Kensington and the dubious distinction of being Jesty's oldest squeeze.'

'He accepted her invitation and went to see her?'

'He did, in the end. Not terribly enthusiastically, I must say. He explained he was doing it exclusively for old times' sake. He was feeling so low and miserable, he said, he couldn't afford to be unkind to anyone, least of all his oldest girlfriend. He'd started trying to be funny once more, which one must take as a good sign. Suggested he might have started recovering.'

'You were never worried he might do something silly?'

'Shoot himself with his army revolver, you mean? It did cross my mind, but no, I can't imagine this particular lovelorn Lothario blowing his brains out with his old army revolver. Still, I am glad he accepted Mrs Luscombe-Lunt's invitation. He needed a distraction.'

'Do drink your cocoa,' Antonia urged.

Payne took a sip, then yawned prodigiously. 'Gosh, I am tired. Is it only midnight? I thought it was at least three in the morning. It's been such a long day. I must have driven like mad.'

'Where is your bowler?'

'Gosh – no idea. Perhaps it's in the car? Hope I didn't leave it in the pub. It would be a bore if I had to phone them and make inquiries.'

'No one would want to steal a bowler. You started telling me about Bettina Tradescant.'

'Oh yes. I thought there was something very fishy about the fashionista. It is my belief Bettina had been inside her brother's room. She wouldn't have known the radiator in his room was the colour of sealing wax otherwise,' Payne explained. 'None of the other radiators at Mayholme Manor is that particular colour. The Master said so and he should know. When she talked to me, Bettina insisted she hadn't been allowed to go to her brother's room, but I am sure now that was a lie.'

'How did she know where her brother's room was?'

'Perhaps Penelope told her? 33 is an easy enough number to remember. Or she might have bribed one of the stewards. She had a row with the Master, but that must have been *later*. Now, why didn't she want to admit she had been to her brother's room?'

'The obvious conclusion is that she felt guilty about something she did there. She couldn't have killed her brother, could she?'

'She might have, but then what did she do with the body?' Payne took another sip of cocoa. 'I suppose someone could have helped her. One of the stewards?'

'Or the Master?'

'Or, as you say, the Master. We keep going back to the Master, don't we? We don't trust the Master. In my opinion the Master is a highly dubious character. His beard is groomed to a point. I suppose the row between him and Bettina could have been staged . . .'

'You said she was in an agitated state.'

'She might have been pretending. She was very pleasant

to me, I must say. She wore a wig that was as black and lustrous as a new piano. She kept pulling her ring up and down her finger.' Payne frowned, remembering Bettina's sluggishly furtive eyes. 'She said she was sure her brother was dead. They are twins, you see.'

Antonia stared. 'Are they?'

'I thought you'd be interested. She told me that she always knew when something awful happened to her brother. She has the telepathy twin thing, or so she claims.'

'Are they identical?'

'Uncannily similar. When I bumped into her, I had the strangest notion that I was seeing Sir Seymour in drag. Perhaps that *was* Sir Seymour in drag? I thought her voice rather masculine. Mightn't Sir Seymour have disguised himself as his sister? That would explain his mysterious disappearance from Mayholme Manor. Just an idea.'

'You suspect that was not really him in the *salle de ciné*?'

'I have no incontrovertible evidence that he *was* there, my love. Any old duffer in a darkened room could claim to be another old duffer.'

'Could that particular old duffer have been one of Sir Seymour's accomplices? Sir Seymour might have asked someone to stand in for him . . . That's the kind of thing one could always get away with in a book,' Antonia said wearily. 'But why should Sir Seymour want to leave Mayholme Manor dressed up as his sister?'

'He might have decided to disappear in order to become a tramp. Apparently Sir Seymour entertained the not entirely rational notion that only as a tramp could one achieve ultimate freedom. He talked to the Master about it. He rhapsodized about life in a cardboard box under a bridge. He might also have wanted to make it look as though his sister had something to do with his disappearance, out of revenge. They hate each other's guts, the Master hinted as much.'

'In that case there will be no body . . .'

Payne gave a portentous nod. '*Twould make a man drink himself dead on gin-toddy – to have neither a corpus delicti nor a body.*'

18

The Water's Lovely

It was the following morning.

Waking up in his bed at Mayholme Manor, Sir Seymour Tradescant grimaced with distaste. He had had a dream, in which his sister Bettina appeared, looking piteous and strangely diminished, her face uncharacteristically free of make-up, a mirror image of his own. Bettina stood beside his bed and held up her hands above her head in some kind of bizarre salutation, the wrists crossed. It had taken him a moment to realize that she had handcuffs on. No ordinary handcuffs, but rather dainty ones, made of fine gold and platinum and encrusted with diamonds. 'The latest fashion accessory,' Bettina informed him. 'Everybody who is somebody has them.' Then, for some reason, she became upset, started sobbing and covered her face with her manacled hands, but he knew she was only pretending – he saw her sly eyes peeping through her fingers.

Sir Seymour felt strangely unsettled by the dream. As it happened, his sister had been very much on his mind. He knew not only that she had come to Mayholme Manor the day before, but that she had been in his room. Nobody had said a word about it, but he found her velvet glove embroidered with roses, with her initials on the hem, on the floor beside his bed. (He'd pushed the glove under his pillow. Could that be the reason for the dream? Didn't old maids put pieces of wedding cake under their pillows in the hope it would make them see their future husband in a dream?)

The illuminated face of the little leather travel clock on his bedside table told him it was twenty minutes past seven. It felt much earlier. It was dark in the room and no matter how he strained his ears, he could hear nothing but silence, the kind of silence described as 'deafening' or more commonly as 'dead'. A bit eerie. Could he have died in his sleep and been transported to some kind of parallel universe –?

Poppycock. Why did he keep harping on death? He wondered if he was perhaps mortally ill, without realizing it, but thought it unlikely. His big toe was fine now. No more pain. Well, he felt a little off colour, that was all. Nothing to make a song and dance about. He always felt off colour in the morning. What was it he had for dinner last night? Quails roasted in a wrap of vine leaves, the blood still oozing from them when cut? Yes. That's what must have given him indigestion. Perhaps he should have followed Henley's advice and chosen something lighter? Oh well, too late now.

That young chap, Mowbray's son, what was his name – Vic? Was he after Penelope? The way he'd kept coming to Half Moon Street. Always there, at one time, not saying much, making sheep's eyes at Penelope. Got on his nerves! Sir Seymour shook his head. Young wife – he shouldn't have got himself a young wife – always some kind of trouble – he should have known he'd reap eternal rue! Well, now that his mother was dead, there'd be no reason and certainly no excuse for Vic Mowbray to be at the house –

Why was he thinking about Vic Mowbray now? What he needed most of all at his time of life was tranquillity. He should endeavour to avoid any kind of worry. That was the way to live to a hundred. What was that joke Mr Lovell had made? Down with Methuselah! Frightfully funny.

Sir Seymour struggled up and turned on his bedside light. He would sit and wait for the steward to draw the curtains. He didn't feel like leaving his bed, not yet. The steward should be bringing his tea any minute now. Tea and paper-thin buttered toast. He didn't like the idea of his bare feet touching the floor. Bettina might have left something in his room – a venomous snake or a poisonous spider or the giant rat of Sumatra – he wouldn't put *anything* past her. She was unpredictable, mad. After his money, like all of them.

Reaching out for the little porcelain dish that stood beside the clock, Sir Seymour picked up his ring and put on his glasses. Once more he tried to put the ring on his finger and failed. Same as last night, dammit. There had been no problem putting on his ring the day before. He flexed his fingers and peered down at them. They neither felt nor looked swollen, but they must be – otherwise why couldn't his ring be fitted on his finger? The band couldn't have *shrunk*, could it? Ridiculous. His fingers did look a bit swollen, as a matter of fact. Was it his heart – his blood pressure? Perhaps he could have a word with Henley, though Henley wasn't exactly a picture of health himself. So fat!

Sir Seymour's eyes remained fixed on the ring. The diamonds sparkled in the lamplight – an illusion of bursting rays – like a shimmering fireworks display. The ring had once belonged to the Duchess of Windsor. A Bond Street jeweller had estimated it was worth at least a million in today's money. Sir Seymour's father had been quite secretive about how he'd come to be in possession of the ring. There was some mystery attached to it. Had Papa perhaps *stolen* the ring from the Duchess?

Was it his fancy or did the diamonds really look dimmer than he remembered them – a little on the dull side? The diamonds appeared to have lost their sheen. Was that *possible*? Like flowers that fade overnight. No – that sort of thing didn't happen to good diamonds. Perhaps there was something wrong with his eyes? He might need new glasses. He wasn't heading for a stroke, was he? Were the first tentacles of Alzheimer's already spreading paranoia and confusion through his brain? Must have a word with Henley. Damned nuisance. He felt . . . well, strange . . . Not himself . . . That bloody dream!

The Master hadn't mentioned Bettina's visit. Maybe he wasn't aware of it, though the stewards were obliged to report all visitors to him. Or perhaps the dear fellow didn't want to worry him? The Master had been extremely concerned when he heard about Sir Seymour's swollen fingers. He had wanted to call Dr Henley at once, but Sir Seymour had assured him there was no real need for it. The Master was the only person who genuinely cared for him!

The night before, in the course of their after-dinner chat, Sir Seymour had been so moved by the Master's concern that he'd hinted at the 'personal consideration' he was leaving him in his will. He had actually named the sum. The Master had inclined his head and his silver beard had bobbed up and down. The Master had been overcome with emotion. Sir Seymour had an idea the Master might be experiencing financial difficulties. He had seen a racing paper on the Master's desk once and on another occasion had surprised him on the blower, placing a bet on Amber Arab. Sir Seymour had been surprised. The Master didn't look like a betting man, but there it was.

Everything else – all his earthly riches – he would leave to Mayholme Manor. He'd meant what he'd said. All he needed to do was pick up the blower and contact Saunders, his solicitor. Money? Why was everybody so fond of money? Bettina kept pestering him for money for some tomfool magazine venture of hers. She expected him to cough up half a million at least. She seemed to believe he could produce banknotes out of a top-hat, like in one of those conjuring tricks, wad after wad after wad –

Sir Seymour started up as he saw a shadowy figure in an orange habit walking towards him. He hadn't heard the door open. Like cats, these fellows. Though this one was more like a rabbit. Like a white rabbit. Sir Seymour peered above his reading glasses. 'You are not Travis, are you?'

'My name is Madden, sir. Your early morning tea, Sir Seymour.'

'Don't think I've seen you before.'

'No, sir. I am new.'

'Do the curtains, would you? Don't stand there, staring. What's the weather like?'

'I am afraid it is rather cloudy, sir.'

'Nothing to be afraid of.' Sir Seymour raised the cup of tea to his lips. 'Not your fault.'

'Is the tea to your satisfaction, sir?'

'Just the right strength.'

'And the toast?'

'Done to perfection. Thank you, Madden.'

'Thank *you*, sir. Would that be all, sir?'

'Yes. No – wait. Run my bath, if you don't mind awfully.'

'Very good, sir.' Madden entered the bathroom and Sir Seymour heard the sound of running water.

Odd-looking fellow – red-eyed – bleached – like a white rabbit, yes. Was he an albino? Would be bad manners asking him, he supposed. A bit disconcerting, having an albino steward run one's bath. What did the fellow want to thank *him* for? Expected to be tipped, no doubt. Well, I won't tip him, Sir Seymour decided. Too early in the morning. Fed up with unctuous flunkeys!

When Madden reappeared several minutes later, Sir Seymour greeted him with a quotation. '*Amat avidus amores miros, miros carpit flores.*'

'Sir?'

'She avidly loves strange loves and picks strange flowers.' Sir Seymour spoke petulantly. He felt a little annoyed that he needed to translate. 'Strange flowers, Madden. That's my sister Bettina. One never knows what she is up to. Like something out of that horror film we saw yesterday. She keeps changing her appearance. She doesn't seem to be happy in her own skin. She calls it "experimenting". You can go now, Madden.'

'Yes, sir.'

'Oh my ears and whiskers, how late it's getting,' Sir Seymour murmured. 'Ha-ha.'

Rising from his bed, he put on his dressing gown and slippers. He was in an excellent mood now. He couldn't quite say why. His moods seemed to change fast. What was that joke? Down with Methuselah! Frightfully funny. He picked up the detective story he'd started reading a couple of days before. He enjoyed reading in his bath. A murder mystery gave you rather a *cosy* kind of feeling. He was extremely careful about what he read these days. No one would ever catch him reading books about the secret disgraces of advancing age, nor about Canadian women finding succour with the pastors of tough industrial estates. There were certain subjects he drew the line at ... What *was* a 'tough industrial estate'?

Henley had told him not to overdo the hot baths. Henley was a fool. All right, there was a compromise – he'd make sure the water was not boiling hot. Lobsters hated boiling water. Ha-ha. The art of compromise. That was what his father had been frightfully keen on. Diplomatists usually were. Cautious fellows, frequently dull since they were always so circumspect. Never said anything amusing. Well, his father had been different. Far from dull. Quite a character, in fact.

It was ten minutes later.

The water, he reflected, was lovely. 'I intend to put all my trust in you,' Sir Seymour told the rubber duck. Jolly invigorating – these new bath salts – a mint-cum-angelica melange. Foam like whipped cream. He'd been extremely fond of whipped cream as a boy. Once his sister had pushed his face into a bowl of whipped cream, then laughed her head off. Made him look a fool.

The bathroom was beginning to steam up. He let the book drop to the tiled floor. Couldn't see properly. He had reached the denouement anyhow. *Such* a simple explanation. He lay back motionless, eyes closed in ecstasy, thinking of breakfast. Felt ravenous, actually. He would phone Saunders after breakfast. Change his will. Should be as simple as falling off a chair –

He must have dozed off and slumped down a bit, his chin and then his lips submerging – the next moment he spluttered and gasped for breath. How easy it was to drown!

'Why didn't you warn me, you silly creature?' Sir Seymour shook the rubber duck angrily. His heart was racing.

Suddenly he saw somebody standing on the other side of the semi-transparent curtain. He squinted. He hadn't heard the door open or noted the sound of footsteps. He was a bit deaf. Figure in orange. The bloody steward! Couldn't quite see his face – why had the silly fellow put up his hood? It was against the regulations, they were *not* allowed to wear their hoods inside.

'That you, Madden? What d'you want? Made me jump. You have no business to be here while I'm in the bath. What the hell d'you think you're doing?' Sir Seymour cried as the figure in the orange habit started lifting the curtain.

Gloves? Why was the fellow wearing black gloves?

19

Alibi

The holiday season had started and at Heathrow Airport the bustle was quite incredible. They had had to come two hours before the flight – not one, as it had been. Penelope Tradescant looked at her watch: nine o'clock. She could do with some more coffee. She'd got up at some unearthly hour. Needed to check in first. How long the queue was!

Her mobile phone rang. 'Hold this,' she told her companion and handed him her overnight bag.

She held the phone to her ear. 'Yes?'

'Lady Tradescant? Oh dear. This is too dreadful!'

'Who is this?'

'I am so sorry. It's Wilfred Cowley-Cowper speaking. From Mayholme Manor –'

'Who? Oh – Master?'

'Yes, yes – oh dear – *yes*.'

He sounded extremely flustered.

'What is it?' Vic whispered.

'Sorry, can't hear you very well,' she said. 'Has anything happened? Not Seymour?'

'Yes! I am so sorry, Lady Tradescant, but I am afraid – it's Sir Seymour – I am so sorry!'

'Seymour? Is he ill?'

'I am afraid I am the bearer of terrible tidings, Lady

Tradescant. The worst possible news. Sir Seymour died this morning.'

'*Died?*'

'What's happened?' Vic asked. 'Who's died?'

'He died forty-five minutes ago. I called Dr Henley at once,' the Master explained, 'but it was too late.'

'Oh, my God. What – but what happened?'

'Sir Seymour didn't feel frightfully well last night. He thought his fingers were a bit swollen – this might have nothing to do with it, mind! I suggested calling Dr Henley, but Sir Seymour insisted he was fine. Well, he died this morning. In his bath.'

Penelope gave a little gasp. 'In his bath!'

'I am afraid so. It's terrible. That's where Travis – one of the stewards – found him when he brought him his breakfast. I am so sorry. This must be extremely distressing!'

'It's a shock . . . My God . . . Seymour . . . Was it a heart attack?'

'Dr Henley is not sure, but he thinks it was a heart attack, yes.'

'Poor Seymour.' She looked across at the darkly handsome face of her companion. Poor lamb, he looked worried, quite distressed in fact. He had insisted on seeing her off. So sweet. She tried to give him a reassuring smile.

'Dr Henley kept warning him against taking hot baths. There may be a PM. I don't know. Dr Henley will need to conduct further examinations.' The Master sounded quite choked. 'It all seems to depend on how conclusive his findings are. He may need to ask for a second opinion, he says. It is all too dreadful for words. I was wondering whether it would be convenient for you to –'

'Of course. I'll be with you as soon as I can.' She looked at her watch. 'I shall take a cab. Thank you for letting me know, Master. I am at Heathrow, as it happens. The airport, yes. I was on my way to the South of France – good thing I never got on the plane!'

'The South of France!' The Master seemed to find this particularly distressing. 'I am so terribly sorry.'

Poor poppet. He was clearly in a state of shock. Penelope had a soft spot for the Master.

'Well, Vic, *c'est la vie*. First your mother, now Seymour. It's awful, I know, though I can't pretend I feel sad for either of them.'

It was half an hour later. They were sitting in the back of a cab and he was holding her hand. He said, 'They'll think it is us, Penelope. *They'll think it's us.*'

'I don't see why they should. Seymour died of a heart attack. That's what the doctor thinks.'

'What if he drowned? He was in the bath, wasn't he?'

'That's a possibility, but I don't see how they could start imagining that we've got anything to do with it. At this point there's no question of anyone suspecting foul play. The fact remains Seymour died shortly after eight o'clock this morning. The Master said so.'

'Eight o'clock? Are they sure? Thank God!' Vic gave a sigh of relief. 'At eight o'clock we were in the cab on the way to Heathrow. Neither you nor I could have been at Dulwich, drowning your husband!'

'Unless one of us managed to be in two places at the same time?' She gave a little smile as she remembered the book of conjuring tricks she had given Seymour. 'Perhaps I am not me?'

'What – what do you mean?'

'Don't look at me like that, silly – of course it's me! I shouldn't be joking, I know, but I can't help feeling very happy. I am free – and I am rich!'

'Will you marry me?'

'I am not sure. Actually, my sweet, I don't think that would be an awfully good idea,' Penelope Tradescant said.

'Why not? You love me, don't you?'

'I adore you.'

'It's interesting, the way you smile when you clearly don't feel like smiling. I caught myself in my shaving

109

mirror doing exactly the same thing the other day,' Vic said. 'It suddenly came to me. We are so similar!'

'We are, aren't we? Practically alike. That can be dangerous,' Penelope said with mock gravity. 'All the more reason why we shouldn't get married.'

'Arise, Sir Nicholas!' It was the dark girl who said it this time and she laid the brush against his left, then against his right shoulder. They were at the same hotel, but the blonde girl wasn't with them.

Nicholas Tradescant went on staring down at his mobile phone. Did he feel sorry – sad? Well, no. He felt – nothing. He felt empty. A bit shaken up, that was all. He'd never loved his father. He had been caned by a servant at his father's orders once. He must have been ten or eleven. He couldn't remember the reason. His father had sat by and watched, while sipping pale sherry. He recalled his father's words. 'Well, Nicky, if you asked me nicely, the castigation could be cancelled.' There had been a smirk on the servant's face. Nicky had clenched his teeth. He hadn't begged for mercy. He hadn't screamed or sobbed. He had stood the punishment out, bloodied but Spartan in his silence. He had then walked stiffly and painfully to his room. He'd wished his father dead, he remembered.

The dark girl put her arm around his neck. 'What are you thinking about, Nicky? Aren't you happy?'

'No.' He frowned. 'We floated an electronically operated boat on the lake once. Many years ago. I was very excited about it, but my father got angry with me, I can't remember the reason, but he told me to go back to the house. He then spent an hour playing with the boat all by himself.'

'What a terrible thing to do! Poor Nicky. Well, your father is dead now and you are one of the richest men in England, aren't you?'

He asked the dark girl where the blonde girl was – did she have any idea?

She shrugged. 'She is a dark horse. Perhaps it was her

who went and killed your father. She said she would, didn't she?'

'Actually it was you who said it.' He gave a faint smile. 'They don't know the exact cause of death yet, but it looks like a stroke.' He glanced down at his mobile phone. There was a message – from his aunt, of all people. What did it say? *Rejoice! Rejoice!*

He shut his eyes. He had started feeling a little queasy.

'I am pregnant and I am absolutely sure you are the father,' the dark girl was saying.

20

Suspicion

'Ah, Master. We meet again. This is terribly distressing,' Bettina Tradescant said.

'Miss Tradescant, my sympathies.' The Master inclined his head in a ceremonious manner. 'A most tragic occasion –'

'Indeed it is. But we need to get these things in perspective. My brother was not exactly a young man. You may not be aware, but there was an awful lot that was wrong with him. An awful lot. Anxiety spells, depression, indigestion, insensitivity, general lack of judgement, deafness. His deafness was much worse than he ever admitted, did you realize? Seymour was terribly embarrassed about his deafness. Seymour was a tormented soul. Not at all what you and I would call a "happy man", so, in a manner of speaking, this is a merciful release.'

'Sir Seymour always said he found great contentment and peace at Mayholme Manor.'

'Well, that was certainly the impression he *chose* to give.' She shook her head darkly. 'You didn't know my brother as well as I did, Master. Seymour believed in sparing the feelings of people he didn't know particularly well.'

How and when she had heard the news, the Master couldn't imagine. Perhaps it was Lady Tradescant who had told her? But he had informed Lady Tradescant about her husband's death only an hour and a half earlier – and Bettina Tradescant was already sitting in his study, wearing profound and rather extravagant mourning, like some Victorian widow! A long black dress with a high collar, black pointed shoes, black hat with two shiny purple feathers, black gloves and two golden crucifixes around the neck. How had she managed it? She must have moved with the speed of lightning. No – impossible!

'I have an admission to make, Master. I have been here for *ages*. I knew of course what I would find, so I came suitably dressed. I am famous for my sense of occasion. I arrived at the crack of dawn and I sat in my car. I was quiet as a mouse. I drank coffee from my thermos flask and read *Vanity Fair*. The book, *not* the magazine. I have been reading it for the past twenty-five years. I admire Becky Sharp terribly. *Such* enterprise. I must admit I prefer the magazine, always useful to know what my rivals get up to, but I doubt if that would have been appropriate in the circumstances. My brother disapproved of what he termed "the world of fashion". Incidentally, I had a mishap in your downstairs lavatory earlier on. I am sure your stewards have informed you?'

'No, they haven't.'

'They should have. Something needs to be done about all those locks and knobs, otherwise one day you may end up with a fatality,' she warned him. 'Next time it will be one of your old buffers! I doubt if any of them has my kind of stamina. I do apologize if I strike you as a little brusque, but I had a bad night. I couldn't sleep at all well, in fact not at all. One of my *tangos nocturnes*. When that happens I tend to lose my temper easily. Everything annoys me. I hope you will forgive me. I explained about the chill the last time we met, didn't I?'

'You did.'

'I can't function if I've got the chill. I simply can't. When did my brother die exactly?'

'Between eight and half-past eight this morning.'

'I locked myself in your downstairs loo at about that time, now isn't that most interesting?' Bettina scowled. 'You are sure Seymour didn't snuff it *in the small hours of yesterday morning*?'

'Quite sure,' the Master said patiently. 'You could ask Dr Henley.' He gestured towards the portly man with the mottled red face, who had been sitting in an armchair beside the window, drinking coffee.

'It isn't so much a question of trust as of principle,' she said obscurely.

Dr Henley rose to his feet with some difficulty. 'Miss Tradescant. How do you do.'

Her leathery skin and somewhat darting eyes gave her an inhuman look, almost reptilian. Later on he was to describe her to his wife as a 'crackling mass of unrelated forces'.

'How do *you* do. One must observe the forms even when one is confronted with the greatest provocation, I am sure you agree? One must assume the appropriate social mask. Fail in that and chaos follows.' For a moment Bettina seemed transfixed by the vague plume of steam that rose lazily from the doctor's cup.

'My deepest condolences.' Dr Henley went on to say that Sir Seymour's death would be a great loss to everybody who knew him.

She gave a gracious smile. 'I don't seriously suspect the Master of deliberately withholding data, it is only that I felt the chill very strongly yesterday. I have had to live with the chill for most of my life. I first became aware of it when I was about four. That doesn't mean I may not have had some sort of prevision. I consulted the Royal Society for Psychical Research about it once, years ago, and they wrote back saying that prevision phenomena happen much more frequently than people imagine. They are awful frauds, mind, still one expects them to offer a competent kind of opinion.'

'As it happens, I am intrigued by psychic phenomena,' Dr Henley said. 'If you don't mind me asking, Miss Tradescant, how does the chill manifest itself exactly?'

'It starts as a painfully persistent thought at the back of my head. Like a drill. It goes the moment I get confirmation. It simply disappears, as though it's never been there, and then I am as right as rain. As light as a feather. The chill can be extremely demanding, almost like a living entity. *Not* a very nice living entity. It has tantrums. It craves attention. It snaps, it growls. No, I made that up.'

'Fascinating. What will happen to it now?'

'You mean now that my twin is dead?'

'Yes. Will it – go away?'

'I hope so. I have no idea. Only time will show. Strictly *entre nous*, I am sick and tired of talking about the chill in the mysterious and exclusive fashion in which Elijah might have spoken of his ravens. Well, it is refreshing to meet a man of science who is not primarily pig-headed. Doesn't happen often, I assure you.' She blew her nose. 'Could Seymour have drowned?'

'I can't say until I have been able to examine the body properly,' Dr Henley said. 'I suspect a stroke or a heart attack. By the time I arrived, Sir Seymour had been taken out of his bath and one of the stewards had attempted artificial respiration, all in vain, sadly. Sir Seymour had high blood pressure. Those hot baths – I did warn him –'

'I am sure you did your best, my good man.' She shook her head. 'I am afraid Seymour was always rather obstinate. Seymour never *listened* to people. He was singularly lacking in what is sometimes called the "imagination of disaster". No question of a post-mortem then?'

'I sincerely hope that will not be necessary,' the Master said crisply.

'It would look bad for you if there were a PM, wouldn't it? I mean bad for the business, Master. It may cause chaps to think twice before they join this so-called "brotherhood". I understand your fees are obscenely exorbitant. But perhaps there were no suspicious features, that's why you are so damned relaxed about it? No signs of struggle – no bruises – broken nails – odd pigmentation – cracked vertebrae?'

'My dear Miss Tradescant!' The Master's face had turned vermilion. 'There is absolutely nothing to suggest that Sir Seymour died of anything but natural causes. Henley, please, would you be kind enough to confirm?'

Dr Henley said, 'No suspicious features.'

'I am terribly glad. You see, I have been in the grip of

115

some extremely complex emotions, that *may* account for my lack of restraint. Somebody told me once that I had a first-rate mind,' Bettina went on with a self-deprecating smile. 'This may sound like an idle compliment, but it isn't. No second-rate mind could have experienced such an intensity of feeling so ... purely.' She adjusted her hat. 'I expect this means, Dr Henley, that your signature on the death certificate is imminent?'

'I wouldn't say imminent, no.'

'But it is only a matter of time, yes? Oh, how I wish I'd been there beside Seymour as he lay breathing his last, holding his hand, stroking his forehead, saying the rosary with him . . .'

The Master frowned. 'I was not aware that Sir Seymour was a Catholic.'

'He wasn't. He nearly became one about fifty years ago, only he hated the idea of turning into a priest-ridden puppet.' Bettina sighed deeply. 'I am in an odd state. I try not to give in to sorrow, you see. It is *such* an appalling waste of energy. You can't get sorrow into shape – you can't build on it, can you, Master?'

'No.'

'Gazing back into the past is equally fatal. I despise women who wallow in their woes! It's women like that who bring womanhood into disrepute. But don't let me detain you any longer with blasts from my feeble trumpet! You should have stopped me! I am sure you are a busy man, Master.' She rose. 'May I see Seymour's body? Would you lead me to it? I want to check something. I will do it very discreetly. I promise I am not going to make a scene. I won't disgrace myself either. I am not in the least squeamish.'

Her large brocade bag stood on the floor beside her feet and she was aware of the Master's eyes fixing on the orange sleeve that stuck out of it. 'Oh, this is one of the frock-coats your boys wear,' she explained amiably.

'It's a habit.'

'Good or bad? Sorry! That was a terrible thing to say. I mean, terrible in the circumstances. The truth is, I simply *had* to have one. I find inspiration for my dresses in the most *unlikely* quarters. My ideas come when I least expect them. Are you by any chance familiar with my latest creation? No? It is a dress that is incredibly soft and limp; it looks almost moist. It brings to mind – rather poignantly – the tongue of a dead kitten. Well! That's *precisely* what gave me the idea.'

The Master tugged at his beard. 'Where did you find the habit?'

'I didn't *find* it. A habit isn't a dog or an umbrella or a one-pound coin. For heaven's sake, Master, don't look so disapproving! It creates *such* tension. There were quite a few of them downstairs, hanging on a rack in the small room, off the hall.' Bettina made a vague gesture towards the door. 'Gathering dust. I was certain you wouldn't mind. To tell you the truth, I didn't really imagine it would be missed.'

Penelope Tradescant stood looking down at the various objects that had been laid on the desk in her late husband's room.

'Snuff-box, monogrammed handkerchief, pocket watch ... Yes ... This is all, I believe. Oh, the ring's not here. Where's the ring, do you know? Seymour's diamond ring. I don't think it's on his finger.' She cast a quick glance towards the shrouded form that lay on the bed.

'The ring?' The Master's hand went up to his beard. 'I think Sir Seymour had some problem with his ring. For some reason he – um – he couldn't wear it. He thought his fingers had become swollen. He said something to that effect last night. The ring should be inside the little porcelain dish over there – on the bedside table.'

'It is not in the dish.'

'How very curious. I am sure it was there last night. Goodness. You are perfectly right. It's not here.'

'It's an extremely valuable ring.' Penelope looked from the Master to the doctor, then towards the steward in the orange habit standing beside the door.

21

Lord of the Rings

Two days later Antonia was sitting at the breakfast table, leafing through *The Times*. When she reached the Obituaries page, she felt her heart jump inside her.

'Sir Seymour has died,' she said aloud. 'Now, what do you make of *that*?'

Then she remembered Hugh was not there to answer her. Hugh had gone to the Military Club the night before to meet an old uncle of his.

She went right down to the very bottom of the obituary and read the last paragraph. It was the cause of death that interested her, naturally, but there was nothing about it. 'Suddenly' was perhaps the only suggestive word, though it meant nothing, really. It was true that people lived longer nowadays, but quite a few gentlemen of Sir Seymour's age – he would have turned seventy in November – did die 'suddenly'. Why assume his death was due to anything but natural causes?

Antonia leafed back through the paper, to page four, where she glanced through the Home News once more. No, nothing about murder of a baronet or accidental death of a baronet or suspicious death of a baronet. Of course not – she'd have noticed it the first time. It was not the kind of thing she was likely to miss. The obituarist did not say where it was Sir Seymour had died either. Chances were that it was at Mayholme Manor, but she couldn't be sure.

What the obituarist did mention, and rather harped on, was Sir Seymour's fabulous financial rating and the fact that the Tradescant family got a mention in the Domesday Book and had once occupied a royal palace. Sir Seymour was survived by his second wife and a son from his first marriage, who now would be the nineteenth baronet.

The capsule-swap at Claridge's. That was where it had all started. The would-be poisoner, Lady Tradescant had claimed, was the housekeeper, Mrs Mowbray. All Lady Tradescant had done was put the antibiotic capsule back into the box. Well, there was no proof either way. Shame that the housekeeper had died and couldn't give her side of the story – she had committed suicide earlier that same day. How convenient that the killer was dead and couldn't be interrogated . . .

Was that a fair observation? Antonia poured herself another cup of coffee. Sir Seymour had died two days after his attempted poisoning and she seemed to assume that Penelope Tradescant was in fact guilty. Well, when a rich old husband died mysteriously, one always started by suspecting the beautiful and much younger wife. Or could Sir Seymour's sister be involved after all? Or his son? Or the Master?

The mass of ideas moved like nebulae inside Antonia's head. She bit into her buttered toast only to discover it was stone-cold. She put it down on her plate and wiped her fingers with the napkin. She was no longer hungry, actually. She thought of the things she needed to do today. Send an email with some queries concerning the proofs to her copy editor rather urgently, as soon as possible. Collect her granddaughter from her primary school at three. Could she really afford to indulge her passion for sleuthery?

There wasn't much to go upon. Events had been related to her at second hand, which was not particularly helpful. No, at *third* hand. Jesty told Hugh, who told her. Lady Tradescant told Jesty, who told Hugh, who told her. How annoying. She was not really in a position to form any valid opinion at all. Hugh had the advantage of having met some of the participants in the drama. Captain Jesty, Bettina Tradescant, the Master. Hugh hadn't met Lady Tradescant, who of course was the principal protagonist, but he had observed the guilty expression on her face.

Hugh had also mentioned one of the Mayholme Manor 'brothers'. A very old man in a wheelchair, a Dr Fairchild, who had been involved in the Nuremberg trials in 1946 in some capacity or other, same as Sir Seymour's father, in fact – but, at this point at least, Antonia couldn't see how Dr Fairchild could possibly matter. The only suspicious thing about Dr Fairchild, she reasoned, was the fact that his room was two or three doors away from Sir Seymour's ... Oh, and he'd *insisted* on being moved to the third floor ...

It was only in detective stories the seemingly irrelevant bit-part player turned out to have done it. Antonia considered that a mere trick, not really fair on the reader. She found herself thinking of Lady Westholme in *An Appointment with Death* – a character who flitted in and out of the story in the most tangential manner imaginable, only to be revealed at the end – logically and entertainingly enough, it had to be said – as Mrs Boynton's nemesis. Antonia had determined never to do that sort of thing in any of *her* detective stories. She believed in introducing the killer no later than page four or five.

She poured herself more coffee. Did Penelope Tradescant tell the truth? Had Sir Seymour died of natural causes? Where had Penelope been at the time of her husband's death?

Once more she wondered if Hugh had read the obituary and, if he had, what he had to say about it.

'Golly. I wonder if he was made away with after all.' Major Payne lowered *The Times*, a thoughtful frown on his face.

'The buttered eggs are bloody marvellous. I couldn't recommend them more,' General Quinton said over his cup of tea.

'Sir Seymour Tradescant's died, Uncle Louis. Did you know him? You used to live in his part of the world at one time, didn't you?'

They were sitting at a round seventeenth-century refectory table in the small green damask dining room at the Military Club, having breakfast.

'Seymour Tradescant? He was at least ten years younger than me, I think. If it's the same chap.' General Quinton tapped his lips with the starched napkin. 'I knew Frances, his first wife. Not terribly well. Splendid old girl. Seymour bullied her mercilessly, they said, but she never complained. Didn't know him at all well. Met him once or twice. Never really felt the inclination. Had one of those mercurial temperaments, or so everybody said.'

'Not a nice chap?'

'Not a nice chap. Enjoyed goading his twin sister into difficulty or disaster *quite* on purpose. Or so rumour had it. Was horrible to his son Nicholas. Don't know if he mellowed with age. A strong element of eccentricity entered into some of his attitudes, apparently. Isn't that an eminently diplomatic way of saying someone's gone mad? Nicholas will be . . . what is the word I want?'

'Pleased?'

'The nineteenth baronet. That's correct, isn't it? The nineteenth, yes. Met Nicholas on a couple of occasions. A thoroughly decent chap. A bit weak-willed, perhaps. Pining for an heir.'

'Sir Seymour married a much younger woman.'

'Ah yes. The second Lady T. At one time everyone was talking about it. Lovely to look at, engaging air of innocence. Always beautifully dressed. After his money of course.' General Quinton paused. 'More than a match for him, they said, so he got what he deserved. She didn't bump him off, by any chance, did she?'

'The paper doesn't say. Are you familiar with Mayholme Manor, Uncle Louis?'

'I thought Seymour lived at Tradescant Hall.'

Before Major Payne could explain, a delicate little cough was heard. 'Sorry to butt in like this, but I couldn't help overhearing. As it happens, I was at Mayholme Manor the other night. Did you say Sir Seymour was dead?' It was a thin, mild-looking elderly man with rimless glasses and a prim mouth, who had spoken from across the table. He sported a rather splendid waistcoat, Payne noticed.

'That's correct. It's in today's paper.'

'I was visiting a friend and was persuaded to stay for dinner. Dear me. *What* a coincidence. I don't like such coincidences at all. I wonder if Sir Seymour died that same night – or the morning after? He must have done – if his death is in today's *Times*. He kept looking down at his fingers, you see – kept flexing them.' The man demonstrated. 'He asked me whether I thought his fingers were a bit swollen.'

Payne gazed at him with interest. 'Really? Did you know Sir Seymour well?' Small world, he thought – talk of serendipitous discoveries!

'We'd never met before. I just happened to be seated next to him. The Master performed the introductions. The Master, you see, always behaves with the greatest good cheer and is graceful and charming and unflaggingly delightful with everyone and everything. The Master's got *style*. Have you met the Master?'

Payne said he had met the Master.

'Mayholme Manor is the most civilized place in the world,' the man in the splendid waistcoat went on. 'I was told that there is *always* a back-up course should the soufflé fall. Bridge after dinner, or else the delights of the *salle de ciné*.'

'You aren't by any chance considering joining the brotherhood?'

'I am still married and not likely to become a widower for some time,' the man in the splendid waistcoat said a touch wistfully. 'They are a most clubbable crowd there. Some of the best families in the land, you know. And the stewards are terribly attentive. That evening, if I remember

122

correctly, we covered an incredible number of topics – a proper debating society! The ballistics of fast bowling, the ancient Haitian monarchy with its Dukes of Marmelada and Limonada, Antonia Darcy's fastidious felons and the Law of Averages. Incidentally, my name is Martindale.'

'Antonia Darcy is my wife ... Are *all* of her felons fastidious?'

'Antonia Darcy is your wife? How perfectly marvellous. Somebody said she operated within a remarkably narrow if exclusive social range – her imagination never moved outside Belgrave Square.'

'I don't think she would like that. It isn't strictly true.'

'I can't think of any other place that's *quite* like Mayholme Manor. *A corner, that is forever England.*'

'I know exactly what you mean.'

'Stewards and style!' General Quinton harrumphed. 'Hotbeds of unspeakable passions and unquenchable animosities, places like that.'

'How interesting, that you should have sat next to Sir Seymour at dinner, Martindale,' Payne said. 'I imagine you are one of the last people to have talked to him before he died.'

'I probably was.'

'Was there anything wrong with Sir Seymour's fingers?'

'Not as far as I could see. But he produced a ring and demonstrated how it wouldn't fit his finger. His little finger. He seemed to have quite an *idée fixe* about it. Only the day before the ring had been on his finger and there had been nothing wrong with it. He described himself as "helplessly perplexed". It was an extremely precious ring, he said. A present to his father from the Duchess of Windsor back in '46, I think he said.'

Payne sat up. That very old chap, whose room was only two doors away from Sir Seymour's, had a portrait of the Duchess of Windsor on his wall ...

'Beware of Greeks bearing gifts,' General Quinton said portentously. 'Stop me if I've said this before, but Mrs

123

Simpson was the greatest mischief-maker the world had ever known. Since Eve.'

'He might have had arthritis,' Martindale said. 'Or some odd form of allergy?'

'I myself suffer from gouty spasms,' General Quinton said. 'Sometimes my feet get so swollen, I can't put any shoes on and have to wear my slippers. To think I used to wear nothing but boots once!'

Major Payne remained silent. The ring had been in the porcelain dish on Sir Seymour's bedside table. He had seen it with his own eyes. He wished now he had taken a closer look at it. The next moment another picture rose before his eyes. The day of his visit – Valkyrian skies – he in his black bowler and rolled-up brolly – Sir Seymour's sister in her ridiculous golfing suit. Bettina had been in a state of some agitation – one of her hands in a glove, the other bare – she had been pulling her ring up and down her finger as they talked – up and down –

Her ring appeared to be – well, *loose*.

He hadn't thought anything of it at the time, but now he wondered.

Bettina Tradescant said she hadn't been allowed to go anywhere near her brother's room, but that was a lie. She *had* been inside Sir Seymour's room.

Two rings, Payne thought – one loose, the other, well, tight. One made for a thicker finger, the other for a thinner, smaller, one.

22

Cruel Intentions

Later in the day he told Antonia about it.

'I believe she swapped the rings. They must have looked identical, otherwise Sir Seymour would have known at once. When it didn't fit, he assumed there was something wrong with his finger, not with the ring. The rather obvious deduction is that Bettina Tradescant had a ring which was identical to the one her brother wore. Her ring was a replica and not worth much while the other one was worth a fortune.'

'Did you say the ring was a present from the Duchess of Windsor to Sir Seymour's father? We can assume that Bettina knew all about it.'

'She is exactly the kind of woman who would idolize the Duchess of Windsor. Actually, she even looks like the Duchess of Windsor. Thin, angular, ugly as sin, one can't imagine her without her *maquillage*, she probably sleeps in it, and, again like the Duchess, she is a fashion fetishist. Yes. I believe she simply *had* to have the ring. Or perhaps there was a practical and purely financial reason for the theft? Maybe she is in debt, needs the money badly and intends to sell it.'

'Did she go to Mayholme Manor that day with the sole object of pinching it then?'

'I believe that was a spur-of-the-moment decision. She

said she had come to check if her brother was dead. She was convinced that her brother had died – she had had the chill and so on.' Payne lit his pipe. 'She goes to his room. Sir Seymour is not there. She spots the ring in the dish on the bedside table. She takes it and leaves her own ring in its place. She then makes a dash for it ... That would explain why she was running as though all the devils from hell were after her and why she nearly smashed my face with the door. She was in a highly agitated state. Well, one possible explanation is that she was afraid of being rumbled.'

'She must have believed her brother wouldn't notice the difference,' Antonia said. 'It didn't occur to her that her ring wouldn't fit on his finger.'

'She made a mistake there. I'd very much like to take a squint at that ring. As you know, my love, I am a great believer in putting theories to the test. I know something about precious stones. I can tell at once if the ring is a fake ... I imagine the young widow's collected all her husband's possessions, including the ring ... Shall I pay the young widow a visit?'

'How would you persuade the young widow to show you the ring?'

'I would introduce myself as the representative of a top Bond Street jeweller. Um. I would say that Sir Seymour had asked me to evaluate the ring. I'll pretend of course that I have no idea that Sir Seymour has died. Ingenious, eh?' Payne puffed at his pipe. 'It would actually be very interesting to meet the young widow. Vis-à-vis.'

'I am sure you would enjoy meeting the young widow enormously. Vis-à-vis.'

'Don't be an ass, darling. My interest is purely criminological.'

'Is it?'

'Nothing but. Who knows, I might even be able to convince Lady Tradescant that the quest for riches is little more than ignoble and illusory. Oh, don't look at me like that! Gives me the creeps. Do let's be sensible and constructive, shall we? Do you think Sir Seymour was killed?'

'I don't know. And I don't care,' Antonia said tersely.

Some twenty minutes later Major Payne's mobile phone rang.

'Hello – that you, Payne?'

'Good lord. Jesty! I've been thinking about you.'

'Did you see today's paper?'

'I did, my dear fellow. He is dead. I know. It's quite incredible.'

'I can't believe it, Payne. We – we expected him to turn up dead, didn't we? And now he's turned up dead. Sir Seymour Tradescant is dead.'

'I know. Well, coincidences do happen –'

'I personally think she is behind it.'

'Who? Lady Tradescant?'

'Who else? She is the most logical suspect. I have had time to think, you see. I am sure she lied to me. That rigmarole – about Mrs Mowbray and so on. I am sure she made it all up. She is a minx. She is a snake, Payne. She is the devil. She –'

'And I was hoping you'd got over her,' Payne said with a sigh.

'I haven't got over her. I keep thinking about her. I can't help it, Payne. I dream about her. I see her in all sorts of different scenarios.'

'You sound as though you might have been drinking.'

'I *have* been drinking. Of course I have been drinking, Payne. Scotch, mainly. I wouldn't have been able to survive otherwise. I tried to speak to her the other day, but met with no success. No one answers the phone. She couldn't have gone away before the funeral, could she?'

'I have no idea.'

'I thought you might be on the case, Payne, that's why I rang you. I thought you might have found *something*.'

'I am not on the case,' Payne said. 'I am not sure there is a case.'

'Of course there is. You don't believe the eighteenth baronet died of natural causes, do you? A clever fellow like you. If you find any incriminating evidence, please let me know at once. I would be most grateful. You will let me know, won't you, Payne?'

Payne promised he would.

'I may actually contact the police,' Jesty said after a pause. 'I may give them a lead or two. Tell them about the curious incident at Claridge's. I may make one of those anonymous phone calls. Or write an anonymous letter or two.'

'You wouldn't stoop that low, surely?'

'I would.'

'Not the conduct of an officer and a gentleman –'

'Don't give me that rot.'

'These things do matter, Jesty.'

'I don't care.'

'What would you be hoping to achieve?'

'I want to make things as uncomfortable for her as possible, Payne. I want her to be harried and grilled and frightened. I want her brought down low, mortified, disgraced, arrested – imprisoned for life –'

If this were a detective story, I would make Jesty the killer, Payne thought. It would be one of those solutions that are described as 'unguessable'. Jesty was the least likely suspect and he would have killed Sir Seymour as a form of revenge on Lady Tradescant – *to get Lady Tradescant suspected of her husband's murder* – because he loved her and she loved him not . . .

23

The Lady Investigates

As they sat having dinner, Antonia said, 'I am as good at telling fake diamonds from real ones as you are. Actually, it would be safer if I went instead. Lady Tradescant might recognize you as Captain Jesty's fellow spy. In fact she is bound to recognize you. She saw you at Claridge's.'

'Only for a split second,' Payne pointed out.

'I am sure she is the kind of woman that never forgets a man's face.'

'You may be right. I hope you are not jealous?'

'I am not going to phone. Better catch her unawares,' said Antonia. 'I will just turn up on her doorstep in Half Moon Street. I will use your top Bond Street jeweller ruse, if I may.'

'You are welcome to it. Don't forget to give a false name. How about changing your appearance in some subtle way?'

'Do you think that would be necessary? She's never seen me.'

'Lady Tradescant may turn out to be one of your greatest fans and recognize you from the photos on the back flap of your books.'

'I hate those photos. They look nothing like me. Besides, I doubt Lady Tradescant is the reading kind.'

'You seem to have got your knife into her. You don't like the idea of me going to see a pretty girl, admit it.'

'I have been thinking, actually. Lady Tradescant is the *most logical suspect.*'

'Jesty also thinks she is the most logical suspect. Perhaps Jesty and you should meet up for tea or drinks and exchange notes? Who knows, you may even take to him. The two of you may hit it off. A lot of women apparently go mad over Jesty.'

It was a morning straight from paradise. The sun, clear of mist, was full and golden in the firmament. Bees hummed among the riot of June flowers. Pigeons cooed. Dupin, Antonia's one remaining cat – Vidocq having died a violent death a couple of months back – strolled across the lawn with feigned nonchalance, his eyes fixed on the fattest pigeon.

Antonia made up her face elaborately, in a manner she had never done before. She then put on a silk dress of a conservative and rather stately pattern, an absurdly smart blue hat and white lace gloves. She had worn this particular ensemble only once before, at the wedding of an impossibly stuffy cousin of Hugh's.

'What do you think?'

'You look imposing,' Payne said.

'I look dreadful.'

'You might be a knight's widow or even a peeress in her own right. The very incarnation of what once upon a time the snobbishly romantic lower-middle classes referred to as a "great lady". You look as though you are heading for the House of Lords or one of Her Majesty's garden parties.'

Antonia scowled at her reflection in the mirror. 'I look older. . .'

'You invite trust, which is exactly what you need today. I won't kiss you because I may smudge your lipstick. Now then. There are two things you need to find out –'

'You would rather kiss Lady Tradescant, wouldn't you?'

'One. The cause of Sir Seymour's death. Two. Lady Tradescant's whereabouts on the morning her husband died.'

She said, 'I will do my best.'

It was an hour later.

Antonia, feeling extremely self-conscious in her white lace gloves and hat, stood in Half Moon Street, outside an elegant Georgian house with neat window boxes of scarlet and pink geraniums. She glanced at her watch. Half past ten. Too early for Lady Tradescant to have gone shopping, or to meet a friend for coffee at Harvey Nicks, or to have her hair done at Luigi's of Mayfair, or whatever it was beautiful rich girls did with their time.

Taking her courage in her hands, she rang the door bell.

A woman's voice answered through the intercom. 'Who is it?'

'My name is Antonia Rushton. I represent Wahlstein and Innocent, the Bond Street jewellers,' she said breathlessly. 'I have an appointment with Sir Seymour Tradescant.'

'I am sorry, but my husband is dead. He died the other day. Didn't you know?'

'Dead? No – no – I had no idea! But – how dreadful! Sir – Sir Seymour spoke to us only three days ago. I am so sorry. We had no idea,' Antonia stammered on. 'Is – is that Lady Tradescant?'

'It is. Seymour spoke to you three days ago? How odd. That's when he died.'

'I am so sorry,' Antonia said again.

'Bond Street jewellers, did you say? What was the reason, did Seymour explain?' Penelope Tradescant asked.

Antonia had worked out the details of her story carefully. 'It was a very delicate matter. It seems Sir Seymour had concerns about his ring. It was a diamond ring of great value. The Wallis ring. That was the name Sir Seymour had for it.'

'I know the ring. What was the problem? No, wait –'

Antonia imagined she heard some other voice whisper in the background.

'I think you'd better come in,' Penelope Tradescant said.

A moment later a humming sound was heard and the door opened.

Penelope Tradescant led the way through a spacious hall, up a flight of stairs and into a magnificent sitting room done in white and Wedgwood blue. One wall was taken up with two large french windows, ceiling high, and opening to a balcony that was filled with flowers. The balcony seemed to extend along two walls of the house.

The room was spotless but there was no evidence of any servants. Who was the person who had whispered to Lady Tradescant earlier on? Apart from the door through which they had walked, there were two more doors. One of them was ajar and now Antonia imagined it swayed slightly. Was someone standing there, listening? Who was it? Penelope's lover? One of her lovers?

Antonia hadn't quite expected her to wear widow's weeds, and she didn't, though Antonia had an idea she would look good in black. Penelope Tradescant was clad in a simple mint-green dress and her hair was pulled back in a pony tail. She looked cool, composed and very young. Her face was fresh and smooth and seemed free of make-up. There was an engaging air of innocence about her. She had perfect bone structure. Hugh hadn't exaggerated. The girl was stunningly beautiful.

'Do sit down – please – Miss Rushton – that's right, isn't it?' Penelope waved towards the sofa. She herself remained standing beside the window, her back to the light. Practising for when her looks start fading, Antonia thought, though that may not be for quite some time yet. 'So, what was it Seymour said about the ring?'

'Well, Sir Seymour rang one of our partners. It was three days ago, rather early in the morning. Mr Innocent's private number, as a matter of fact – Sir Seymour was a most valued client.'

'I was not aware that Seymour had dealings with your firm. Wahlstein and Innocent, did you say? Never heard of you before. Never knew you existed.'

'Sir Seymour wasn't a regular customer, but he has bought things from us in the past,' Antonia explained. 'The last time was twenty years ago, actually.'

'Oh, I wasn't married to him then. What did he want you to do exactly?'

'Well, Sir Seymour asked us to look at a ring. He wanted it carefully examined. He said the band seemed to have suddenly – shrunk. He couldn't fit it on his finger. He suspected that the ring – a very valuable ring that had belonged to his father – had been stolen and replaced by an identical-looking replica.'

'He suspected the Wallis ring was a fake? This is extremely interesting,' Penelope said. 'Go on.'

'Sir Seymour believed that the substitution had taken place the day before. He was perturbed, puzzled, really, that's why he needed an expert opinion.'

'How terribly curious – but there is something even more curious,' Penelope said slowly. 'You see, the Wallis ring was *not* among my husband's effects, which I collected on the day he died. It seems to have disappeared.'

'*Disappeared?*'

'Yes. The Master ordered a search, over which he presided in person. They searched high and low, the stewards, the Master and the doctor, but they found nothing. The Master suggested that the ring might have fallen down the drain and he promised to have a plumber round to check. He promised to report back to me.'

'Is the ring insured?'

'I believe it is – it's got to be. I don't know. Seymour never told me. I will need to check with Seymour's solicitor. This is one complication I could have done without.' Penelope's hand went up to her forehead. 'I am sorry. Things at the moment are at sixes and sevens, as you can well imagine. It looks as though there won't be a PM, but the situation may change. I would hate it if the police got involved.'

'Oh dear. I hope not! Why should they want a PM?' Antonia opened her eyes wide. 'Hope you don't mind me asking?'

A door was heard slamming and Penelope gave a little gasp. At once she smiled and apologized. 'Sorry. There's a draught somewhere. I am all alone. This whole business has made me jumpy. I haven't been sleeping properly.'

Only now Antonia noticed the dark smudges under the young woman's eyes.

There must be another exit, she thought – probably to the garden at the back? Whoever was in the flat had now left . . .

'I thought I could cope with a crisis, but I am not very good at it,' Penelope said. 'It feels as if I am trapped in some horrible dream. I was at Heathrow, you see, standing in a queue, thinking of France, really looking forward to it, when I got the Master's call. A friend was seeing me off. The Master told me they had found Seymour dead in his bath. If the call had come two hours later, I wouldn't have got it. I would have been on the plane! Then I would have had to jump on the next plane back to England.'

'Thank God for small mercies,' Antonia murmured sympathetically.

'We turned round and walked back to the taxi rank . . . As luck would have it, we got the same cab that took us to the airport, can you imagine? The cabbie gaped at us. He was extremely curious – wanted to know why we were going back — what had happened – he kept asking questions. I hated explaining but –'

So Penelope had an alibi for the fatal morning. She couldn't have been in two places at the same time. Unless she had faked her alibi somehow? She wasn't anybody's idea of a cold-blooded murderess. She had an air of sweetness and vulnerability about her. In addition to her stunning good looks. Antonia could see how easy it would be for middle-aged fools like Hugh and Captain Jesty to swoon over her.

'Dr Henley believes Seymour had a heart attack or a stroke, brought on by the hot bath, but he said he would need a second opinion. He's managed to speak to another doctor now,' Penelope was saying. 'It's someone who visits Mayholme Manor twice a month. There've got to be *two* signatures on the death certificate. That's the procedure . . . I haven't even started thinking about the funeral . . . All kinds of people keep ringing asking me about the funeral . . . I don't seem to know any of them!'

'It must be terribly nerve-racking.'

'I am sure I will survive,' Penelope said with a smile, but her eyes looked suspiciously bright.

'Of course you will,' Antonia said firmly. Poor girl, she thought.

'Shall we have coffee?'

'That's very kind of you, Lady Tradescant. I shouldn't really impose on your kindness at a time like this –'

'Oh nonsense. I won't be a minute.' Penelope started walking towards the door.

No, she didn't give the impression of being hard or calculating or predatory – wasn't that what gold-diggers were supposed to be? Antonia had come prepared to dislike and distrust Penelope Tradescant, but now she found herself warming to the girl. Something of the lost soul about her, despite her air of cool poise and sophistication . . . She clearly needed to talk to someone . . .

Antonia glanced at the little table beside the sofa. Cards were laid out on it. Patience. The Queen of Spades looks a bit like me, Antonia thought. She has a similar sort of hat on, how ridiculous. The Joker sported a natty little moustache and a red hussar's uniform and was depicted in the act of strangling a plump woman whose expression was one of unbridled ecstasy. *A lady killer.* A literal kind of joke. Antonia smiled. That's Captain Jesty, she decided. Poor lovelorn Captain Jesty. Hugh said Jesty hadn't got over Penelope . . .

Beside the cards lay a cardboard wallet. *British Airlines.* Antonia picked it up quickly and took out its contents. A plane ticket. *23rd June. Heathrow London–Paris. Flight time: 10.30 a.m.*

Lady Tradescant would have had to be at Heathrow two hours prior to the flight. She had taken a cab. The same cab, as it happened, had then delivered her back. It could all be checked of course. The cabbie had been curious and asked questions. The cabbie would certainly remember the beautiful young widow. He would also remember her escort. Who was her escort? Her lover?

Penelope appeared with a tray containing two steaming bone-china mugs.

'Here you are. I didn't put out any sugar. Is that OK?'

'Yes. Thank you.'

'I have decided to come clean. I believe I know who the thief is. Only one person could have swapped the Wallis ring with an identical-looking replica with a smaller band.' Penelope took a sip of coffee. 'It's Bets. Only she could have done it.'

'Bets?'

'Seymour's sister Bettina. I call her "Bets". She's always been mad about the Wallis ring. She had a replica made a couple of years ago. As it happens, I helped her with it. Seymour refused to lend her the ring, so she asked me to take photos of it, from every possible angle. Which I did. She then gave the photos to some jeweller, who used them to produce the replica. She paid something like a thousand pounds for it. The real thing of course costs much more.'

'The substitution wouldn't have been noticed had the band been the right size.'

'You are absolutely right. Well, Bets got it wrong there. Too impatient, never thinks things through properly. She's always been like that.' Penelope smiled. 'She is a great friend. I have tremendous affection for her. She's done so much for me! She "discovered" me. I used to work for Bets' mag. *Dazzle.*'

'I thought you might be a model. You have the look.'

Antonia nodded. 'My daughter-in-law is a former model.' It felt good *not* to have to tell lies all the time, she thought.

'Bets is wonderful. She is generous to a fault, the sweetest, kindest person who ever lived! She is his twin, but she couldn't be more different from Seymour. Most people say she is a lunatic. I personally think she is a genius.'

'To either sort morality is meaningless,' murmured Antonia

'Bets is one of the last true originals. She's got ideas. But she needs money, a lot of money,' Penelope went on ruefully. 'She is terribly keen on starting a magazine, you see. She's told me all about it. When she became the editor of *Dazzle* she moved it away from the usual debs-and-dowagers milieu – she embraced instead an edgier, more outré fashion arena. She showed no particular respect for the old Establishment! I was a nobody when she discovered me. She is remarkably broad-minded. She is unlike anyone else in the business. She *deserves* to have her own mag. All she needs is the capital!'

'She seems have found it now . . .'

'As far as I am concerned, she is welcome to the Wallis ring. I don't want that ring. I believe it's cursed. She can keep it. Seymour is dead, so it couldn't matter less. It would solve all her problems. In fact I am glad she took it! It was naughty of her, but I won't read the riot act to her.' Penelope laughed. It was a most attractive laugh.

'Well, I am glad the mystery has been resolved,' Antonia said brightly.

'Yes, thank God. I shall phone the Master and tell him to call off the search. I'll tell him – what shall I tell him? I'll make up some story. I'll say – I'll say I've found the ring in the lining of Seymour's coat. How about that?'

'But, Lady Tradescant, what about the other ring – the replica? Where did *that* disappear?'

'The replica? Oh, who cares!' Penelope waved her hand dismissively. 'It cost only a thousand pounds. Perhaps one of the stewards pinched it. Not worth making any fuss about it, really.'

The next moment the door bell rang and she went to answer it.

No servants, Antonia thought. She's got rid of her servants. Coming from a humble background, Penelope didn't believe in the exploitation of the masses? The cynical explanation would be that Lady Tradescant didn't want anyone to know what she got up to in the privacy of her town house. Did she perhaps receive visits – from men?

As though on cue, Penelope reappeared in the company of two pleasant-looking youngish men in well-cut suits.

'I am so sorry, Miss Rushton. These gentlemen are policemen. They want to talk to me about something rather urgently.'

Antonia rose to her feet. 'Yes, of course. Will you be all right?'

'Of course I'll be all right! It's some routine inquiry – isn't it?' Penelope turned to one of the men.

'I will find my way out.' Antonia walked briskly out of the room.

24

The Adventure of the Audacious Eavesdroppers

Major Payne sat in a deckchair in the garden. He was speaking into the phone. 'Hope I am not interrupting your tête-à-tête with Lady Tradescant?'

'You are not. I left a minute ago.'

'So she agreed to talk to you?'

'We had coffee together. She was perfectly amiable. She's got an alibi for the fatal morning.'

'Of which no doubt you are highly suspicious?'

'I am not, actually. She does seem to have genuinely been "elsewhere".'

'That indeed is what "alibi" means ... Jesty won't like it ... Where was she?'

'Heathrow Airport. I saw her ticket. She was in a check-in queue when she received the sad news.'

Payne asked her whether she had got to see the ring.

'No,' said Antonia. 'The ring has vanished.'

'The replica – what we believe to be the replica has vanished?'

'Yes. Apparently it wasn't in Sir Seymour's room when Penelope went to collect his possessions.'

'It would be interesting to know if Bettina Tradescant was at Mayholme Manor on the morning Sir Seymour died,' Payne said thoughtfully.

'You think Bettina did it *twice*? You believe she stole the original ring *and* the replica?'

'It's perfectly possible. Um ... It occurs to her that her brother will realize the ring is a replica and that he will guess she is behind it. So she goes and steals the replica, believing one of the stewards will be blamed for it. She reasons that without the replica Sir Seymour can prove nothing that will count against her.'

'Do you think she might have killed him too?'

'Well, yes. Say, Sir Seymour catches her red-handed and kicks up a stink. He threatens to call the police. Things get out of hand and she kills him. She is ever so slightly mad. It's definitely worth checking if she was at Mayholme Manor on the fatal morning. What was the cause of death, did Penelope tell you?'

'Sir Seymour apparently died in his bath. It's difficult to imagine Sir Seymour and his sister having a row and then he goes and takes a bath while she is still there, in his room?'

'Perhaps she left – and then, after a couple of minutes, *came back* ...'

'Hugh, two policemen came to see Penelope while I was still there.'

'Really?'

'Yes – but it had nothing to do with Sir Seymour's death.'

'How do you know? They couldn't have let you stay on and listen while they interrogated Lady Tradescant.'

'No, but I managed to hear what they said.'

'Did you eavesdrop?'

'Well, I happened to be standing outside the drawing-room door and –'

'You eavesdropped! In your stately hat! You stooped and listened at the keyhole! I bet you tried to hold your breath? Well, I suppose we've come to a point where, as they say, the gloves are off and Queensberry rules no longer apply ... What did the plod want with Penelope?'

'It's a completely new development. It has nothing to do with Sir Seymour's death, at least I don't see how –'

Antonia broke off and Payne heard her speak to someone. The next moment she said, 'Sorry, Hugh, I'll get back to you later.'

'Who's that with you?' Payne asked but she had rung off.

Who was the man who had spoken to her? Payne was sure it was a man's voice that had addressed her. He felt vague stirrings of anxiety. No – what could possibly happen to Antonia in the very heart of Mayfair – in broad daylight?

For several moments he sat very still, watching their cat stalk a dove.

He wondered what his next move should be. Another visit to Mayholme Manor seemed to be indicated . . . He'd need to find out whether Bettina had been there on the morning of her brother's death . . . *Yes* . . . Where were his car keys?

This time he didn't so much as glance at the frieze with the bubble and the eerily featureless figure inside it. As he crossed the hall and went up the stairs, Major Payne was struck by the thought that this was a silence more profound and mysterious than the mere absence of noise. He met no one on the way.

He was soon inside the antechamber that led to the Master's study. He was put in mind of a superior dentist's waiting room. William Morris wallpaper. Table lamps. A sofa upholstered in dark red. A bowl containing several exquisite roses. (Viscountess Folkestone?) The door to the Master's study was ajar. He heard the Master's voice raised in dismay.

Payne listened.

'He *wouldn't*? But you said he would, Robert. Didn't you say he would?'

'I did say it, but he wouldn't. He gave every indication he was going to play ball. I never imagined he'd dig in his heels like that. I am awfully sorry, Wilfred. Didn't seem that sort of chap at all.'

'What is it this Lyndhurst is supposed to have found?'

'Bruises on the right shoulder – black marks. Hardly perceptible to the naked eye, but Lyndhurst thinks they are suspicious. He believes they may be the result of violence. I pointed out that the body of an elderly man could be bruised easily, and in peculiar ways –'

'What's he suggesting exactly – that someone *drowned* Sir Seymour in his bath? That Sir Seymour was pushed under the water and held there? What a fool. People should endeavour *not* to use their intelligence when they have so little of it.'

'Lyndhurst appears most anxious to speak to the police.'

Outside the door Payne stood still and inclined his head forward, not daring to breathe. It occurred to him that he was in exactly the kind of situation Antonia had found herself in a little earlier. How odd. We are two parts of a whole, he thought.

'We can't afford to have the police here. Any whiff of a scandal would cause irreparable damage. It would destroy me. I wouldn't be able to survive the pressure. I am not a strong man, Robert, you know that perfectly well. It would drive me to the brink. It would be the end of *everything*.'

'Lyndhurst insists there should be a PM followed by an investigation.'

Payne found he was leaning on the polished table that stood outside the study door and now he frowned down at the pile of newspapers and magazines. He noted mechanically that the top paper was two days old.

'Didn't you try to impress it on that mule that it would not be a frightfully good idea?'

'I did my best, but he remained adamant. He's dug his heels in.'

'You couldn't have tried hard enough!'

Payne's eyes remained fixed on the newspaper. *Memorial Service*, he read. *Friends and relatives of Petunia Luscombe-Lunt, who died tragically in the Alps on 12th June –*

The name rang a bell. Did he know a Petunia Luscombe-Lunt? Now where . . .?

'I agree it was a mistake bringing Lyndhurst in –' Dr Henley broke off. 'I think there's someone at the door.'

Payne straightened up. His cover had been blown. The blasted newspaper had rustled. Well, time for action. If he was to bluff his way through, he mustn't hesitate for a second. Pushing the door, he sauntered into the Master's study.

'Good afternoon,' he said. 'So sorry – I don't suppose this is a frightfully convenient time?'

The Master was sitting at his desk, Dr Henley in one of the large armchairs. The Master's hand was at his throat. He was a peculiar colour.

'I am afraid it is not,' the Master managed to say. 'You haven't got an appointment with me, have you?'

'No. We have met before, actually. You seem to have forgotten, but I was here a few days ago.'

'Good lord.' The Master's eyes bulged a little. 'Major Ponsonby, was it?'

'Payne, actually.'

'Major Payne. Yes. That is correct. You were writing a new history of Mayholme Manor. Hope you won't think me frightfully rude, but may I suggest you call sometime later? Dr Henley and I happen to be in the middle of an important discussion.'

'I have a confession to make,' Major Payne said gravely. 'I am *not* writing a new history of Mayholme Manor. I am not a writer. I am a private investigator.'

There was a moment of paralysed silence. The Master had flushed an alarming shade of carmine. 'It has nothing to do with poor Sir Seymour, I trust?'

Payne said that it had *everything* to do with poor Sir Seymour. '*Not* with his death as such –'

Dr Henley rose to his feet by executing the three or four distinct movements into which the portly gentleman of advanced middle age tends to divide a simple physical effort. 'I am afraid I must go, Master. Prior engagement.' He produced a silver pocket watch and shook his head. 'Completely slipped my mind.'

143

Talk of rats leaving sinking ships, Payne reflected as the door closed.

'A truly remarkable fellow, Henley. This place would never have been the same without him. I admire him immensely,' the Master said. 'Such style. Such panache.'

'I have been employed by Nicholas Tradescant. *Sir* Nicholas Tradescant, as he now is –'

'Such vigour, such vitality, such intense *joie de vivre*. You should see him in the garden, hacking away at hedges. He does it with a kind of savage grace,' the Master gabbled on. 'He does it with brutal brio.'

'Sir Nicholas has asked me to investigate the theft of his father's ring.' Payne wondered if the Master had started feigning madness. Or could he have lost his mind for real?

'Henley is noted for his easy superiority of manner. Henley belongs to that rare breed of men who can command respectful attention in *any* kind of milieu. Henley would feel equally at home on a battleship, at a cricket test match or at the Savoy Grill. Anyone meeting Henley for the first time might be excused for mistaking him for minor royalty.'

'Sorry, Master, but would you mind terribly if I asked you a couple of questions?'

25

Playing Happy Families

'I do apologize. I made you jump. You don't know me. Are you a friend of Penelope's?' It was a good-looking young man with feverish black eyes who had addressed her. He couldn't be more than twenty-one or twenty-two, Antonia thought. His hair was dark and almost shoulder-length. He looked like a cross between Prince Valiant and Rudolf Nureyev, she decided.

The next moment she frowned in a puzzled way. 'I think we have met before – haven't we? Your face looks familiar.'

'I think you saw me earlier on, as you walked to the house. I was in my car.' He pointed. 'You passed by. I have been sitting there the whole morning, watching the house. Who is the man? There is a man with Penelope, isn't there? You must have seen him. He was with her, wasn't he?'

'What man?'

'Not at all her type, but he is clearly allowed access. Something I am not. Not any longer.' The young man spoke bitterly. 'He had dark glasses on but took them off. Brown hair, round eyes, shining upper lip. She opened the door for him – that was earlier on, a couple of minutes before you came. He is there, isn't he? In the house. He hasn't come out yet, so he must still be inside. Didn't you meet him? Didn't she introduce him to you?'

'No. I didn't meet anyone. Lady Tradescant said she was

145

alone in the house.' That slamming door. There had been somebody there. Antonia was sure of it, though she decided to say nothing about it.

The young man passed his hand over his face. 'Sorry. You probably think I am mad. I haven't been very well. I want to know what Penelope's doing. So much has been happening. Do you know Penelope well? I haven't seen you before.'

'No, I don't know her very well,' Antonia said.

'Who were those two men I saw go into the house ten minutes ago? Did Penelope introduce them to you? Sorry. I don't suppose firing questions at you will endear me to you, will it?'

'Did you say you were a friend of Lady Tradescant's?'

'Well, I was *much* more than a friend, but things – things seem to have changed. Not my fault. I've done nothing. I don't know why she turned against me. My name is Victor Levant. I am the son of their housekeeper. The Tradescants' late housekeeper.'

'You are Mrs Mowbray's son?' Antonia looked at him with interest.

'Yes. Did you know my mother?'

'I didn't. But I have – heard about her. I know she – she died. I am sorry.'

'My mother died last week. That's when things started going wrong. I don't really understand it. There was a terrible accident. Did Penelope mention the accident?'

'No. I read about it in the paper. I am so sorry.'

'May I talk to you? My car is over there. *Please.* We could sit inside.' He pointed. His car was some distance down the street. 'I need to talk to someone. I don't know anybody in England. Only Penelope – and now she's turned against me! You look like a very nice woman. I am sure I can trust you.'

'You should do nothing of the sort.' Antonia smiled. 'Appearances can be extremely deceptive.'

'I've been sitting in my car, watching the house, waiting for Penelope to appear, only she refuses to speak to me.

146

She tells me to go away. I don't know what I've done. I really don't.' The young man's voice shook. 'Everything was fine and then she – she suddenly changed. Shall we go to my car?'

'OK, let's go to your car.' Antonia didn't think he was dangerous. She didn't think he was deranged, just very young, very upset, very confused and, clearly, extremely unhappy. He didn't seem to have had much sleep recently, poor boy, judging by his drawn pale face and bloodshot eyes. 'I am sorry about your mother,' she said after they got inside the car.

'It was terrible, the way she died, but I hardly knew her. Not at all in fact. As it happens, we were reunited only a couple of months ago.'

'You have lived abroad of course. Your accent . . .?'

'Canadian. I was given away for adoption when I was a baby, you see, so I spent most of my life abroad. Canada. My adoptive parents were very nice people. I don't think my mother – my real mother – was a very nice person. Would you like a cigarette?' He produced a packet. 'I'll have to smoke, hope you don't mind. Very few people in England smoke, I notice.'

'No, thank you. You go ahead. I am used to it.' She watched him light a cigarette. 'My husband smokes. He smokes a pipe and occasionally cigars.'

Vic Levant said, 'You see, my mother – the one who died – didn't want any children. She gave birth to a number of children, a great number of children, but she gave them all away. She kept producing children and giving them away. She gave us all away. Got a lot of money for us.'

'Oh dear. Do you know your real father?'

'No. I don't think I'd have had much to say to him. He was all for it, apparently. It was my mother's idea, but he went along with it. Children for sale. He encouraged my mother to produce as many as she could.' Vic drew on his cigarette. 'I only came to England last year. My adoptive parents are both dead now. As I said, they were very nice people. I sought my mother out, don't know why.'

147

Antonia looked at him. 'Was that how you met Penelope?'

'Yes . . . She was at the house that day . . . That was the best thing that ever happened to me . . . She was so sweet.' Suddenly his features hardened. 'She let those two men in. I saw them go in. She's been seeing other men. I saw her talk to a black man. And there was the one she let in. I know I am right to be jealous. I don't know what's happening. I really don't. I thought we were good together, but then it all changed so suddenly. Overnight, literally . . . I wonder if it's my fault . . . It happened on the day her husband died . . . I'm not making much sense, am I? She suddenly said she didn't want to see me any more!'

'Did she give you any reason?'

'She said it wasn't safe. She said we mustn't be seen together. She said we mustn't see each other. She said I might get into trouble with the police – because of what happened to her husband. That was nonsense of course – I was nowhere near her husband when he died. She then said she needed time to think. She came up with all sorts of excuses! She said we'd better not see each other till after the funeral at least – I am sure you know her husband died?'

'I do.'

'Those two men – you saw them, didn't you? You must have seen them! You were still with her when they went in, weren't you?'

'I was, yes. I saw them.'

'Oh – there they are!' Vic pointed. 'Coming out of the house.'

They watched the two men walk up to a car that had been parked at the other end of the street.

'Both are dark . . . She likes dark men. She told me.'

'Those are policemen, Mr Levant.'

'*Policemen?*' He stared at her. 'Are you sure?'

'I am sure.'

'What did they want from her? They don't think she – that she had anything to do with her husband's death? She couldn't have. She was nowhere near Mayholme Manor that day. She was at Heathrow when she got the call.'

'You were with her?'

'Yes! Somebody phoned her from Mayholme Manor and told her Sir Seymour had died. The Master. She'd asked me to see her off. She was on her way to the South of France.'

'Well, that eliminates both of you from the suspects' list then,' Antonia said lightly.

'Did the police think it was me who killed Sir Seymour? Was it me they wanted to talk to Penelope about?'

'No. It's nothing like that. You are being paranoid now. I don't think they know you exist. Besides, no one's suggested yet that Sir Seymour's been killed. You have nothing to fear. Did you say you went to Heathrow only to see her off? You weren't going to the South of France with her then?'

'No. I wanted to go, but she said no. She said she didn't want people to start gossiping. Anyway, she never went to the South of France. She had to come back. She had to go to Mayholme Manor. Are you sure the police don't suspect Penelope of having something to do with her husband's death?'

'Positive, Mr Levant. They never mentioned Sir Seymour's death.'

'What did they want then?' Vic persisted.

Antonia hesitated. 'Well, they seem to think she had something to do with your mother's death.'

26

The Bad Sister (1)

'Such occasions are invariably wearing and troublesome. This must be terribly unsettling for you personally, Master. Being put on the spot can't be much fun.'

'Fun is the very last word I would use to describe my sentiments at the moment.'

'You'd be perfectly justified if you refused to answer my questions and showed me the door this very instant. You are under no obligation to talk to me. Private detectives after all are not the police.'

'I'd rather deal with you than with the police,' the Master said after a pause.

'Would it put your mind at rest if I told you that I have managed to establish a strong presumption as to the culprit's identity?'

'That would very much depend on who you believe the culprit is.' The Master picked up a silver paper knife, tried its point with his forefinger and put it down again.

'It is not you – nor is it anyone else directly associated with Mayholme Manor.'

'This sounds reassuring,' the Master said cautiously.

'I have reason to believe that it was Sir Seymour's sister Bettina, who stole her brother's ring on the afternoon of June the 22nd,' said Payne. 'That was the day I paid my first visit to Mayholme Manor.'

He hoped it wouldn't occur to the Master to ask him

why he had come at a time when no crime was yet known to have been committed. 'Miss Tradescant managed to sneak up to her brother's room without anyone noticing her,' he went on quickly. 'Sir Seymour, as we established, was in the *salle de ciné* at the time. The reason for her visit is not yet clear. She saw his ring inside the porcelain dish on his bedside table and took it. It is known, I believe, as the Wallis ring. Bettina left her ring in its place. Her ring was an exact replica of the original, only it was smaller. And, one can assume, much cheaper. She was hoping that her brother wouldn't notice the difference.'

'Sir Seymour should never have left such a valuable ring lying about.'

'I agree. There should have been a barbed wire entanglement round it.'

'So *that's* why the ring didn't fit his finger! He was worried silly. He was convinced there was something wrong with him. He believed his fingers were swollen.'

'What I want to ascertain now, Master, is whether Miss Tradescant was here on the morning her brother died as well. That was when the *second* theft took place. That was when the replica disappeared.'

'She was here,' the Master said promptly. He clearly felt no misgivings about implicating Bettina. 'She'd been here since dawn, she said, sitting in her car outside, waiting for a "confirmation". She was convinced her brother was dead.'

'So she could have slipped in, gone to her brother's room and pinched the replica.'

'What would she want the replica for?'

'The replica constituted evidence that pointed to her,' Payne explained. 'It must have dawned on her that if her brother's ring was too loose for her finger, the replica would prove too tight for his finger and that he might work out what had happened soon enough. So she decided that the replica had to disappear.'

'Miss Tradescant made a complete nuisance of herself that morning. She was dressed in black from head to toe.'

The Master winced at the memory. 'She managed to get herself locked inside one of the downstairs lavatories. For half an hour, or so she claimed.'

'Really? How did that happen?'

'Oh, something had gone wrong with the lavatory door lock, or the door knob remained in her hand, some such rigmarole. She banged on the door and screamed to be let out, she said, but no one came. Well, all the stewards are upstairs at that hour, that's our busiest time, you see, so I am not surprised that no one heard her. When she was eventually released, she came to see me. It was the same cranky old story as before. She was convinced her brother was dead, the chill had made that perfectly clear, and so on and so forth. As it happens, this time she'd got it right. Sir Seymour *was* dead.'

'It's odd that she'd got it right . . . That could have been a coincidence of course . . .'

'She stole one of my stewards' habits,' the Master said.

'She stole one of the stewards' habits?' Payne's eyebrows went up. 'Those orange things?'

'Yes. It was in her bag. She said she thought it might provide her with inspiration for a dress – some such nonsense. I wouldn't be at all surprised if she turned out to be a kleptomaniac as well.'

'Who found Sir Seymour's body?' Major Payne asked after a pause.

'Travis, one of the stewards. He'd gone up with Sir Seymour's breakfast.'

'And who was the last person to see Sir Seymour alive? Travis again?'

'No. That must be the other chap. Um. Madden.' Once more the Master picked up the paper knife. 'He is newish. I took him on at Dr Fairchild's recommendation. We don't really need any more stewards, but sometimes one does do things to oblige the brothers. Old men are noted for their whims and caprices. Dr Fairchild has been most generous to Mayholme Manor. Madden had worked for Dr Fairchild, it seems – his personal valet, something like that.'

'Dr Fairchild's valet? And now he is a steward here? How terribly interesting. Dr Fairchild is the gentleman in the wheelchair, correct? Pebble glasses – looks bleached? He insisted on being moved from the ground floor to the third floor, giving some silly reason for it? He had a portrait of the Duchess of Windsor on his wall, I noticed. The Duchess is depicted wearing a dress strikingly embroidered with wreaths of black pineapples.'

'Your powers of observation, Major Stratton, are quite remarkable.'

'Payne. I couldn't help noticing that Dr Fairchild's new room was only two doors away from Sir Seymour's . . . Did they know each other well?'

'Not at all well. They'd never spoken to each other, to my knowledge.' The Master frowned. 'Some time ago Sir Seymour imagined Dr Fairchild was staring at him. He said he didn't like it.'

'So Dr Fairchild's former valet was the last person to see Sir Seymour alive . . .'

'I am sure it is not as sinister as you make it sound, but, yes, it was Madden who brought Sir Seymour his early morning tea and drew his curtains.'

'I would very much like to have a word with Madden.' Major Payne rose to his feet. 'And with Dr Fairchild, if possible.'

'Well, Madden is most likely to be in Dr Fairchild's room.'

As he strolled out of the study, Major Payne paused once more by the little table with the newspapers. The paper on the top was still crumpled, the ink a little smudged where he had put his hand.

Memorial Service – friends and relatives of Petunia Luscombe-Lunt –

The next moment he remembered. *Got* to be the same woman. Couldn't be two women with a name like that. The Law of Probability was against it. It was her. Jesty's Pill. Jesty's oldest squeeze.

Petunia Luscombe-Lunt appeared to have perished in an accident while hiking in the Alps. Poor old Jesty. Unlucky, oh so unlucky, in love! RIP Pill, Payne murmured. He made to go, but suddenly he stopped again, turned round and picked up the paper once more.

Something had caught his attention . . .

But – but that didn't make sense. An utter impossibility, in fact. The date was wrong. There must be some mistake, surely?

27

Mystery Monk

Vic Levant went on staring at Antonia. An unworldly, unhappy, deep-thinking boy, she thought.

'The girl apparently suggested that Lady Tradescant killed your mother by pushing her from the top floor.' Antonia halted. 'You look shocked. I am sorry. Perhaps I shouldn't have told you.'

'That's OK. It's all rubbish,' he said dismissively. 'What did Penelope say?'

'Her reaction was very much like yours. She actually laughed. She said the whole story was a fabrication, from start to finish.'

'How seriously are the police taking the story?'

'My impression was that they were just making a routine inquiry as they invariably do whenever a member of the public reports a suspicious death.'

'There was nothing suspicious about my mother's death. That was an accident.'

'So you said. Did you know this girl?'

'I did. Not very well. She was one of the Tradescants' two maids.'

'The policeman said her name was Daisy. Daisy Warren? Or was it McLaren?' Antonia felt she couldn't very well admit she had been listening at the keyhole.

'Daisy, yes. Don't know her surname. I only knew her as Daisy. She was a troublemaker. That's exactly the kind of thing she would do. I mean lying – gossiping – spreading stories. I am not really surprised.'

'Did she have any reason to hate Penelope?'

'Well, Penelope intended to sack her and Daisy was well aware of the fact.'

'I wonder ... I wonder if that had anything to do with you?'

'All right. Daisy had a crush on me. She kept following me about whenever I was there. She started telling everybody I was in love with her and that we were going out together. She then started spreading rumours about Penelope. She said Penelope had lots of lovers and had been unfaithful to Sir Seymour from the very start of their marriage, which was all nonsense. I mean Daisy couldn't possibly have known anything about it. She had been in Half Moon Street only a couple of months.'

'I see,' Antonia said.

There was a pause. He sighed. 'Maybe Daisy did tell the truth after all . . .'

'About Penelope pushing your mother to her death?'

'No, no – about Penelope having lovers. OK. Those two men might have been policemen, but what about the man with the short brown hair and the dark glasses? She let him in. I never saw him come out. He was nothing to look at, which is odd because Penelope is always so particular about looks. He had this determined air about him. He licked his lips as he went up the steps. He had a shining upper lip. I watched him. He is crazy about her. I could tell. It was obvious!'

'That's jealousy talking. You shouldn't really be spying on people, or stalking them. You may get yourself into serious trouble.'

'I don't care.'

'You couldn't possibly know that man was crazy about her merely by looking at him through your car window.'

'I could.'

'Now, *do* be reasonable –'

'There is a door at the back of the house. It leads to the garden,' Vic Levant said thoughtfully. 'There is a small gate in the garden wall. He probably went out that way.'

Out in the corridor Payne bumped into the steward called Travis, whom he remembered from his first visit to Mayholme Manor. Travis appeared to be engaged in dusting. At least he wore rubber gloves and brandished a feather duster. The sound of a Hoover at full throttle came from somewhere above.

'Ah, Travis. Just the man I wanted to see.'

'Sir?'

'I understand you were the person who found Sir Seymour's body?'

'Yes, sir.' Travis's expression did not change.

Payne explained that he was a private investigator. 'The Master said I could go round and ask people some questions.'

'Is it about Sir Seymour's death, sir?'

'Actually, I am investigating the disappearance of Sir Seymour's ring. What time did you go into Sir Seymour's room on the morning he died?'

'It was twenty-five past eight. Sir Seymour always had his breakfast at half-past eight.'

'What did you do exactly?'

'As Sir Seymour wasn't in his room, I placed the breakfast tray on his bedside table. I assumed he was still having his bath. He had a bath every morning. I usually called out, *Your breakfast, Sir Seymour*. He would say something like, *Jolly good show*. But this time there was no reply. I didn't think anything of it at first. Sir Seymour was a bit deaf, you see. So I made to leave the room, but then thought I'd better check if he was all right.'

'You went to the bathroom?'

'Yes, sir. Sir Seymour was lying in the bath. Floating, like. Face upwards. His eyes were open. It looked as though he was staring at the ceiling. I could tell at once that he was dead, though I did check his pulse. Then I raised the alarm.'

'I don't suppose you noticed whether Sir Seymour's ring was in the little porcelain dish on his bedside table?'

'It wasn't, sir,' Travis answered promptly. 'The ring wasn't there.'

'You sure? You strike me as sturdily confident.'

'I am sure, sir. When I put down the breakfast tray, I happened to look inside the dish. I saw Sir Seymour's cuff-links and a tie-pin, his silver pencil, also a pair of matching pearl studs, but there was no ring.'

'Did you notice anything else that might be termed "out of the ordinary" – either in Sir Seymour's room or in the bathroom?'

'No, sir. Everything was as usual . . . Sir Seymour died of a heart attack, didn't he, sir?'

'This, at the moment, is the official version. Did you, by any chance, see any strangers around the building that morning?'

'Well, I saw someone I took to be one of the fellows go across the hall downstairs. The person was wearing one of our orange habits, but had his hood up. I failed to see the person's face. Wearing the hood inside the building is against the regulations, that's why I took note. The person was wearing gloves, which, again, is against the regulations.'

'You are wearing gloves now.' Payne pointed to the bright yellow gloves on the steward's hands.

'No, not gloves for cleaning, sir. Proper gloves. Leather. Black.'

'When exactly did you see this person?'

'About quarter past eight. I said hello, but got no answer.'

'Where did he go?'

'The person walked out of the front door. I glanced out of the window. There was a sort of a mist outside. We often get a mist in the morning these days. I can't say which way the person went . . . A couple of minutes later I heard Miss

158

Tradescant screaming to be let out of the toilet . . .' Travis's eyes narrowed. 'The front of the person's habit looked *darker* . . . As though –' Travis broke off.

'As though it had been splashed with water?'

'I don't know, sir. I asked the other fellows later on, whether it had been one of them, but they all said no.'

'You kept saying "person", Travis. *Could* it have been a woman?'

Travis seemed to come to a decision. 'Actually, sir, I am convinced that it was Madden I saw.'

Payne's left eyebrow went up. 'Madden? Why do you think it was Madden?'

'He was Madden's height. Madden often walks about the building with his hood up. *And* he likes to wear gloves, sir. He seems to imagine it is funny, and he doesn't say hello or acknowledge you in any way. Madden frequently acts in a superior manner. Well, Madden doesn't really belong to Mayholme Manor. That's why I still think of him as a stranger.'

'He is Dr Fairchild's former valet, isn't he?'

'He is not Dr Fairchild's valet, sir. He is Dr Fairchild's grandson.'

'His grandson? How do you know?'

'Both are albinos, sir, though of course one always thinks Dr Fairchild is so very pale because he is so very old. That's what alerted me in the first place. I also happened to over-hear a bit of conversation between them. I was passing by Dr Fairchild's room a couple of days ago and the door was open. They were both inside. Dr Fairchild said, "Don't be an ungrateful beast. Everything will be for you." They were sitting one opposite the other and Madden had crossed his legs. *Not* like master and servant. Madden gave a mock bow and said, "My gratitude knows no bounds, Grandpa." They went quiet the moment they saw me.'

'Have you by any chance observed anything else recently that was unusual, Travis? Concerning this pseudo-servant – Dr Fairchild – any link between either of them and Sir Seymour?'

'I wouldn't call it a "link" exactly, sir, but when Sir Seymour's sister came the first time, I saw her bump into Madden. He asked her whether she had the Master's permission to walk about the premises and she told him to mind his own business. He tried to block her way and she hit him on the head with her handbag and called him a "whey-faced son of a worm". Madden told her she would be sorry. And she said, "I am absolutely terrified. What would you do? Have me hanged?" And Madden said that perhaps he would.'

'Most amusing. Suggestive too. Thank you, Travis. Well, I think it is high time I met the mysterious Madden and his grandpa.'

A minute later Major Payne entered the lift. He pressed the third-floor button.

He examined his clues. The Wallis ring – the portrait on the wall – the fact that Dr Fairchild and Sir Seymour's father had been in Nuremberg at the same time – the unreasonable request for a change of rooms – the introduction of the grandson into the set-up . . .

28

Major Payne Pulls It Off

Dr Fairchild cut an absurdly dandified figure in his silk polka-dot dressing gown and polka-dot scarf. He sat in his wheelchair as though it were a throne.

'I have never met you before, but I can't help being impressed by your reasoning. Touché – as we used to say at the fencing club.' He took his silk handkerchief out of his breast pocket and proceeded to unfurl it. He produced some sparkling object, which he held up between his forefinger and thumb.

'Would you believe me if I told you I'd been waiting for an opportunity to get rid of the ghastly thing? Here you are, kind sir.' Stretching out his claw-like hand, he placed the ring in Major Payne's hand with a ceremonious gesture. 'This, I suppose, is how legends of chivalric quests for lost grails are born. Wouldn't you say?'

'Lost *and* pilfered.'

'The idea of a pilfered grail appeals to me greatly.' Dr Fairchild nodded. 'You do say the most entertaining things. This ring is a replica, as I am sure you are aware, and, as such, is of no use to me or to my grandson. Sorry – I shouldn't make his decisions for him. You don't by any chance want the ring, do you, Madden?'

'I don't,' Madden said.

Dr Fairchild turned back to Payne. 'Madden does not

want the ring either. I suppose you intend to take it back to Tradescant?'

'Sir Seymour is dead.'

'Of course he is. My short-term memory is not what it once was. Well, the ring is my rightful possession and Madden pinched it at my request, but I am not sure he killed Tradescant. I never asked him to.'

'One of the other stewards believes he saw Madden going out of the building at about the time Sir Seymour died, with his hood up and wearing a pair of black gloves,' Payne said. 'There was a wet patch on the front of his orange habit.'

'There are occasions when Madden does things impulsively and sometimes he does choose to act on his own initiative. If Madden killed someone,' Dr Fairchild went on in a thoughtful voice, 'he would do it quietly, without losing his temper. He would do it with a sense of mission. Madden is a former commando. He was in the Foreign Legion, but he was too squeamish about blood and blades, so that necessitated his departure. He would never use a knife. He faints each time he cuts himself shaving. Can't stand cuts, can you, Madden?'

'I don't faint.'

'All right, but it makes you feel ill. When he brought me the ring, Madden didn't say a word about finding Tradescant's dead body. I heard about it later on, from the Master. I personally don't believe Madden drowned Tradescant, that's how it was done, wasn't it, though I have an idea that he *might* have seen the killer.'

'I saw no one,' Madden said.

'I knew the ring was a fake the moment I looked at it. One glance was enough. *Such* disappointment. You can keep it, if you like. Do with it what you will. Dispatch it to your favourite charity. Or present it to your wife with my compliments. If you have a wife.'

'I have a wife,' said Payne.

'I thought you might. You don't look *le célibataire-par-excellence* type at all.' Dr Fairchild's pebble glasses flashed

162

in the light. His irises were pink, Payne noticed, with dark red pupils. 'What reason would you give if I asked you why you were here?'

'I have been investigating the disappearance of the Wallis ring.'

'Sleuthing capers, eh? Are you really a detective? How terribly exciting. You are certainly endowed with a God-like inquisitorial omniscience. What was your very first ratiocinative feat? I am sure you remember. Come on, out with it.'

Payne cleared his throat. 'I must have been twelve and deeply steeped in the Sherlock Holmes stories. I got it into my head that one of my aunts' butlers wasn't a real butler. I had noticed the fellow lean against the sideboard once too often. I also noticed that he tended to look bored while the family ate and talked and he did nothing to conceal it. I saw him yawn. When I told my aunt about it, she said she was aware of the lack of reverence, but she dismissed the whole thing as a mere "sign of the times". It was the early '60s, you see. The end of the old order – some said it was the end of civilization as we knew it. But then my aunt's butler disappeared with the family silver and soon after the police discovered that he was in fact a professional burglar. I don't think he was ever caught.'

'I like it when criminals don't get caught.' Dr Fairchild nodded. 'There were an awful lot of detective agencies before the war. Not so many now, I understand. I wonder why. Fewer befuddling felonies? The police getting more efficient? Can't be that, surely? I don't suppose it was our dear Master who hired you?'

'No one hired me.'

'I never thought I'd live to meet one of those amateur sleuths whose work is their own reward! I must say I am terribly impressed at the way you rumbled us. I expect you own a detective agency? You don't? That makes it even more remarkable! An air of adventure hangs heavily about you. I used to read a lot of Buchan, you know. Richard Hannay. Sandy Arbuthnot. I believe you are the same kind of fellow. You belong to the *breed*. Do let's have some decent conversation, shall we? It's a long time since I have had a decent conversation with a man of such quality. I can't afford to be bored at my time of life. I will be ninety-two in November. Or is it ninety-three? What was it the poet Herrick said?'

'*Gather ye rosebuds while ye may?*'

'That's exactly the line I had in mind. The more I get to know you, the more my admiration grows. Madden hates capping my quotations. Madden is a clever boy. He reads books and watches television, but he is sullen, oh so sullen. He refuses to provide me with stimulating conversation. Consequently, all I do is sit in desolation, totting up my sins and misdemeanours.'

'It will soon be time for your medicine,' Madden said, his eyes on the clock.

'My theory is that Madden saw Sir Seymour's killer and struck up some sort of a deal with him. Did you see the killer, Madden?'

'Perhaps I did.'

'Never a straight answer! The potentate of prevarication, that is Madden. Madden is not his real name, but he chose this name when he came here, so let's stick to it. Our choice of names reveals something about us. My grandson's real name is unusual, one might even say rather an exotic one, but since I have been sworn to secrecy, I will not reveal it. What is *your* name?'

'Payne.'

'Is that your real name?'

'It is. Major Payne.'

'Major? I never cared much for the military, for majors least of all, but you seem different. You must have deduced that I am not terribly happy with Madden. I wish you could swap places with him, now why don't you? There is a grudge-bearing, vindictive side to Madden. Takes after me, I suppose. I have done some fairly dishonourable things in my life, Major Payne, though *not* for money. Never for money. Well, I intend to send Madden packing.

164

I have no more use for him. Madden lives in what used to be my flat in Cavendish Street, but that's not good enough for him!'

'I never said that.'

'No, but you think it, Madden. You think it. I can read your mind.'

'No, you can't.'

'On the other hand, it might look a little odd if you went off too soon. There'd be whispering and conjecture and wild canards. Madden failed to bring home the bacon. To think that that was why I arranged for him to be here in the first place. I called him the moment I saw the ring on Tradescant's little finger. It was one of those one-in-a-million occurrences. Me bumping into my former enemy's son and him actually wearing the Wallis ring!'

'Sir Seymour's father was your enemy?'

'My bitterest enemy, yes. Are you interested in extraordinary coincidences, Major Payne?'

'I am. Very often they turn out not to be coincidences at all. You asking for a room on the third floor, for example. Only two doors away from Sir Seymour's room. That was not a coincidence at all.'

'Of course it wasn't. That was part of the *plan*. Well, I simply *had* to have the ring. Ultimately, the ring would have gone to Madden.' Dr Fairchild sighed. 'Madden is forever complaining that I am not leaving him much in my will. I am sorry to have to say this, but Madden is a greedy pig.'

'I didn't fail to bring home the bacon,' Madden said.

'I don't know why I keep getting cross with Madden. It reduces me to tears each time I do. It's my age, must be. Senescence setting in. The twilight of the gods. Drooling delirium. The Grim Reaper at the Pearly Gates. Do you believe in a future life, Major Payne?'

'I do.'

'I don't. Never have. Life is a matter of cosmic hazard, its fundamental purpose mere self-perpetuation. One beautiful day our so-called wondrous world will simply drift

165

into frozen silence, the human species will disappear and they won't be missed for the simple reason that there will be nobody and nothing out there to miss them. Even if there were such a thing as reincarnation,' Dr Fairchild went on, 'I would hate it if I had to return to the earth as someone else.'

'That is because you could never like anyone else enough to want to be them,' Madden said.

'Bitter, oh so bitter. Isn't it funny that, had we been Muslims, we wouldn't have dreamt of referring to bacon and pigs? Do you suppose Muslims have any pig expressions in their languages, Major Payne?'

'I would say it was highly unlikely.'

'No one in the Pashtun Pass would ever think of getting as sozzled as a sow, *inshallah*?'

'They wouldn't do that anyway, since they don't drink. You seem to forget that that is their other big taboo.'

Dr Fairchild bestowed on Payne a glance such as perhaps might be due to a performing circus animal of extraordinary accomplishments. 'Would you care for a drink?' He waved his claw-like hand towards the old-fashioned cocktail cabinet. 'We've got some first-class whisky. Or would you like some tea? I never know the time. What's the time?'

'It's time for your medicine,' Madden said.

'No, thank you,' Payne said. 'I am all right.'

'According to a rumour circulating among the brothers at the moment, the Master bumps off those of us who have remembered him in their wills. Somebody died four months ago, chap called Fenelon, distant relation of the Bishop, I believe, and, apparently, he left the Master something like ten thousand pounds. Not an exorbitant amount, but enough to allow our Master to indulge his luxurious tastes ... That ring looks awfully pretty, doesn't it? What are you going to do with it?'

'I haven't decided yet.'

'Shame it isn't the real one. Must have cost a couple of hundred pounds to have a replica like that made. The real

Wallis ring is a 3.7 carat diamond cocktail ring made of gleaming white gold and pavé-set diamonds. Worth a king's ransom. I've got it all written down somewhere. So Sir Seymour's sister beat us to it, eh? Did you hear that, Madden? That old hag beat us to it!'

Major Payne's eyes had strayed to the portrait of the Duchess of Windsor on the wall. 'Did you know her well?'

'Let's have a drink and then – then I will tell you a story. We *must* have a drink.' Dr Fairchild clapped his hands. 'Madden – malt.'

29

Something Like a Love Affair

'I first met Mrs Simpson, as she then was, in the early days of January 1936. She had gone to Hungary for what they used to call in those days "a discreet nose job". She had chosen the Streilitz, a little-known, but rather exclusive, clinic overlooking Lake Balaton. Grey Gothic gables, curtains the colour of old blood, chill choking fog, a general air of desolation – you get the picture. My elder brother Lucius – another Dr Fairchild – had been specializing under the legendary Dr Horthy. I was not a doctor yet. I was barely twenty. It was the year of the Abdication. It was my brother who operated on her. My brother had invited me to spend Christmas with him. Mrs Simpson had been at the Streilitz a fortnight.'

'She wasn't there incognito?' Payne said.

'I believe she was, though it fooled no one. Imagine Charlie Chaplin, Mickey Mouse or old Musso going somewhere incognito.' Dr Fairchild cackled. 'Her face was terribly well known. Her picture had been appearing in most of the Continental papers for quite some time. The affair with the Prince of Wales had already become public property. Well, the nose job had been a complete success. Lucius was rather proud of it. Mrs Simpson put in an appearance only after the bandages were removed and all the bruises gone. She was *not* an ordinary woman, Major Payne. Shall we drink to her?'

'I am not at all sure we should. Wasn't she devious and deceitful? An adventuress and an arriviste?' Payne blustered blimpishly. He hoped he wasn't overdoing it. He had an idea that Dr Fairchild might enjoy a challenge.

He was right. Dr Fairchild cackled, clapped his hands and cried, 'Encore!'

'She was self-willed, power-hungry, false and manipulative. She stole our King by means of a technique known as the "Shanghai clutch". She threatened our national security. She should have been sent to the Tower. They should have had her drawn and quartered.'

Dr Fairchild raised his glass. 'To a great American lady.'

'There is no such thing as a great American lady. It is a contradiction in terms,' said Payne teasingly. 'Great ladies do not occur in a nation that is a little more than two hundred years old.'

'Ah. She looked radiant that night. There might have been minor scars but they were completely invisible under her artful make-up. It was some sort of a cocktail party. Two of the women – the wife of a White Russian admiral and an American socialite – curtseyed to her. The moment she appeared, there was a sudden concerted silence. Isn't that what is said to mean that an angel has passed overhead? I think there were three Englishwomen present, but they stood looking down their noses, as though they'd smelled a bad egg. Mrs Simpson was unflaggingly pleasant to everyone.'

Madden, Payne noticed with some amusement, blew out his cheeks, rolled up his eyes and stared at the ceiling. Madden must have heard the story hundreds of times already.

'She wore a most striking dinner coat, Mainbocher, I believe, which gave the impression of having been made of spun glass. Her hair too was like glass, smooth and shiny. Below each cheekbone, there was a slight hollow, a miracle of delicate modelling. I am sure you've noticed how fame makes some people so familiar that when one encounters them in the flesh, their real, physical presence

169

seems a little eerie? I remember shivering. I couldn't take my eyes off her. She was incredibly thin and angular, yet she moved around the room in a fluid and serpentine kind of way. She exuded great strength and authority. She brought to mind one of those pagan goddesses. She –'

'*She* – who must be obeyed?'

'Interesting you should say that, Major Payne – in view of what happened later on. We shook hands. She gazed at me rather fixedly, I thought. I was far from handsome, but I suppose I was rather unusual-looking on account of my extreme whiteness. I was wearing a white dinner jacket too – that must have made me look like a ghost. Or like a moth.'

'Wasn't your brother an albino?'

'Oh no. Lucius was perfectly normal, if normal is the word. Makes you wonder about nature's caprices, doesn't it? Mrs Simpson lingered beside me. Our conversation was a series of civil banalities, but then I happened to quote Goethe in German – *Entbehren sollst Du!*'

'You want me to deny myself?'

'Mrs Simpson said she had a lot of German friends. Von Ribbentrop, no less. The German ambassador to London at the time, that's correct. Our conversation at that point became more specific.' Dr Fairchild raised the whisky glass to his lips. 'We discovered a shared fascination with Germany. The conversation turned to politics. We agreed Herr Hitler was doing a first-class job. I then confided in her my intention to join the BUF.'

'The British Union of Fascists?'

'I was young and innocent. I believed in purity,' Dr Fairchild said dreamily. 'Still do ... There was a large mirror on the wall above the fireplace and I happened to see our two reflections. Well, we looked different from everybody else in the room. We looked – alien. We might have been fabled monsters that had crept out from the depths of Lake Balaton. I suddenly had the oddest of feelings – *that we belonged together*. Maybe I was a little drunk, but I felt ready to do *anything* for her.'

'Are you ready for your medicine?' Madden asked.

'I was an incurable romantic, Major Payne, with a bias towards the bizarre. The Duchess – as she was to become in later years – stood for everything I admired and yearned for. Mystery – oddity – danger – the ultimate challenge. Well, something happened later that night –' Dr Fairchild broke off irritably. 'What *is* it, Madden?'

'Your arm, please.' Madden had produced a syringe and an ampoule.

'Are you sure it's time? Oh, very well. *Castigo corpus meum.*' Dr Fairchild started rolling up his sleeve. 'Madden has had medical training, so I hardly ever feel a thing. Ouch! *Not* so good this time, Madden. What's the matter with you today? This – this feels different somehow. Why does it feel different, Madden?'

'I have no idea. You don't think I am trying to poison you, do you?'

'That remains to be seen. More whisky, Major Payne?'

'No, thank you.'

'We danced. *These foolish things remind me of you.* That was the tune they played. Mrs Simpson led – a bit like a man. I didn't mind. It was a foxtrot, I think, or do I mean quickstep?' Dr Fairchild's eyelids flickered. He yawned. 'It isn't time for my nap, is it?'

Madden said nothing. He was watching Dr Fairchild closely.

'After we finished dancing –'

Dr Fairchild broke off. The gleam faded from his eyes, and they became dim and extremely tired. A spasm seemed to twist his body. His eyelids flickered once more, closed, and his head lolled and fell forward.

30

The Great Escape

'What did you give him?' Payne asked.

'Something to shut him up. He was overexcited. He was talking too much. Showing off. It is bad for him to meet new people, really. His blood pressure tends to go up. He keeps waking up during the night, asking for things, which is a fucking nuisance. You look disappointed, Major Payne.' Madden smiled. 'You don't really want to know what happened next, do you?'

'As a matter of fact I do.'

'She went to his room that night and they became lovers. Grandpa was an incredible lover. Casanova would have been jealous of his technique. Grandpa and Mrs Simpson went on meeting in secret after their respective returns to England. Their affair was unflaggingly intense and earth-shatteringly passionate, but when she married "David", it all had to end. They kept in touch over the years. Corresponded. Spoke on the phone. In 1937 she ordered him to write a series of obscene poison pen letters to the Duchess of York and Queen Mary, which he did. When the war started in 1939, they were on Hitler's side. Grandpa managed to keep his allegiances secret and he worked his way to the very top of the medical profession. He got several important government jobs –'

'Sorry to interrupt, but how does the ring come into all this exactly?'

'Bored already?' Madden grinned. 'And this is only the potted version! OK. Fast forward to 1946. The war is over. The Duchess of Windsor and "David" are languishing in the Bahamas. "David" is the Governor. She finds Nassau nauseating, the back of beyond, a pitiful place, the pits. She has started finding "David" dreary. She is in fact at her wits' end. She rants and raves against "David's" family. She is obsessed with not being an HRH. She brims over with bile. She mourns the German defeat. She chants *lamentoso* – the dirge of suicidal despair. The Nazi defeat and the capture of Ribbentrop in particular have sunk her in the deepest depression.'

'Ah. The Nuremberg trials. Something happened in Nuremberg, correct?'

'It did. Grandpa found himself part of the British team, which was dispatched to Germany to make sure interrogations and executions were properly conducted. Grandpa was appointed by no less a figure than Sir Dick White, the head of Counter-Intelligence in the British Zone of Germany. The Duchess was thrilled when Grandpa was then given "charge" of Ribbentrop, former German ambassador to Britain and Hitler's foreign minister. Ribbentrop, you will remember, had been declared a war criminal and sentenced to hang.'

Payne thought back to what he had read about Mrs Simpson's involvement with Ribbentrop. Prior to the war she was said to have acquired classified information via the King, which she then passed on to Ribbentrop, who paid her directly from German funds in Berlin. Hitler's aim seemed to have been to get the King interested in the Fascist cause.

'How terribly curious ... Two of the Duchess's former lovers brought together in the most extraordinary of circumstances ... Perhaps the Duchess had something to do with it?'

'Grandpa claims he managed to get close to Ribbentrop by buying gallons of vodka for one or two top-ranking Russian officials. That was what the Duchess had instructed him to do, yes. She had already placed a special "fund" at

Grandpa's disposal.' Madden looked at Payne. 'I must warn you Grandpa is not a particularly reliable narrator.'

'What did the Duchess want him to do exactly?'

'To help Ribbentrop escape from prison.'

'You are not serious,' Payne said.

'It does sound fantastic, I agree. The most awful rot. I don't believe any of it myself. There are actually several versions of this story, depending on what mood Grandpa happens to be in. I am going to stick to the most popular version, shall I?'

'Please do.'

'Grandpa notices that the prison padre, a Pastor Turgau, looks a bit like Ribbentrop and at once he hits upon the bold notion of substituting one for the other. The substitution is to take place on the morning of the execution. Pastor Turgau is a little thinner than Ribbentrop, he is also older, but Grandpa doesn't consider that a problem since everybody knows that people lose weight and age prematurely in prison, especially if they happen to be on death row, awaiting execution. Father Turgau's eyebrows are bushy, of the "caterpillar" variety, and he sports a mane of grey hair. Ribbentrop, on the other hand, is practically bald, with no eyebrows to speak of. But there are such things as artificial eyebrows and trimmers –'

'How in heaven's name could Dr Fairchild have persuaded the pastor to shave his eyebrows and allow his head to be placed inside the hangman's noose? But perhaps persuasion doesn't come into it?'

'It doesn't. The plan – code name, the Great Escape – is to have Pastor Turgau injected with a hallucinogenic, mind-altering drug. Grandpa insists it would have been one of the earliest uses of LSD. The idea was to reduce Turgau to a gibbering wreck moments before he was taken to the scaffolding. Now do not interrupt. Pastor Turgau has an established routine of visiting each one of the war criminals in their cells every morning. He prays for them, in some cases with them. He invariably starts by falling on his knees, shutting his eyes and bringing his hands together. When he goes into Ribbentrop's cell, he finds there not

174

only the condemned man, but Grandpa as well. Ribbentrop is lying on his bunk –'

'What about the soldiers guarding him?' Major Payne protested.

'Untrustworthy Russian guards.' Madden waved his hand dismissively. 'Highly corruptible. Would sell their mother and father for a glass of fiery water. There are two of them and they are only too willing to be bribed. Please do not interrupt, or I'll never be able to finish. I fucking hate this story. Dr Fairchild informs Pastor Turgau that Ribbentrop has been taken ill and he says he has just given him an injection. Indeed Dr F. is still holding the syringe in his hand. The poor padre suspects nothing. He has no means of knowing that the syringe is for him. The moment he kneels and shuts his eyes in prayer, the syringe is plunged into his neck.'

'How perfectly simple and straightforward.' Payne stole a glance at his watch.

'Once Pastor Turgau is incapacitated, the swap takes place. Cassock, wig, dog collar, caterpillar eyebrows and black cap for Ribbentrop. Turgau, on the other hand, is shorn of his mane and eyebrows and put into Ribbentrop's prison uniform. Then, jabbering incomprehensibly and gesticulating wildly, in the grip of what appears to be a hysterical fit, he is led to the hangman. Meanwhile Ribbentrop, in the guise of Turgau, leaves the prison building. A car is waiting for him outside. A false passport and a plane ticket are handed over to him. Then the usual destination. Brazil or Argentina. It is the Duchess's funds that make it all possible.'

'And what exactly are the Duchess's motives? I refuse to accept it is love. A less lovable person than Ribbentrop, one could hardly imagine.'

'Well, Grandpa thinks that was her way of cocking a snook at the Establishment. She never forgave Britain for her non-HRH status and her and the Duke's exile. She bore them a grudge to the end of her days. According to one version of the story, the Duke was part of the conspiracy. He knew of the scheme from the very moment of its inception and approved of it whole-heartedly.'

175

'To imagine any such scheme could ever possibly have succeeded, one needs the mental equipment of the White Queen in *Alice* . . .'

'Grandpa insists that it *would* have succeeded – if it hadn't been for the intervention of Sir John Tradescant.'

Payne nodded. 'I'd started to wonder where exactly Sir Seymour's father came in.'

'Sir Seymour's father was my grandfather's nemesis. A somewhat flamboyant figure notable for the tortured splendour of his moustache and the diamond stud in his tongue at a time when pierced tongues were not the commonplace they are today. As it happened, Sir John was also part of the diplomatic troupe that had arrived in Nuremberg. He and Grandpa were friends to start with, they played bezique together, but it all went wrong when Sir John took the wildest of fancies to the ring. Sir John, apparently, had a thing about jewellery, which amounted to an overpowering fetishistic obsession. Grandpa says Sir John coveted the ring with Gollum-like intensity.'

'The Duchess of Windsor had already given the ring to your grandfather? *Before* the task had been accomplished?'

'Yes. The chronology of the story's events is somewhat shaky, you have noticed. The Duchess had the ring delivered to Grandpa by a messenger. It was a token of her trust. The proper reward, she said, would follow. What that might be she never specified. Each time Grandpa tells the story, he changes some of the details. The crux of the matter is that Sir John Tradescant found out what Grandpa was preparing to do and used this knowledge to blackmail him. He demanded the Wallis ring in return for his silence.'

'How did he find out what Dr Fairchild was preparing to do?'

'Sir John had a queer womanish streak in him. He was the worst busybody who ever lived. Sir John contrived to eavesdrop on a telephone conversation between Grandpa and the Duchess. According to another version of the story, Sir John stole some of Grandpa's papers and read a letter written to him by the Duchess. Sometimes Grandpa says

Sir John stole his diary, which contained all the details of the Great Escape.'

'Sir John threatened Grandpa with exposure?'

'Yes. He said he would bring the matter to the attention of the authorities unless Grandpa gave him the ring. Well, those were harsh times. Collaborators and fifth columnists got hanged at the drop of a hat, as I am sure you know. Showcase trials were all the rage. Lord Haw-Haw and so on. Grandpa says he had no other option but to play ball.'

'What did Sir John do *after* he got the ring?'

'He proceeded to demolish the Great Escape plan, that's what. He made sure the complicit Russian soldiers guarding Ribbentrop were replaced by incorruptible British ones and that there were four of them instead of two. He also informed Pastor Turgau that his services were no longer needed. Consequently, Ribbentrop's hanging took place exactly as scheduled.'

'I believe Ribbentrop's hanging was badly botched? It took him at least five minutes to die? I read about it somewhere. He kept writhing and making terrible noises. All rather gruesome.'

'Grandpa says that that was also Sir John Tradescant's doing. Sir John bribed the hangman to "botch" the hanging. He instructed him to prolong the end for as long as was possible. That was the kind of thing Sir John got a kick out of.'

Payne said, 'It's a fascinating story. It might make a good film.'

Madden glanced across at Dr Fairchild who was sleeping with his mouth open. Madden's expression was hard to fathom.

There was a pause.

'I say, old boy, I don't suppose you'd tell me if you saw anything of interest in Sir Seymour's room at the time you pinched the ring, would you?'

'On the contrary, Major Payne. I have every intention of telling you. I did see something of interest. Let's go to my room,' Madden said. 'I don't want us to interrupt Grandpa's beauty sleep.'

31

What the Steward Saw

Madden's room adjoined his grandfather's. It was very small, hardly larger than a cupboard. Everything in it was narrow. The bed was narrow. The bedside table was narrow. The chair was narrow. The table lamp was incredibly narrow. The Gothic window that overlooked the chapel was narrow. It felt like entering some modernist installation, Payne thought.

'Don't you get a little claustrophobic here? No dreams of premature burials at night?'

Madden shrugged. 'It's better than a prison cell.'

'Have you been in a prison cell?'

'Perhaps I have. What exactly would be the cause of death if one did get buried prematurely? Asphyxiation?'

'You could be brain dead through oxygen starvation after only a few minutes,' said Payne.

His eyes fixed on the pile of books that lay on Madden's bedside table with some surprise. They were not the kind of books he would have associated with Madden, but then he had no idea what kind of books he would have associated with Madden. Madden was an enigma.

'Do you like Charlotte Brontë, Madden?'

'Not in the least. She was an unpleasant example of spinsterhood, a raving, craving maenad seeking self-immolation on the altar of her frustrated passions.' Madden waved towards the narrow chair. 'Take a pew.'

'What about Austen?'

'Under the mask of an impartial observer, Aunt Jane was nothing but a prying, sub-acid busybody in everyone's flirtations.' Madden had perched on the edge of his bed.

'One wonders what a clever fellow like you is doing in service.'

'I am not really in service. Never been. I am here at Grandpa's behest.'

'The Master tells me you were the last person to see Sir Seymour alive.'

'That's not strictly true.'

'Oh?' Payne looked at him.

'I brought Sir Seymour his early morning tea. I drew his curtains. He asked me to run his bath, which I did. He then came up with a quotation.'

'What kind of quotation?'

'*Amat avidus amores miros, miros carpit flores.* I left the room soon after.'

'But you returned for the ring?'

'I did. Some quarter of an hour later I went back. The door to the bathroom was ajar. I thought I heard the sound of water splashing. I didn't think anything of it. I went straight to the bedside table, took the ring from the china dish and I put it into my pocket. When I looked towards the bathroom again, I saw someone standing beside the bath. The man was wearing an orange habit and he was looking down at something in the bath. I couldn't see the person's face. The person had the habit hood up, which at once struck me as unusual. I also caught a glimpse of the person's hands in black gloves. The gloves were dripping water.'

'Sir Seymour's head was held under water till he drowned. He must have put up a bit of struggle, which would account for the splashing sound you heard ... The killer didn't become aware of your presence?'

'No.'

'What did you do?'

'I was standing beside the window. I quietly sneaked behind the window curtains. A good thing because the next moment the person came out of the bathroom. The front of the habit looked darker. It had been splashed with water.'

'I see.'

This, Payne reflected, tallied with what Travis had told him earlier on. Travis too had seen the mysterious steward. Travis had thought that it was Madden.

'The person quickly walked out of the room. I waited a couple of moments, then came out from behind the curtains and went to the bathroom. Sir Seymour was lying in his bath. His eyes were open. He was dead.'

'You checked his pulse?'

'I did. I checked his wrist and his neck. As Grandpa informed you, I have had medical training. I don't make mistakes about things like that. There was no pulse.'

'You didn't raise the alarm?'

'No. I had Sir Seymour's ring in my pocket. I feared I might get myself in trouble. So I left and went to Grandpa's room. I knew that Travis would discover Sir Seymour's body when he brought his breakfast to him at half-past eight. Which he did.'

There was a pause, then suddenly Major Payne laughed. 'Sorry! It's just hit me that all along there was a witness to the murder!'

'I didn't witness the act of murder per se.'

'You saw the killer's face . . .'

For some inexplicable reason, Madden's expression changed and for a moment it looked as though he was going to be sick. His hand went up to his upper lip, then it covered his mouth.

'What's the matter?' Payne asked, concerned.

'Nothing.'

Payne looked at him curiously. There was a pause. 'Would you recognize the person if you saw him again?'

'I would. Actually, it's not a him. It is a her.'

'Oh? A woman? You sure?'

Madden said slowly, '*I know who the killer is.*'

'You do?'

'It was Sir Seymour's sister. Miss Bettina Tradescant.'

32

The Bad Sister (2)

'You are positive it was her?'

'One hundred per cent. I know what Miss Tradescant looks like.'

'There was something of a contretemps between you and her, wasn't there? You questioned her right to roam round the premises and she challenged your authority. One of your fellow stewards told me about it.'

'I would have known she was Sir Seymour's sister even if I'd never seen her before,' Madden pointed out. 'They look uncannily alike.'

'Well, by her own admission, she was near the scene of the crime at the crucial hour. She had been at Mayholme Manor since early morning, apparently. She told the Master she had been sitting in her car. What was the time when you saw her come out of Sir Seymour's bathroom?'

'Some minutes after eight. Five or ten past.'

'Would you be prepared to repeat your story to the police, if necessary?'

'I would,' said Madden.

Two hours later Major Payne and Antonia sat at St James's restaurant, on the fourth floor at Fortnum and Mason's, having tea and comparing notes.

'He saw her coming out of the bathroom. She was

dressed in a steward's orange habit. Or so he claims.'
Payne took a sip of tea. 'It fits in with what the Master told
me about Bettina having an orange habit in her bag when
he met her later on.'

'And Travis saw a figure wearing a wet habit cross the
downstairs hall and leave the building at quarter past
eight? It all tallies perfectly.'

'Indeed it does. All perfectly damning.'

'So it was the bad sister who did it?'

'Bettina had a good enough motive for her brother's
murder. She benefits from Sir Seymour's will. It seems he
intended to cut her out. Penelope might have told her
about it, so Bettina goes and kills him before it is too late.
Makes perfect sense.'

'You said you were not entirely convinced by Madden's
account?'

'One should be suspicious of light-fingered gentlemen's
gentlemen on principle . . . I am trying to keep an open
mind, my love . . . Well, Madden had a reason to hate
Bettina . . . He'd been humiliated by her . . . She'd banged
him on the head with her handbag while another steward
watched . . . At one point Madden started acting rather
oddly . . . He suddenly looked ill . . . His hand went up to
his upper lip . . . I don't know what it all means, though I
feel something stirring at the back of my mind . . . This is
an amply mystificatory affair and no mistake. I am sure
we'll get to the bottom of it soon enough, never fear . . .
May I eat the last smoked salmon sandwich? Would you
mind dreadfully?'

'Eat them all, if you must.'

'May I kiss you?'

'No, not now. Not *here*, Hugh – with the pianist and
everything. OK, but be quick about it . . .'

'You don't want the cucumber sandwiches either?'
Payne said a moment later as he straightened his tie. 'You
used to adore cucumber sandwiches.'

'No one could possibly "adore" cucumber sandwiches
. . . I am not really hungry.'

182

'You should make sandwiches like that at home.'

'I did make sandwiches like that the last time your aunt paid us a visit . . .'

'You should do it more often.'

Antonia picked up her teacup. 'What's the tune the pianist's playing?'

'"These Foolish Things". Dr Fairchild danced to it with Wallis Simpson. Or perhaps he didn't. There is a strong possibility he made up the whole thing. He seems to be a notorious Munchausen. *A cigarette that bears lipstick traces,'* Payne hummed. *'An airline ticket to romantic places.'*

'These would make good clues in a detective story,' Antonia said. 'A lipstick-smeared cigarette stub and a plane ticket to Tangiers are discovered beside a dead body. It's the lipstick that's going to be the clue . . . *Is* Tangiers romantic?'

'I don't think so . . . The cigarette was actually smoked by a man . . .'

'Wearing lipstick?'

'No. He had been kissing a woman wearing lipstick.'

'*No.* He had been kissing a woman who had been kissing a man wearing lipstick.'

'Some chaps do wear lipstick.' Payne nodded sagely. 'It means nothing at all.'

'Actually,' said Antonia, 'I've got an extraordinary story to tell as well. It concerns Penelope Tradescant.'

'I am all ears.'

Antonia took a sip of tea. 'One of the Tradescant maids, a girl called Daisy Warren, went to the police and reported that, on the day of Mrs Mowbray's fatal fall, Mrs Mowbray and Lady Tradescant had a serious argument about something. They "exchanged words". It sounded extremely serious, Daisy insisted, though she couldn't say exactly what the argument was about.'

'Nothing to do with Mrs Mowbray and the accounts? Mrs Mowbray, if I remember correctly, had been caught cooking the accounts earlier that morning?'

'It wasn't to do with the accounts. Mrs Mowbray was threatening to tell her son something. Daisy had no idea what. Lady Tradescant and Mrs Mowbray then started walking up the stairs. Daisy heard Lady Tradescant say they needed to discuss the matter in private. It was the *two* of them, and not only Mrs Mowbray, as originally stated by Lady Tradescant, who went to the top floor. Some quarter of an hour later Mrs Mowbray fell to her death.'

'Daisy suggested Lady Tradescant pushed Mrs Mowbray from the top window? That it was with that purpose in mind she took her to the top floor?'

'Well, the policemen simply presented Penelope with the facts. They were extremely tactful about it. It was clear from the way they spoke to Penelope that they weren't taking Daisy's story really seriously. It was all in the nature of a routine inquiry, they kept repeating.' Antonia took a sip of tea. 'Or maybe they were only *pretending* not to be taking the story seriously. Might have helped if I'd been able to observe their faces, but of course I couldn't.'

'This is extremely interesting.'

'Vic said the allegations were all rubbish.'

'Ah. *The* lover.'

'Maybe not *the* lover. Vic suspects Penelope has other lovers. At least one other lover. He believes there is a new man in Penelope's life. Someone who is nothing special to look at, apart from a shining upper lip. Vic is very jealous, poor boy. Actually I thought there was someone at the house on the day of my visit, so he may not be completely wrong. Daisy was very jealous of Penelope. She had had a crush on Vic, apparently. She regarded Penelope as her rival. That, I suppose, seems a very good reason why she should have made up the story.'

'Shame Daisy had no idea what it was Mrs Mowbray was threatening to tell her son.' Payne bit into a fresh sandwich.

'As a matter of fact,' said Antonia, 'I have a theory what it might be about. It is a bit far-fetched but perfectly possible. Rather fascinating. Shocking too, in a way. Of course

I have no proof. It's only a theory. I wonder who would know,' Antonia went on thoughtfully. 'Mrs Mowbray, most certainly, but she is dead. Who else is there? Would Bettina know?'

'Know what?'

When Antonia eventually told him, Payne whistled. There was a pause.

'Sometimes your hunches let you down, you know. Resemblances can be jolly deceptive.' He cleared his throat. 'Remember Major Nagle?'

'I remember Major Nagle.'

'Who was actually not Major Nagle. If *only* I'd been in the library with you that day, you wouldn't have made *any* mistakes.'

'It ill becomes you to be pompous and patronizing.'

'I do believe you said something a minute ago,' said Payne, 'which fits in with something else that's been nagging at me . . .'

'Isn't that always the way with us?' Antonia sighed. 'I think we should speak to Bettina Tradescant. I have an idea she might know. Whether she'd be willing to spill the beans is a different matter. Penelope described her as a "great friend". It was Bettina who "discovered" Penelope, put her on the catwalk and so on.'

Payne glanced at his watch. 'She lives in Rutland Gate. Let's see if she'd agree to speak to us about such an uncomfortably personal matter. I have a feeling she would. Eccentrics aren't as easy to shock as the rest of us mere mortals.'

33

A Guilty Thing Surprised

The door was opened by Bettina herself. She was wearing a clinging medieval-style gown of dull green brocade. Her faded brown hair – if indeed that was her hair and not another wig – was parted in the middle and brought down over her ears. She had the look of an ageing Madonna, an effect somewhat spoilt by her lapis-lazuli blue parrot earrings.

She didn't seem to find their unexpected visit at all strange. She seemed genuinely pleased to see them. She invited them in and led the way into a room painted pale gold and furnished with cherry-wood Victorian pieces. Although the afternoon was warm, logs were burning in the grate of an elegant arched fireplace, and there was a bowl of green tulip-buds on a low table beneath one brightly twilit window.

'Belinda du Broke's boy is always welcome here. Hugh, wasn't it? The last time I saw you, you were wearing a black bowler!' Bettina wagged her forefinger at Major Payne. 'The trouble with black bowlers, Hugh, is that they can create a false impression. *You could have been taken for an Ulster Protestant.* Belinda married a man young enough to be her son. Fellow called Talleyrand-Vassal, if one has to be precise. She must have had you a bit late in life.'

'Rupert Talleyrand-Vassal was my *step*father.'

'Do sit down. Make yourselves comfortable. Let me light

these scented candles – *there* – drat, I always scorch my fingers – delicious smell, don't you think? How about a little drinkie *à trois* – or are you here strictly on business? This is not a bad dress, my dear,' Bettina told Antonia. 'It suits your colouring admirably. I imagine you live in the country?'

'Hampstead.'

'I grew up in the country and I hated it. The annual clay pigeon shooting used to upset me more than words can express. Once my father tricked me into eating strawberries soaked in ether. He said it would be like kissing snow, but it was nothing of the kind. My twin brother – he is dead now – made my life hell. I loathed that guileless limbo between girlhood and adulthood. Do remind me of your name, my dear. Antonia? Women with classical names are almost invariably bitches. Ah, the Claudias, the Helenas and the Cassandras I have crossed swords with! I dare say you do seem an extremely nice woman. You have a generous mouth, though your lipstick is a shade too pale. Be bold, that's my advice. You won't regret it.'

Bettina held up her right hand and twiddled her fingers admiringly. She was wearing the ring, Payne noticed. *The* ring. The unique Wallis ring, which she had stolen from her brother. She seemed completely unselfconscious about it.

'Did you manage to see my brother that day, Hugh? You seemed intent on bearding him in his lair.'

'No. I didn't see him.'

'Seymour apparently died the *next day.* Seems I was wrong about it.' She sighed. 'So much wasted energy! Unless the Master perpetrated a deception? In my opinion, the Master is the one to watch. Never trust a man with a beard, unless he is a king. That's what my father used to say. Are you sure you don't want a drink? I have some apple-green liqueur, which I find delicious but no one else seems to like it. I have no idea what's in it. *Not* apples. A most interesting flavour. You haven't come to ask questions about the funeral, by any chance?'

'Not quite –'

'The funeral seems to have been postponed indefinitely.

187

I am not sure whether I should attend. It would be hypocritical of me if I did, don't you think? They haven't yet issued a death certificate. Penelope is naturally worried, poor girl. The contents of the will haven't been revealed to any of us either. I tried to pump old Saunders about it on the phone, but he was terribly tight-lipped about it. I suppose you know that Seymour intended to leave all his money to that ghastly place?'

'To Mayholme Manor? Really?'

'Yes, Hugh. Really. He told Penelope about it. He was mad about that place. He brought home one of those orange habits once, she told me, and had been using it in lieu of a dressing gown. I still like the colour, mind. Isn't it a blessing Seymour snuffed it before he could change his will? There *may* be a post-mortem. Heaven knows what they hope to discover. Have you met Penelope?'

'I went to see her this morning,' Antonia said.

'You went to Half Moon Street? How perfectly splendid. Good to know Penelope has loyal friends who stick by her at times of trouble. She phoned me an hour ago, actually. She took me to task about something I did.' Bettina laughed. 'I must say she was extremely sweet about it. She is a dear, dear child.'

She twiddled her fingers once more, causing the Wallis ring to flash in the lamplight. She seemed to expect them to make some comment. She must have had the band narrowed, Payne thought.

'That's a beautiful ring,' he said.

'Yes, isn't it? It belonged to Papa, then to my brother. Now it's mine,' Bettina explained nonchalantly. 'Finders keepers, losers weepers.'

'This sounds like some private kind of joke.'

'It's a Van Cleef and Arpels. I intend to sell it eventually, but the future belongs to me, as they say, to carve as I wish, so I would like to wear it a bit longer. Papa's passion for jewels knew no bounds. In one extraordinary photo he is wearing at least ten tiaras, about twenty necklaces, fifty bracelets, a dozen diamond clips – *and very little else*. My poor mother had her garden, but I do believe there was talk in the servants' hall. Whenever a piece of jewellery caught Papa's fancy, he simply *had* to have it. He couldn't rest, he got tension headaches. He was like a magpie. He'd go to the most extraordinary lengths to acquire it.'

'We actually wanted to –'

'My family is *not* a healthy family. I am terribly glad I haven't got any offspring. Nicky – my nephew, you know – has had no children either, which I always thought a jolly good thing, but now, it turns out, he's expecting not only one but *two*. By *deux putains*. Nicky phoned me earlier on. He seemed deliriously happy. A blonde and a brunette, he kept repeating. First one told him about it, then the other. He was a bit drunk, which is understandable. He intends to divorce his wife as soon as possible, so some good is going to come of it after all. He wants to do the honourable thing and marry both girls, or so he says. I suppose it *could* be done it if they all went to one of those sultanates?'

'We wanted to talk to you about Penelope,' Payne said.

'Poor Penelope is completely out of her depth. Well, that's how *I* would feel if I knew that by Hallowe'en I was going to be one of the richest girls in the land. We arranged to have tea at Claridge's tomorrow, so I expect she'll tell me all about it.' Bettina turned towards Antonia. 'You said you saw her this morning. How did you find her?'

'She seemed fine. Two policemen came while I was there,' Antonia went on quickly, fearing another interruption. 'They wanted to talk to her about Mrs Mowbray.'

'The housekeeper woman? But Mowbray is dead!'

'The police were interested in Mrs Mowbray's children,' Antonia said boldly. She wondered if there would ever be a time when she wouldn't have to tell lies.

Bettina inserted a cigarette into a short silver cigarette holder and rattled a silver match-box. 'No more matches. Light, anyone? Do you mean the police *know*?'

Payne produced his lighter.

'I am afraid they do.' Antonia hoped they were talking about the same thing.

189

'Well, it was bound to come out sooner or later. Couldn't matter less this day and age. Who cares about lowly origins any more? If we lived in the Victorian age, a novel might have been written about it. *Lady Tradescant's Secret*. Something on those lines. People say I was born with a silver spoon in my mouth and where did *that* get me? I imagine the police have come across papers and things proving beyond any reasonable doubt that they are mother and daughter?'

'Yes.' Oh dear. So I was right, Antonia thought.

'Mowbray was an unsavoury character, though I dare say I admired her chutzpah. Did it all for the money of course, what else? A survival technique, some may argue. They haven't been able to track down the *other* children, have they? Though why should they want to do that? At one time Mowbray had quite a farm of little ones, I understand. She was almost indecently fertile. Is childbirth too awful, my dear?'

'Mine was very painful,' Antonia said.

'I knew it! I don't think Penelope would mind paying for her mother's funeral, if that is indeed what this is all about. She is a good girl. I hope she finds some nice young man soon enough.'

'You seem to know her well,' Payne said.

'She has been scarred badly, poor child. Such an *unsettled* kind of background. When I first met her, she was the proverbial wild girl, you see. Doing really crazy things, dressing up in outrageous costumes, going on hair-raisingly reckless capers, taking incredible risks. She's changed since. She is a different person now. She could easily have been vain, frivolous and foolish, but she is in fact frightfully intelligent. I love her to bits. She is the daughter I never had.'

'When did she learn that Mrs Mowbray was her mother?' Payne asked.

'Her adoptive parents told her at some point, gave her the name and so on. Penelope then got it into her head to seek Mowbray out. Well, eventually they met and she and

190

Mowbray hit it off, it seems. Got on like a house on fire. To start with, at least. Penelope was already married to Seymour. It was Penelope who got her mother the job in Half Moon Street. She is a very kind-hearted girl.'

'Did Penelope ever try to get in touch with any of the other children – her brothers and sisters?'

'If she did, she never told me. Apparently there are Mowbray children all over the place. Australia, Canada, the Middle East, someone in Kenya – adopted by a missionary couple. Penelope has inherited her mother's business sense, I think. What other reason could there have been for her marrying Seymour? I must admit I encouraged her. Marry him, I said, make sure he leaves you *everything*, then have him bumped off!' Bettina gave a loud laugh.

'How many children did Mrs Mowbray sell?'

'Don't know the exact number. An awful lot. Started producing them at the age of sixteen, apparently. Thirty, thirty-five thousand pounds sterling, that's what she charged per child, I do believe. Not bad. That was quite a lot of money at one time, especially for that class of person, but Mowbray's husband blew it all, on drink and gambling and trips to Thailand. One shudders to think what he was after in Thailand, though that's neither here nor there. Then the husband died, of his excesses, one imagines, that's why Mowbray needed to get a job. To tell you the truth, I never really liked her. A calculating, grasping sort of person. Hard as nails and as dishonest as they come.'

'*Not* the kind who commit suicide?'

'Was it ever suggested she committed suicide, Hugh? I thought that was an accident. She was probably drunk when she fell to her death. I am not sure she drank, but she might have. Anyhow, good thing she's gone, if you ask me. I feel absurdly relieved.'

'Why relieved?'

'Why? Now that Mowbray is dead, there will be fewer chances of any Mowbray children going to Half Moon Street. Fewer chances of Penelope meeting one of her brothers and falling in love with him.'

'What do you mean?'

'I am a crazy old thing, I know, but I used to wonder what would happen if one of the Mowbray boys decided to track his mama down, the way Penelope had done. What if he turned up in Half Moon Street and met Penelope? Two good-looking young people. Passionate, impulsive. Apparently *all* the children were exceptionally good-looking. What if neither Penelope nor the boy realized they were brother and sister?'

'Go on.' Antonia's heart was thumping in her chest.

'It is a most *unlikely* kind of scenario, I must admit, but I suffer from insomnia, what I call my *tango nocturne*, so there is very little for me to do at night, but indulge in strange and frequently lurid thoughts. Is incest still the ultimate taboo, I wonder? What do you think, Hugh?'

'I am sure that for most people it is.'

'Can't be worse than cannibalism, surely? The Bible's full of incest. Adam and Eve's children did it – must have done, when you think about it – then the children's children must have done it – I mean, who else *was* there? This now is the apocalyptic scenario. One of Mowbray's sons has tracked her down, but of course, like Penelope, he uses the name of his adoptive parents. He speaks with an American or New Zealand accent. He arrives at Half Moon Steet. It happens to be Mowbray's day off. It is Penelope who opens the door. The boy doesn't tell her whose son he is.'

'Why not?'

'Say, Mowbray has instructed him *not* to tell since the master has strictly forbidden relatives of members of staff to come into the house. And of course Penelope introduces herself as "Lady Tradescant". The Mowbray boy and Penelope are violently attracted to one another. They start an affair –' Bettina broke off with a little cry. 'My dears, the look on your faces! One might have thought that it really happened.'

'Well, it did happen,' Antonia said as they were driving back to Hampstead. 'That's what I thought. The circumstances of their meeting may have been different, but the fact remains that they did become lovers. I noticed the resemblance, but of course I couldn't be sure. Well, now we know for sure they are brother and sister. Poor Vic.'

'People often choose partners who look like them, haven't you noticed? I don't think it's a conscious thing,' Payne said. 'Liz Hurley and Hugh Grant might have been brother and sister.'

'Perhaps it happened *exactly* as Bettina suggested . . . He introduces himself as "Vic Levant". He speaks with a Canadian accent. His mother is not there when he and Penelope first meet.'

'Penelope must have realized what had happened the moment Vic told her whose son he was. He was visiting his mother, remember? So it seems Penelope plunged into the affair with her eyes open while he remained in the dark. Poor chap. I imagine she fancied him wildly. She doesn't seem to be a particularly responsible or moral person.'

'Bettina did say that Penelope liked doing wild and reckless things. Perhaps it gave her a thrill – the secret knowledge she was breaking one of the greatest taboos?'

'How long did the affair go on for?'

'A couple of months. It's just ended.' Antonia frowned. 'She must have persuaded him not to tell his mother about it.'

'Mrs Mowbray must have realized what was going on,' Payne said.

'Yes. I don't suppose it would have been possible for them to keep it secret from Mrs Mowbray. Not for long. And what does Mrs Mowbray do when she tumbles to the fact that her son and daughter are having an affair? I can't quite see her as being outraged, horrified or disgusted – can you?'

'No. I wonder if she struck some sort of a deal with Penelope? Perhaps she asked for hush money? In return for not telling Vic. Penelope doesn't want to end the affair. Penelope is enjoying herself too much. She allows herself to be blackmailed for a while, but then –'

193

'Then Mrs Mowbray becomes a liability?'

'Yes. Mrs Mowbray keeps asking for more and more money. When she cooks the accounts and Sir Seymour sacks her, she asks Penelope to do something about it – persuade Sir Seymour to give her another chance. Penelope refuses. Penelope has had enough of her mother. Mrs Mowbray threatens to tell Vic ... Maybe she threatens to tell Sir Seymour as well?'

'Yes. Vic is a sensitive decent soul,' Antonia said. 'The type who would almost certainly have broken up the affair in horror and revulsion if he had learnt the woman he wanted to marry was his sister.'

'He wanted to marry her?'

'Still does! That's what he told me. He sounded extremely serious about it.'

'Bettina said Penelope was like her mother in some respects. Perhaps she takes after her mother in *every* respect? Calculating, amoral, as well as immoral, hard as nails.'

'Hugh, what if that girl told the truth after all? I mean Daisy Warren. She reported to the police that she overheard an argument between Mrs Mowbray and Penelope. Mrs Mowbray was threatening to tell Vic about *something*. Daisy had the impression it was something *important*. She then saw Penelope and Mrs Mowbray go up the stairs. Shortly after, Mrs Mowbray fell to her death from one of the top-floor windows ... *It all fits in.*'

There was a silence. Major Payne spoke.

'What I think we should do is go back to the very start of this affair. We need to re-examine all the known facts. We should look closely at the order in which certain events took place. We should also give the death of Petunia Luscombe-Lunt some very careful consideration ...'

34

The Face of Trespass

It was the following morning. Feeling dizzy and dazed and looking incredibly haggard after yet another *tango nocturne*, Bettina Tradescant had managed to drag herself to her study.

She sat drinking strong black coffee and talking into the telephone.

'What do you mean, sweet child, you have no such friend? She said she was a good friend of yours. Her name is Antonia, but I found her frightfully decent. She is Hugh Payne's wife, you know. He is a Talleyrand-Vassal. Odd thing, names. You were never a St Loup before you married, but you chose a name *that suited you*.'

'There's some misunderstanding, Bets.' Penelope Tradescant's smile was half exasperated, half amused. That happened often when she talked to her patroness. 'I have no friend called Antonia Payne. Nor Antonia Talleyrand-Vassal.'

'But you *must* do, Pen dear. Why should she lie? She was a very pleasant woman, if a little primly dressed.'

'Wait a minute. A woman called Antonia did come yesterday, but she said that she worked for some Bond Street jewellers. She introduced herself as Antonia Rushton. What she wanted to talk about was Seymour's ring.' Penelope frowned. Something was going on.

'Well, she said nothing about the ring, though I dare say

both she and Hugh stared at it a good deal. She mentioned the police. She was apparently there when the police came to see you about your late *femme de ménage*, correct?'

'She was, but –'

'There you are! So it's the same woman! Sorry, my dear, I keep forgetting that Mowbray was your mama.'

'This woman – Antonia – wasn't there when the police talked to me,' said Penelope slowly. 'She'd gone by then.'

'Well, she seems to know *all* about you. She knows Mowbray was your mama. This is all terribly confusing and I've got a headache. What I am trying to say, Pen, is that she *must* be a good friend of yours.'

'The policemen came to talk about my mother's death. If they knew we were mother and daughter, they said nothing about it. How did this woman know about it?'

'Don't ask *me*. I have no idea.'

Penelope Tradescant put down the phone. A sudden, terrible sense of loneliness and shame possessed her and she stood very still, her hands clasped before her. Then the feeling passed. Once more she picked up the receiver and dialled a number.

'It's me. Something's up. Listen. You don't happen to know a woman called Antonia, the wife of someone called Hugh, do you? It's all very odd. She came here pretending it was about Seymour's ring. She's been pumping Bettina – Seymour's sister – for information. I think she has been nosing round, finding things out. I don't like it, Beau.'

'Nosing around? Did you say "Hugh"? I wonder now –'

As they were having breakfast, Antonia asked, 'What was it that put you on the right track?'

'I believe it was the curious incident of Petunia Luscombe-Lunt's phone call.'

'But Petunia Luscombe-Lunt is dead! You just checked – she couldn't have made that phone call!'

'That was the curious incident.'

Payne then told Antonia what he planned to do.

'He is dangerous, Hugh. Must be. A man possessed. He's already committed a cold-blooded murder. He didn't hesitate to drown a helpless elderly man in his bath.'

'I am perfectly aware of it, my love. Well, he is a driven man.'

'Do you think Madden will cooperate?' Antonia asked after a pause.

'I don't know. He is a very strange fellow. A first-class liar, among other things. He might already have dispatched his "grandpa" beyond the land of Morpheus and into Hades – or wherever it is old sinners like Dr Fairchild go.'

Getting into his car, Payne drove to Mayholme Manor once more.

This time he saw a police car parked outside the main entrance. So, he thought, it's begun for real.

He didn't meet anyone as he crossed the hall and went up the stairs. The door to Dr Fairchild's room was closed and he knocked on it. The door opened and Madden appeared.

'Major Payne? I thought you were the police,' he said expressionlessly.

'May I?' Payne went past Madden and entered the room. 'I hope you don't mind frightfully.'

'I do mind frightfully.'

'You haven't yet told the police your story then? Of the person you saw emerging from Sir Seymour's bathroom?'

'No, I haven't. The police inspector and his sergeant are with the Master. The news is that they have decided to conduct a PM on Sir Seymour's body.'

'You and I are perhaps the only people who know for certain that Sir Seymour was killed. I have always liked the idea of being ahead of the Law. Where is Dr Fairchild?' Payne had seen the empty wheelchair.

'He felt rather unwell last night and was taken to the

197

hospital. I am afraid the excitement of meeting you proved too much for him.'

'Nothing to do with whatever it was you pumped into his bloodstream?'

'I don't know. It is true that I gave Grandpa a slightly larger dose than usual.' Madden spoke absently. 'He seems to be responding well to treatment. They told me he was having an inhalation session. He is taking lungfuls of pure oxygen out of a special oxygen tank. Oxygen relieves stress, purifies the blood and revitalizes all the internal organs. The whole thing costs a fortune of course. I expect Miles will soon be back as good as new. On the other hand he might not be.' Madden walked up to the window and stood there, looking out.

Payne said, 'I don't believe it was Bettina Tradescant you saw coming out of Sir Seymour's bathroom, Madden.'

He didn't turn round. 'It was Miss Tradescant I saw.'

'Perjury is a very serious offence. You are lucky I am not the police. But the police may come knocking on this door any moment now.'

'I am not afraid of the police. I will try to make myself scarce before they decide to talk to me.'

'As an albino you might find it difficult to hide,' Payne pointed out.

'Difficult but not impossible. Why do you think it wasn't Miss Tradescant I saw?'

'I managed to establish that between five to eight and twenty-five minutes past eight, which is the approximate time of the murder, Bettina Tradescant was confined to the downstairs lavatory. The door handle had got broken off and remained in her hand. She couldn't get out.'

'How did you establish that?'

'At least three stewards ran to her rescue and they are prepared to testify to it, if necessary. They all happened to notice the time.'

'Why would I keep insisting it was her I saw coming out of the bathroom?'

'That was your revenge for being hit across the head with a handbag. Sounds petty and trivial put like that, but then quite a lot of crimes are committed for incredibly petty and trivial reasons. Dr Fairchild did say that you had a grudge-bearing, rather vindictive side to you.'

'Grandpa thinks he knows me *so* well.' Madden's pale lips twisted into a sardonic smile.

'I suppose he does, even though he is not your grandpa.'

'What do you mean?'

'This is none of my business of course, but I have been wondering. It isn't only that you slipped up and called him "Miles". The clues are mainly psychological. The kind of waspish badinage and droll teasing he subjected you to while at the same time he was clearly upset by your lack of attention suggested an abandoned lover rather than a grandfather. His obsession with the Duchess of Windsor was also suggestive. After all, she was the fag-hag par excellence. She had some unusual affairs – the notoriously homosexual Jimmy Donahue, the Duke himself, according to some sources, and so on.' Major Payne regarded Madden thoughtfully. 'This raises a curious question – are albinos exclusively attracted to albinos?'

'No, they are not, if you must know, but it helps,' Madden said sullenly. 'We have been together for thirty years. I was eighteen when he picked me up. He was not always like that. I mean a perfect nuisance to others and an abject misery to himself. There was a time when he was fun to be with. Well, he is *old*.'

'I suggest we don't waste any more time, Madden. Sorry. "Madden" is not your real name, I keep forgetting. I won't press you to tell me your real name – that is of no importance.'

'Madden *is* my real name. Miles was being silly. You don't really think I killed Sir Seymour, do you?'

'As a matter of fact, I don't. You saw someone come out of Sir Seymour's bathroom – *not* Bettina. A man wearing an orange habit and black gloves. The times tally,' Payne went on in a thoughtful voice, 'You said you saw him at

199

about ten past eight. Travis saw a figure answering that description cross the downstairs hall at about quarter past eight and go out through the front door. You said that the front of the person's habit was wet. This is also confirmed by Travis.'

'Why are you so sure it was a man?'

'That's what you said first. You first referred to a "man", then you switched to a "person".'

Madden shrugged. 'A slip of the tongue.'

'The man's face is the very essence of the unmemorable. He has brown hair and round eyes. He also had a little moustache, which he has since shaved off since he feared a moustache would help identify him. He shaved it off in a hurry earlier that same morning. He was nervous because of what he was going to do, so he wasn't careful enough and cut himself. On his upper lip there was a nasty little scar.'

'You are making things up as you go along, aren't you?'

'*Tout au contraire.* Haven't you heard of the art of deduction? When I asked you to describe the person in the orange habit,' Payne went on, 'your hand went up to your upper lip and your face twisted. For a split second it looked as though you were going to be sick. Dr Fairchild did say you were squeamish about blood and blades – that's why you left the Foreign Legion. You reacted to the memory of that nasty little scar you spotted on the man's upper lip. The scar has now almost healed and is no longer visible, but the killer still has a shining upper lip, or at least did yesterday.'

'Actually, I saw no one. You are wrong about everything.'

'You are changing your story yet again?' Payne shook his head. 'Is that wise? As a matter of fact, I came to ask for your help.'

'I have nothing more to say to you.'

'You'd rather speak to the police inspector? Bloodied but unbowed, eh?'

'If the police ask me about it, I'll say I saw nobody.'

'What about the ring? What if I told them that it was you who stole the replica?'

'It would be your word against mine. Miles – if he is still alive – will say it never happened. Miles loves me. There are no other witnesses.'

'You don't want to hear my proposition?'

'No. I am not interested. What proposition?' Madden crossed his arms.

Payne told him.

'I see. Sleuthing capers. Setting traps. It's the kind of thing that never works in real life. The answer is *no*,' Madden said.

'No?'

'No.'

'I must say I am disappointed, old boy. You sure you won't reconsider?'

'Adieu, Major Payne.'

Payne turned round and walked to the door. I will have to think of something else now, he thought gloomily.

35

The Sting

Some thirty-five minutes later Madden produced his mobile phone and dialled a number he had never called before.

A man's voice answered.

Madden's expression did not change. He said, 'I am ringing in connection with the murder you committed on the morning of 23rd June.'

'Sorry?'

'I saw you.'

'Is that some sort of a joke?'

'I saw you kill Sir Seymour Tradescant. He was in his bath. You drowned him.'

There was a pause. 'Who are you?'

'One of the stewards at Mayholme Manor. At the time of the murder I happened to be in Sir Seymour Tradescant's room. I had concealed myself behind the window curtains.' Madden spoke slowly. 'You came out of the bathroom. Your gloves were dripping with water. You were wearing a steward's habit. The front of the habit was wet too. It was ten minutes past eight.'

'Sorry – you must have got the wrong number.'

It was at this point, Madden reflected, that the man should have rung off if he was innocent, if he really believed he was the victim of a hoax. Only he didn't ring off.

A little smile hovered round the edges of Madden's lips. 'You walked across the room fast and went out. You were seen by another steward downstairs. He didn't see your face, but I did.'

'How did you get my phone number?'

'That's not important. I know your name. I also know your address.'

'What do you want?'

'An arrangement?'

'What kind of an arrangement.'

'Money.'

'How boring. How much?'

'Five thousand pounds. No, seven.'

'I haven't got so much.'

'Your girlfriend has money.'

'All right. Where?'

'Claridge's – at three?'

'*Claridge's?*'

'It's in Brook Street,' Madden said. 'Off New Bond Street.'

'I know where Claridge's is. Won't it be better if we meet somewhere outside? In some park?'

'*No.* Claridge's. I will wait five minutes and if you are not there, I will call the police and tell them what I saw,' Madden said.

'No need to take that line. Very well. Where will you be? How will I recognize you?'

'In the foyer. Don't worry about recognizing me. I know what you look like. Make sure you have the money. Cash. Hope your scar has healed. Can't stand blood,' Madden added as an afterthought.

36

To Fear a Painted Devil

It was now twenty-five minutes past three in the afternoon and another summer day of unparalleled loveliness.

Major Payne and Antonia had had what he called a 'Proustian' luncheon: asparagus, *boeuf en daube*, strawberries and cream cheese. They were now sitting in striped deckchairs under a large striped umbrella, having coffee. Their garden looked at its best, *embaumé* with roses and honeysuckle, clematis, lilies and wild snow-white convolvulus. Bees buzzed, excited by the variety of scents.

Major Payne was wearing a white Panama hat, smoking his pipe and doing the *Times* crossword puzzle. Antonia had dispatched her proofs and was reading a book. Antonia's cat Dupin had just climbed to the very top of the ancient maple tree in pursuit of a crow. The maple tree had been one of the special 'features' that came with the house.

'*Paints one's relatives in waterproof material* ... Second letter "I".' Payne looked up. 'Any idea?'

'How many letters?'

'One ... two ... Seven. Relatives is "kin", I suppose ...'

'You paint in oils ... Oh, that's very easy. *Oilskin*,' said Antonia. She picked up the coffee pot. 'Would you like more coffee?'

'Of course.' Payne penned in the word. 'What about this one? Um. *Deadly danger in Eden – not entirely unexpected.*'

'Hugh.' Antonia had shaded her eyes and was gazing across the garden towards the french windows, which the sun's rays had turned to pale brass. 'I think there is someone in the drawing room.'

The next moment they saw a woman's figure come through the window. Very tall and buxom, with a narrow waist. The woman's face was deeply tanned, almost the colour of mahogany. Her glossy jet-black hair fell in waves and reached down to her waist and she wore a broad-brimmed hat. Enormous golden earrings hung from her earlobes. Her lipstick was a light shade of purple. She was wearing large sunglasses in golden frames. She was dressed in a shimmering silk tunic of fluorescent green and magenta red trousers. She wore high-heeled sandals. Her appearance was exaggeratedly outlandish, histrionic, somewhat grotesque.

Also, sinister.

Payne rose to his feet. He cast a discerning eye over her. Larger than life. Carmen Jones meets Carmen Miranda? With a dash of the '70s thrown in? Highly conspicuous. He didn't think the conspicuousness was accidental. Deadly danger in Eden, eh? His gaze remained fixed on the woman's leather bag that was slung casually over her right shoulder.

They had been expecting a phone call. Not a visit.

'Your front door was open. I rang the bell but you didn't seem to hear,' the woman said, speaking with an accent he could not quite place. 'I do hope you don't mind? I know it isn't the done thing –'

'It isn't,' Payne said. 'You are absolutely right. I don't think we have ever met, have we?' He was standing beside his deckchair, his hands in his trouser pockets, feeling oddly vulnerable. That bag. She's got something. It's the way she clutches at it.

'I needed to talk to Antonia. To both of you, in fact.' The woman smiled. 'I would like to know why you have been poking your noses into my affairs and trying to cause mischief.'

'Lady Tradescant,' Major Payne murmured. 'Why the masquerade?'

'I like experimenting with things,' Penelope Tradescant said lightly. 'Hangover from my modelling days.'

'It seems more like an attempt to change your whole appearance beyond the possibility of recognition.'

'Do you really think so? Major Payne, isn't it? You seem to have caught the sun since I last saw you at Claridge's. Of course I only saw you for a split second. It suits you, if you don't mind me saying so.'

'Won't you sit down?' Antonia waved towards the third deckchair. The afternoon was still warm but she suddenly felt chilled. *It is the bright day that brings forth the adder and that craves wary walking.* It was the disconcerting feeling of the familiar suddenly becoming unfamiliar – as well as horribly menacing. Antonia decided not to offer her coffee.

Penelope sat down. She held her bag on her knees.

'You insinuated yourself into my house under false colours. You came pretending to be the representative of a jewel firm. What were you hoping to find out? You listened outside the door, didn't you? While I talked to those two charming policemen.'

Penelope was gazing in Antonia's direction but it was Payne who spoke. 'Murder is a serious business. Sometimes we employ unorthodox methods.'

'Murder? What murder?'

'There were two murders. Your housekeeper, who was also your mother, and your rich old husband.'

'Mrs Mowbray's death was either an accident or suicide,' said Penelope. 'It hasn't yet been established which. I don't think it ever will be. But perhaps you know something I don't? Please enlighten me.'

I hate doing this, Payne thought. He cleared his throat.

'You had been considering getting rid of your rich old husband for some time. You knew that it had to be done soon – before he changed his will and left his not inconsiderable fortune to Mayholme Manor. The opportunity presented itself on the morning Sir Seymour ordered your mother out of the house. Your mother had been blackmailing you over your affair with your brother. You are a fast and efficient thinker. You hit on the idea of killing your husband and making it look as though the housekeeper had done it as one final act of revenge – before committing suicide. Two birds with one stone. You pushed Mrs Mowbray out of the top window of your house. Sir Seymour's infected toe suggested to you the manner in which he was to be dispatched –'

'Poor Seymour. That infected toe gave him hell.'

'Sir Seymour had been taking antibiotics – one capsule every six hours. The course was nearly over,' Payne went on. 'There were only two capsules left. They were inside the silver snuff-box, which Sir Seymour carried in his pocket. You managed to get hold of a bottle of nicotine. Also of an antibiotic capsule, the kind Sir Seymour had been prescribed. You filled the capsule with a deadly dose of nicotine. You then placed the nicotine bottle inside your mother's cupboard for the police to find. For some reason you never got an opportunity of effecting the substitution at home. Maybe Sir Seymour never let the box out of his sight?'

'My dear Major Payne. You sound like one of those impossible oracles. And you look so infuriatingly pleased with yourself! As if you have just clean bowled an opening batsman facing your first ball!'

As far as cricketing metaphors went, that wasn't too bad. Payne picked up his pipe and started filling it with tobacco from his pouch. 'It was only at Claridge's that you managed to swap the capsules. Unfortunately, you were seen. Captain Jesty had been spying on you from behind a potted palm and he saw exactly what you did.'

She gave an exasperated sigh. 'I made it abundantly clear to that tedious man that it was *the other way round*.'

'Jesty was smitten by you. He was unable to tear his eyes off you. When you realized that there had been a witness to the switch, you lost your poise and for a moment you looked the picture of guilt. I can testify to it since I was there too. I rarely have occasion to doubt the evidence of my eyes. What happened next was very interesting.' Payne stroked his jaw with his forefinger. 'Very interesting indeed.'

'What happened next, Major Payne?'

'You got into the taxi with your husband and accompanied him on what was to be his last journey to Mayholme Manor. In the course of your journey you managed to get hold of the snuff-box. Did you pick his pocket? Or perhaps you simply asked him to hand the snuff-box over, so that you could admire its filigree? A rather magnificent seventeenth-century snuff-box, isn't it? You had the antibiotic capsule ready and you contrived to put it *back* into the snuff-box – having extracted the lethal capsule first.'

'So *that's* what I did!' Penelope clapped her hands. 'I had no idea.'

Payne lit his pipe. 'You must have felt great relief. I can imagine the thoughts that passed through your mind. Your husband would *not* die, there'd be nothing in the papers about it, and the intrusive stranger with the snub nose and the silly moustache would not be reporting to the police the suspicious incident he had witnessed at Claridge's. What you did *not* foresee was that Captain Jesty would try to blackmail you into becoming his paramour.'

'A paramour . . . Do you always use such quaint words?'

'You agreed to meet Jesty and the very next day the two of you had lunch at Quaglino's. By the end of that lunch, Jesty's infatuation had transcended into a full-blown obsession. Dangerous things, obsessions. Get in the way of rational thinking. Jesty poured his heart out to you. He told you he adored you. He thought you were a goddess. He wanted to be your slave. You made it clear you were not interested. You remained distant and unresponsive. You turned down his advances. You made nonsense of his blackmail attempts by presenting him with an entirely different and, I dare say, rather convincing version of what had taken place at Claridge's.'

'I told him that he had misread the situation completely.'

'You told him you never wanted to see him again. You looked as though you despised him. You informed him you were leaving for the South of France.' Major Payne paused. 'I bumped into Jesty outside Mayholme Manor later that same day. He was in a terrible state. He looked ill. We had a drink together but it didn't help him much. He said he wanted to die. He had fallen in love with you. Life wouldn't be worth living if he couldn't have you, there'd be no point for him to go on. But then – out of the blue – you phoned him.'

37

The Deadly Joker

Penelope Tradescant shook her head. 'I never phoned Captain Jesty.'

'I saw his face light up. He looked incredulous at first, then delighted. No. "Delighted" is too mild a word. He was transported with joy. He started saying your name – but broke off after the first syllable. *Pe*. I think that some preservation instinct impelled him to pretend it was not you but someone else. Maybe something in your voice alerted him to the dangerous enterprise you had in mind for him?'

'What dangerous enterprise?'

'I wouldn't go so far as to insist that Jesty possesses a sixth sense, or that he might have had some sort of pre-vision – I will leave that kind of thing to your patroness Bettina. Still, it is curious. I asked Jesty whether it was you on the phone. He shook his head. He assumed a crest-fallen expression. He said it was one of his old girlfriends. His oldest squeeze. *Petunia*. Same first syllable as your name, see?'

'Your ingenuity leaves me gasping.'

'It is Jesty's ingenuity one should be gasping at. Jesty managed to put on a jolly convincing show for my benefit. He played the vapid lady-killer to perfection. Pill, darling, what a beast he had been, *mea culpa*, darling, and so on. You were probably surprised, but I am sure you realized soon enough there must have been a good reason for the charade. You told him you wanted to see him. You invited him over to Half Moon Street that night, didn't you?'

'I never phoned Captain Jesty,' she said again.

'His story, after he rang off, was that Petunia – a Mrs Luscombe-Lunt – had asked him round to her place. He said he didn't really want to go, he didn't feel like it, but would do it for old times' sake. He then flew into the night. Well, on that occasion he managed to pull the wool over my eyes. At that point I had no idea that it couldn't possibly have been Mrs Luscombe-Lunt who phoned him.'

'Why not?'

'Petunia Luscombe-Lunt couldn't have phoned him for the simple reason that she was dead. Jesty wasn't aware of the fact. That's where he slipped up. He hadn't seen Petunia for some time. The poor woman had perished about ten days earlier, on 12th June, in an accident in the Alps. I read about her memorial service in *The Times* a couple of days later, entirely by chance. That, you see, was when I had my very first inkling of the truth.'

'What *you* believe to be the truth,' she corrected him.

'This whole awful business starts and ends with you, Lady Tradescant,' Payne said. 'Jesty did your murder for you, at your request. He went and drowned your husband. He shaved off his moustache first. He thought he would be too conspicuous otherwise. Only he did it a little too rashly and cut himself. He had a nasty little scar on his upper lip on the morning of the murder. It probably got infected because it turned a vicious kind of red. It could be spotted from a distance. Like the mark of Cain.'

'This is actually terribly amusing.'

'You managed to assess Jesty's possibilities pretty accurately. You saw his murderous potential. You and he are a bit alike. More than a bit. Amoral, unprincipled, callous, single-minded, reckless. Am I missing something? I believe you are the cleverer of the two, but we must give Jesty his due. He played the part of the embittered jilted suitor to perfection.'

'Immoral? Impulsive? Well versed in the art of dissimulation? Evil?'

'Evil,' Payne echoed. 'It is the kind of word that conveys the same sort of sense, largely meaningless, amorphous and diffuse, as applied to love. In fact it nearly misses being an anagram of love, have you noticed? Everybody seems to believe they know what "evil" means but none could have defined it with any degree of precision ...'

'I must say I have never before met a metaphysical Major!'

'My aunt has always been extremely interested in the lethal and erotic possibilities of the set-up known as folie à deux.' Payne stroked his jaw with his forefinger. 'She would be thrilled if I told her that the murder of Sir Seymour Tradescant was the direct consequence of a folie à deux.'

'I fear the sun might have proved a little bit too strong for your poor head.'

'Jesty made it clear that he was mad about you and would do anything for you – *anything* – if only you were to favour him. Well, you were brought together at the right psychological moment. The failed murder of your husband was still very much on your mind. You were angry with the "spoiler". I don't think you are the kind of person who gives up easily. You had a brainwave. *Why not use the spoiler – he owes it to me – he seems right for the job – why not make him do it?*'

'I think your cat wants to join us.' Penelope Tradescant was looking in the direction of the maple tree. 'What's her name?'

'It's a he,' Antonia said. 'His name is Dupin.'

'Well, you were right about Jesty. He *was* the right man for the job. Vic Levant is also very much in love with you,' Major Payne went on, 'but somehow I don't think he would have agreed to kill your husband.'

Penelope frowned. 'What do you know about Vic?'

'Apart from the fact that he comes from Canada, that he is the son of your late housekeeper, that he is your brother

212

and, until recently, your lover, nothing at all. I don't doubt you were fond of him, but with Jesty on the scene, Vic had to go. You had already decided that Jesty was your man. Perhaps his Casanova credentials played their part too?'

'I believe Captain Jesty was with you the morning I paid you a visit,' Antonia said, 'but he didn't stay to be introduced. The door slamming – remember?'

'Is that *all* the evidence you could produce that links me to Captain Jesty? A slammed door? A shaved moustache?' Penelope Tradescant laughed. It was a very attractive laugh.

'Vic saw Captain Jesty going into your house. He would certainly recognize photos of him. Minus the moustache. Vic commented on Captain Jesty's shining upper lip,' Antonia said.

'Poor Vic. I doubt if he would make a good witness. I am concerned about him, you know. Didn't you find him a trifle on the febrile side – a shade unbalanced? He's been stalking me, you see. He keeps phoning. He wouldn't accept no for an answer. He is far from reasonable. He has developed the annoying habit of bursting into tears when least expected.' Penelope shook her head. 'The police would take a very dim view of it, if I were to make a report. Poor Vic needs psychiatric help . . . What a clever-looking cat! Perhaps he is a detective too?'

'He is named after a detective,' Antonia said, feeling a little foolish.

Dupin had walked up to Penelope Tradescant and was rubbing against her legs. She scratched him behind his ears and made him purr. And I always thought you such a good judge of character, Payne thought, annoyed by what he perceived to be Dupin's treachery. He snapped his fingers and called out, 'Dupin! Come here at once!'

'He is not a dog, Major Payne,' Penelope Tradescant said. 'All right. I admit Captain Jesty has been making rather a nuisance of himself. So what? Say, I made the mistake of letting him into my house on one or two occasions. That proves nothing. Nothing at all.'

'Jesty was at Mayholme Manor on the morning of the murder,' said Payne. 'One of the stewards saw him come out of Sir Seymour's bathroom. Jesty was wearing an orange habit. He had clearly decided that he could be taken for one of the stewards. The front of the habit was wet with Sir Seymour's bath water. It was you who gave him the habit, wasn't it? Sir Seymour had brought the habit home and had been using it as a dressing gown. But perhaps Jesty has a cast-iron alibi for the morning of Sir Seymour's murder?'

'Perhaps he has. Why didn't the steward try to stop him? Why didn't he raise the alarm? Why didn't he tell the police at once? He hasn't told the police yet, has he?' Penelope's voice rose. 'Do you really believe the police would take his account seriously?'

'They might.'

'You have no case. There is nothing either of you can do. Your case is as flimsy as the little piggy's house that was made of straw.' Penelope Tradescant glanced at her watch, then rose to her feet. 'I need to go home to change. I have a flying lesson at five. I am buying one of those light two-seater planes.'

'You came here with the intention of ascertaining if we had any serious evidence against you and your accomplice. Luckily for you – perhaps luckily for us as well – we haven't.' Payne spoke a little wearily. 'Am I right in thinking there is a gun inside your bag?'

'A gun? Oh yes. I completely forgot about it.' She opened her bag and produced a small, rather elegant-looking revolver. 'I've got a licence for it. I only carry it for protection. I hope I'll never need it, but who knows? We live in troubled times.'

'If things had turned out differently, would you have shot us – and our poor cat as well, perhaps? I believe you would. Your outlandish outfit makes it clear that you didn't want to be recognized if someone saw you enter or leave our house.'

'I would never have shot your cat,' Lady Tradescant said. 'Never. Such a *clever*-looking cat.'

Payne's mobile phone rang.

It was Madden.

Madden had had second thoughts. He had called Payne back. Madden had agreed to cooperate. It was on Payne's instructions that he had called Captain Jesty and pretended to blackmail him.

Payne had contemplated a trap. Jesty's compliance would have constituted proof of guilt.

'He didn't turn up,' Madden said. 'He must have realized that you were behind the ploy, that you were trying to get him and I was merely your instrument. You shouldn't have suggested Claridge's.'

'Damn. I meant to say the Savoy.'

'I recorded our conversation on my mobile,' Madden said. 'Wouldn't that help?'

'Most enterprising of you, my dear fellow. Well, let's see what the police will make of it,' said Payne.

He was not particularly optimistic.

38

Nemesis

The police made very little of the recorded conversation between Captain Jesty and the steward Madden. They did not think it was the kind of evidence that would be considered acceptable in a court of law. They agreed to listen to the story the young man called Vic Levant had to tell, but that too failed to impress them.

A jilted lover, as Major Payne pointed out, rarely makes a reliable witness. Not even when he happens to be the culprit's brother.

So it was that Sir Seymour Tradescant's huge fortune passed into the hands of his murderers. Evil appeared to have won. Nevertheless, Nemesis did have the final word, and when Major Payne and Antonia read in the morning paper that Lady Tradescant and her friend Captain ('Beau') Jesty had been killed in the accidental crashing of Lady Tradescant's two-seater plane in a field near the M25 on 30th August, they knew that Justice was satisfied.

There were signs of autumn in the air and their garden looked silvery with faint dew.

'Well, that's that, I suppose,' Payne said, putting *The Times* down.

'It's the kind of deus ex machina solution I would *never* have chosen for any of my detective novels,' said Antonia as she helped herself to more coffee.